EXIST

BOOK 6 BEYOND THE THAW

TAMAR SLOAN

HEIDI CATHERINE

SEQUEL HOUSE

HAWK

*H*awk's eyes spring open.
It's today.

Which makes it the first day of the rest of his life. Or perhaps the last day of his former life.

Actually, it's both.

He slips out of bed, wondering where he'll sleep the next time he closes his eyes at night. At least he knows it will be next to Sam. And Mercy. He needs to remember to keep her close, too. She's going to feel lost without Luca to bat her eyelashes at. But in time, she'll find her feet. It's what she does best.

Hawk tiptoes to the door of his family's hut and leaves quietly.

Which is what he does best.

It's dark outside. Not even the birds are awake yet. But soon they'll be flitting around Askala as people emerge from their huts, ready to greet the sun.

He makes his way down the track that leads to the beach, wanting some time by himself before he has to say his goodbyes to his family. Because once he climbs aboard the boat with the five other Seekers, it's quite possible he'll never be alone again.

Feeling like he's choking, Hawk tugs on the leather strap he's wearing around his neck. His father gave him a large silver pendant after the Announcement, making him promise to wear it always. Wren wears one just like it. It's how people used to communicate when their words were separated by too many miles. Ravens would carry messages, seeing the sun glint off the pendant as a signal to land.

Maybe he can see if Sam or Mercy want to wear it.

Breaking through the trees, he feels the soft sand underneath his feet. Wearing shoes has been difficult since he stood in that bucket of acid water in the second test of the Proving. A test that was only a week ago yet feels like forever. Time has a habit of stretching out like a bow when the days are filled with fear.

Because there's no doubt that's exactly what the Proving had been about for everyone involved. Fear of failing. Fear of not failing. Fear of who may or may not pass or fail with you. For Hawk it was fear of not knowing what path he wanted to take, only that whatever it was, he wanted to walk it with Sam.

He got everything he wanted in the end. A chance to take Askala's message beyond their shores. And with not just Sam, but Mercy as well.

And Gust, Nikita and Siena…but he hasn't given them too much thought. Especially Gust.

The sound of the ocean draws Hawk forward as if it's calling his name. But he stumbles on a fallen tree branch. Waving his hands, he tries to steady himself, ending up crashing to the sand and landing heavily.

He shakes his head, wishing Sam were here to see that. It might make her feel better about all the times she's unintentionally ended up sitting on the ground when all she'd been trying to do was walk.

"That's got to be you, Hawk."

Hawk groans as he realizes it hadn't been a tree branch that tripped him up.

2

"And that's got to be you, Luca."

"What are you doing walking out here in the dark?" Luca sits up and Hawk can just make out his form in the shadows.

"Same thing you're doing." Hawk brushes some sand off his hands and stands. He and Luca were never best friends. He doesn't see any reason why they should start now.

"You must be happy with yourself," says Luca, pulling himself to his feet.

Hawk walks toward the water without answering. He hadn't come down here for a fight.

But it seems Luca has more to say as he follows him to the shoreline.

"You do realize that every token you gave Sam was a nail in her coffin," says Luca.

Hawk rolls his eyes. They don't even use coffins in Askala. Or nails.

"Why do you underestimate her so much?" Hawk asks. "She's stronger than you think."

"It's you who's doing the underestimating." Luca picks up a rock and tosses it into the ocean. "But it's the Outlanders you're underestimating. If you'd seen what I've seen—"

"Give it a rest!" snaps Hawk. "Yes, we all know you're the high and mighty explorer who's roamed the Outlands, fending off danger at every turn. Have you ever stopped to think that maybe you're not the only one who feels the need to do more with their life than...this?"

As if on cue, the sun pokes out over the horizon, its golden light shining like a halo. A flock of birds soar across the sky in a vee formation, taking turns to be the leader in just the way Askala's leaders do. The strongest at the front, forging the way, until they grow weary and someone else takes their place while they gather their strength to lead again.

"You know I'm searching for someone," says Luca.

"Even though you have a perfectly good mother right here."

Hawk shakes his head. "Nova's given you everything, yet you behave as if it's not enough."

"She has. But you're right. It's not enough." Luca's voice is heavy with emotion and Hawk decides to drop it. He's got no idea what it would be like to grow up with a family that's not your own.

"Well maybe it's not enough for me, either," Hawk says. "I need to do more with my life than I can here."

"I get that." The shadows shift from Luca's face and Hawk sees his dark eyes are locked on him. "But do you have to take Sam with you?"

"That's Sam's decision." Hawk sighs. It doesn't matter how many times he says this, Luca's just not prepared to listen. "It's true that I voted for her, but she decided to become a Seeker all on her own."

"If you pull out, then she will, too." Luca touches Hawk lightly on the arm. "I know she will. So will Mercy. They only feel safe because you'll be there."

"And I'll keep them safe." Hawk shakes off Luca's hand. "You might not like me, but you know I'll do that."

Luca sighs. "You don't know what the Outlanders are capable of."

"My father was an Outlander!" Hawk throws out his hands. "And Wren! And Jagger! We have plenty of Outlanders living amongst us here. One more, now that Charity's joined us. And they've all been capable of assimilating to our peaceful life. They all saw the way forward. Every single one of them. But the time has passed where we can just sit here waiting for more of them to wash up on our shores. We have to go to them. Reclaim one piece of land at a time. Convert each heart, one by one, until the Outlands no longer exists."

Luca doesn't say anything for a few beats and Hawk crosses his arms, glaring at the sun as it lifts above the horizon. So much for a few quiet moments alone!

"You know, Hawk," says Luca. "That was the most words I've ever heard you say at once."

"And did you listen to any of them?" Hawk glares at Luca, who shrugs before walking off.

Hawk lets out a long breath, trying to force the annoyance from his chest. Luca is without question the most frustrating person Hawk's ever met. And that includes Gust. It's just as well that after today, he's never going to have to deal with Luca again.

He sits down on the cool sand and looks toward the Newlands, the never-ending plume of thick gray smoke pouring into the morning sky. Soon, that will be his home. Soon, that smoke will stop. Soon, the island will be allowed to regenerate and thrive as the people realize they depend on it for their survival.

Urgh! This pendant! How can anyone possibly breathe with a noose around their neck?

Hawk tears the leather strap from his throat and dangles it from his fingertips, watching how the pendant catches the morning sun and reflects the light onto the sand in colorful rainbows. He can see why a bird might be attracted to it.

How can Luca think he's naïve to the risks in the Outlands? And how arrogant of him to think he's the only one capable of finding his way out there. He was the same age as Hawk is now when he first left in search of his mother. If he can survive, then Hawk can, too.

Someone sits down beside him and Hawk sighs, his breath catching in his throat when he sees it's his aunt. It's more popular out here this morning than the ballroom on Announcement day.

"Wren," he says. "What are you doing here?"

"I'm scared." She tucks her knees up to her chest.

Hawk's brows shoot up. He's never known his aunt to be scared of anything.

"You'll look after Mercy, won't you?" she asks. "Because I've made it very clear to her that she needs to look after you."

Hawk smiles. At last, someone who can see the female Seekers through a clear lens. Hawk might be twice their size but that doesn't mean he's twice as capable.

"We'll look after each other," he says. "I promise."

"You have a kind heart." She reaches for his pendant, not asking why he's taken it off, and turns it over in her hands. "That's why I worry about you."

"Kindness is the foundation of Askala," he says, repeating what his mother always tells him. "It's the gift we'll be bringing to the Outlands."

"Screw kindness!" Wren clenches her fists around the leather cord. "You need to be strong."

Hawk's jaw falls open. He knows his aunt is tough, but he's never heard her speak like this before.

"You do whatever it takes to survive out there." She grips his arm. "You lie if you need to. You kill if you must. There's no room for kindness in the war that's coming."

Hawk's not sure what to say to this new side of Wren. He's heard stories of how fierce she'd been when she'd arrived in Askala, killing a giant leatherskin singlehandedly before washing up on shore and showing everyone here that size is no indicator of courage.

"There's no war coming, Wren." He puts his hand over hers and squeezes it. "This is different. And there's always room for kindness."

She shakes her head. "Not always. If it's a choice between you or them, you must choose yourself. Always. Killing a man is difficult. You can't hesitate. I did that once and it nearly cost us all our lives. When you line up your shot, you take it. Do you understand?"

Hawk nods, even though he hopes he never understands what she just said.

"This isn't a game." She passes him back the pendant. "It never has been. I swear if anyone touches Mercy, I'll come over there and kill them myself."

"You won't need to." Hawk's voice is weak, lacking the conviction needed to persuade Wren of something he's not entirely sure he can promise. He can't watch Mercy every moment of every day.

"You've got to be kidding me!" Wren shoots to her feet faster than an arrow.

"What?" Hawk stands beside her, following her gaze into the morning sky.

"A raven," she breathes. "It's one of my father's."

"How can you tell?" He squints at the black bird, which looks exactly like any other raven he's ever seen.

"Hold out your pendant," she says, flipping her own out from the neckline of her shirt. "He's seen us."

The raven circles for a long while, then swoops down and lands in front of them. It's then that Hawk sees what's different about it. There's a note tied to one of its feet.

Wren crouches down, tugging at the hem of Hawk's shirt, encouraging him to do the same.

"Who's the note for?" Hawk asks, his brow furrowing.

"I don't know." Wren holds out her palm, rubbing her fingertips with her thumb. "But I'd like to find out."

The bird hops closer. It's an impressive size for a raven, with glossy feathers the color of night and a sharp beak that Hawk's not entirely sure he wants to get too close to.

Wren reaches out and unties the note, tucking it under her arm as she shows the bird her empty hands.

The raven tilts its head in disappointment.

"Sorry," says Wren. "No crickets today."

Flapping its wings and letting out a caw of disgust, the bird lifts into the sky and heads back out across the sea.

"I can't believe it," says Wren, stretching back up into a standing position. "They're using ravens again."

"Who is?" Hawk cranes his neck as he tries to see the note Wren's unraveled. None of this is making any sense.

Wren holds out the parchment and Hawk's disappointed to see it's in some kind of code.

"Can you read it?" he asks.

She nods. "Stage one complete. The Falcon is dead. Commander's instructions to follow."

The words send an icy chill down Hawk's spine. Who in sweet Terra is the Falcon? "I don't understand. What does this mean?"

Wren looks up from the note, blinking at him as if trying to clear the fear from her eyes. "It means I was wrong. The war's not coming. It's already here."

SAM

"*Y*ou can't go, Sam."

Sam glances down at where her mother has gripped her hand, stopping her in the middle of the path. They're on their way to the meeting of the leaders.

They're on their way to the vote.

Sam frowns. "But I was voted as a Seeker. I was chosen to go."

Her mother bites her lip. "Yes, I know that. But with everything we've just learned, and Seb..."

Sam's frown deepens. Seb had been paler than usual this morning, but that could be caused by anything. A poor night's sleep. His loss of appetite last night.

The upcoming vote.

Sam twists her hand so she's holding her mother's. "Seb will be fine. He's got you and Dad to look after him."

"And who will you have?"

Her mother's face is tight with worry, her hand gripping Sam's so hard it almost hurts. But Sam shakes it off as she steps back.

"Why does everyone think I need looking after?"

The hurt that not even her own father wants her going flares like a cut that was just reopened. Not only that, he asked Luca to sabotage her.

Sam's hands clench. "Did it occur to you that maybe I can do this?"

She's the one who still made it through. Enough people put tokens in her urn to enable her to be here.

Her mother's face softens as her hand reaches out. "Sam, of course we believe in you. It's just that the Newlands are more dangerous than we realized."

But Sam jams her hands on her hips. "You didn't stop Luca from going."

And neither did Sam, no matter how much it broke her heart to watch him leave. Hawk was the one who held her as she cried at the prospect of never seeing her brother again.

Her mother shakes her head. "That was something Luca needed to do. You knew that."

"Exactly." Sam lifts her chin, waiting for her mother to see their hypocrisy.

This is something Sam needs to do.

Her mother's shoulders sag. "This is different, Sam. Luca had some idea of what he was up against. He was prepared."

"Don't you see? I've been preparing for this my whole life! I didn't know it at the time, but this is exactly what I'm supposed to do."

All her knowledge, if it's not for sharing, what else is it good for? The people of Askala already know its value and what they're supposed to do with it.

It's the people beyond their borders who need it.

And the very planet they're standing on.

Sam reaches out to her mother, just like she did a moment ago with her. "This is what you raised me to do, Mom. To fight for this."

Her mother's eyes flutter closed before opening again, full of desperation and tears. "Please, Sam. We're begging you."

Sam stills. She's always done what they've asked of her. Always. Making her parents proud is all she's ever wanted.

But how can she be proud of herself if she stays?

How can she watch Hawk leave?

She shakes her head. Her parents may not agree with the decision she's about to make, but maybe one day, they'll be proud. "I'm a Seeker. I want to go."

Her mother's shoulders droop so low, Sam wonders how she doesn't buckle. "Then you need to understand that we're going to do everything we can to stop this from happening." Her eyes beseech Sam's. "We love you, we're desperate."

"But...that's selfish. All I want is your support."

"Love isn't as clear cut as that, Sam. You leaving could be seen as selfish."

Sam takes a step back, stumbling a little. Her mother reaches out, but Sam brushes her hands away. Is her mother saying Sam's doing this for herself? To prove she can do it?

To be with Hawk?

Turning away, Sam takes a step further down the path. "If I stay, you'll lose me anyway."

Without looking to see what impact her words have, Sam continues to their destination.

Sam's first meeting of the leaders.

She's dreamed of this moment. Imagined it. Used to look forward to it...

Only one generation ago it was called the High Bound meeting, but Bound and Unbound no longer exist. Nor does the great big ship the meetings were held in.

Now, a large circular table has been built under the canopy of the trees not far from the ballroom, wooden stools circling it.

It's peaceful. It's beautiful. It holds the hearts and minds dedicated to Askala.

And Sam's here. Taking the seat beside her mother, joining her father and everyone else she's looked up to her entire life. And just like she hoped, Hawk and Mercy are there with her. Mercy's with her parents. Hawk's sitting quietly on Sam's other side.

Except, this isn't a dream come true. They're not deciding on the future of Askala.

They're deciding hers.

And every Seeker who passed the second Proving.

She wasn't supposed to be here. They were all meant to be on their way to the Newlands by now.

Her father stands, and the shuffling around the large table instantly comes to a halt. "Thank you for coming here at short notice. With the new information we've received, there are decisions to be made."

Sam's hands tighten in her lap. The decision whether the Seekers should even leave.

Her father indicates to Wren and she stands. "As you all know by now, a note was intercepted this morning. It speaks of stage one being complete and to wait for the Commander's further instructions."

An unsettled murmur drifts around the table. People glance at each other, their sense of peace suddenly feeling fragile.

Wren's gaze connects with each person. "The Outlanders are planning something. I believe they're preparing for war."

Dex rests a hand on her arm. "We don't know that for sure. But it's certainly worrying." He glances at Mercy on his other side. "The Newlands are far more dangerous than we anticipated."

Sam's father nods. "We need to discuss whether it's safe for the Seekers to go there."

Hawk stills beside Sam. There hasn't been time to talk, but she knows all his dreams are riding on the vote that her father will propose.

Sam freezes. What will Hawk do if they're told the Seekers must remain in Askala? Will he leave anyway?

If he does, Sam will have to choose.

Her father's gaze falls on Luca across the table. "Luca, could you tell us what the Seekers can expect when they arrive in the Newlands?"

Her brother nods and stands as if he was expecting this. Tension winds through Sam's gut. Why does it feel like they're being ganged up on?

Luca clears his throat. "The Outlanders who arrive here aren't the same as the people the Seekers would meet out there. They haven't just been offered a safe haven and unlimited food. They're desperate and accustomed to using violence to get what they need." His gaze falls on Mercy. "Women are the most vulnerable. They're seen as a possession. More of a commodity to be traded."

A few women inhale sharply. Mercy simply lifts her chin, holding Luca's gaze.

Luca's brows twitch down as he looks away. "They fight first, ask questions later. And now that we know they're planning something, they're going to be less likely to want us over there. They'll see it as a threat." His gaze clamps onto Sam. "That's why they didn't welcome us when we went to the Newlands. Why they walked us out with spears."

Sam's hand flutters in her lap, wanting to press it against her cheek. The swelling and bruising are subsiding, but the ache still clings.

Except one moment of anger isn't enough reason to quit. Doesn't Luca see? The only way the people of the Newlands can learn Askala isn't a threat, that there's so much they can learn from each other, is to show them.

Grace seemed like someone they could reach. Maybe even Raiden.

And imagine what would happen if the Commander listened? If he were helping spread the message...

Her father's pale as he nods. "Did you know about this new Commander?"

"I'd heard whispers, but I didn't believe it was true," Luca says heavily. "Since Ronan died, they've fought amongst themselves too much. They were never that coordinated."

Dex leans forward. "And this Falcon they mention. Have you heard anything about him before?"

Luca shakes his head. "I'm guessing it's code for something."

The Falcon is dead.

Everyone's mulled over that puzzle. Obviously, the Outlanders were waiting for that to happen. Whatever it is. And it's now cleared an obstacle for whatever they're planning.

Sam has to hold herself in place. She wants to stand, to shout at every worried face.

They're running out of time.

Luca sits down and the happy chatter of birds sounds strange in the thick tension.

Sam's father stands again. "In light of this new information, I propose a vote. I believe it's too dangerous to go ahead with our initial plan. I believe there should be no Seekers."

Sam's mind screams a denial. Except, even she can see that quite a few of the others agree. One or two are already leaning forward, preparing to vote.

Diesel frowns as he presses his hands onto the table. "So you put us through all that for nothing?" His voice rises. "Bryan and Simon died during those tests!"

A few gazes slip to focus on the timber in front of them. Simon's father chose to resign as leader after he lost his son.

Sam's mother nods, her eyes overflowing with empathy. "That's why we're proposing this. We've lost too much already."

Sam can hardly breathe. Her mind is in overdrive. They can't have come this close only to lose everything they worked for.

Suddenly, the thought of remaining in Askala is the last thing Sam wants.

Nor is it what Hawk wants. Or Mercy.

Sam shoots to her feet. "But how else can we teach them? How else will they learn there's another way to live?"

Mercy straightens, too. "You're the ones who wanted to take Askala's message beyond our shores." Her gaze sharpens. "It seems to me we need the Seekers more than ever."

Hawk stands. "They're right. We can do this."

Sam's chest fills with pride. Only a few words, but the ones that count.

Diesel's brows hike up. "So the Seekers still wish to go to the Newlands?"

A multitude of faces turn to look at the other three Seekers.

Siena looks a little pale. "I made a commitment, I'll see it through."

Gust glances around, looking like he's trapped. He swallows. "Of course we wish to go," he squeaks.

Nikita glances at him in surprise. She straightens her shoulders. "We're the best of the best."

Except it almost feels like there's an "aren't we?" at the end.

Sam looks around. So many familiar faces. Zali. Jagger. Aarov. And now the new generation who joined along with her. Diesel. Juno. Ekon. The Seekers' future lies in their hands.

Each and every one of them look away.

No!

Hawk tugs on Sam's hand, pulling her back onto the stool. She looks at him, and he holds her gaze. His eyes are stoic. Determined. He's telling her something.

We'll go anyway.

But can Sam do that? Once the leaders have voted, can she go against their decision? Openly defy her father?

Even if it means losing Hawk when she's only just discovering what he really means to her?

Jagger stands, his face determined in a way Sam hasn't seen before. "You need to realize that complacency is dangerous. You can't just wait for the Outlanders to come to you. Askala has what many others want."

Sam's father's hands sweep out. "And they are welcome to share everything we have."

Jagger shakes his head. "Not everyone wants to share, Kian. Resources means power. We must stick to the plan."

Zali gasps and every head turns to her. "You want to send the Seekers there, despite what we have learned?"

Jagger shakes his head. "I don't believe remaining here and hoping this all goes away is the best for Askala and its people."

Zali lifts a trembling finger, pointing it at him. "You wanted these tests. You convinced us they were necessary." Her eyes widen. "And that raven was sent to someone in Askala."

There's a collective intake of breath around the table.

Wren pushes up, her hands fisted on the wooden tabletop. "What are you suggesting, Zali?" she asks quietly.

Sam's own eyes widen. Wren sounds...dangerous.

Zali's hand flutters to her throat. "I wouldn't accuse anyone without evidence. I'm just conscious that Jagger used to be one of Ronan's men. That he would have Outlander sympathies."

"Ronan was my father," Wren grinds out. "What does that make me?"

Jagger lifts a hand in a conciliatory gesture. "Askala saved me. It showed me we have a responsibility to more than just survive. Of course I want others to learn that." He looks to each of the Seekers. "Askala taught me that we can't just think of ourselves."

A few people nod, but Zali looks away as she sits down. Several people gaze at Jagger as if they're seeing him in a new light.

Sam frowns. Everyone knows the story that Jagger risked his life for Askala. He saved Wren's life and countless others.

Is Zali suggesting he did that so he could infiltrate Askala? Become a spy?

It doesn't feel plausible...but then again, no-one hypothesized that a new Commander would rise up.

And that the Outlanders have been planning something for far longer than they realized.

Wren glares at them, one by one. "Jagger and I were some of the first Outlanders who showed you what Askala could do. Don't ever forget that."

Dex places his hand over Wren's and just like magic, her body unwinds. She collapses onto her seat, glancing at him. He nods in understanding, squeezing her hand.

Sam's father stands again, the movement slow and stiff as if he's aged a century over the course of this meeting. Just like Dex and Wren, his hand is clasped tightly in her mother's.

"We will vote," her father announces. "All those who believe those chosen as Seekers should stay in Askala, please raise your hand."

Sam's already done the math. It's the first thing she did as everyone took their place around the table.

There are twenty-four leaders. That means they need thirteen people to vote in their favor. With six Seekers, they're almost halfway there.

Her father's hand is the first to rise up, his anguished gaze holding hers. Sam's eyes sting as she watches her mother's hand join his as it reaches for the green canopy above them.

Dex is next, followed by Zali. Sam glances at Wren, noticing she's chewing her lip. With a sigh, she raises her hand.

Mercy shakes her head. "No, Mom." Her whispered words are heavy with betrayal.

More hands lift above grave faces. Sam's heart plummets painfully with each one.

Like a tide she can't stop, Sam watches as eleven hands rise into the air. She holds her breath when there are no more. The wave of votes has come to an end.

Except then her gaze flies to her brother.

Luca hasn't voted.

Please, Luca.

Luca's gaze darts to their father before returning to hers.

Please.

He mouths two words. "I'm sorry."

And then his hand joins the others.

It's a tie.

MERCY

*M*ercy walks back to the hut with her parents, her arms firmly crossed. This isn't how today was supposed to turn out. Right now, she should be climbing aboard a boat and heading to the Newlands. Not going home to wait for the re-vote to be called.

Ties are always difficult in Askala. It's far easier in the years when there's an odd number of leaders. But they can't exactly rig the Proving to avoid even numbers. Some years it just doesn't work out.

"Nobody's going to change their vote," says Mercy, aware that she's pouting. "And then what happens?"

"Someone will change their vote," her mother says. "Someone *always* changes their vote. You'll see."

"How about you change your vote?" Mercy suggests, knowing she's wasting her breath.

Her mother raises her eyebrows. "Or how about you do?"

"Not. Happening." Mercy's footsteps turn to stomps. "We're needed out there. The contents of that note are only further proof of that."

Her parents look at each other in that frustrating way they do when they're communicating without words. Sometimes Mercy swears they're two parts of the same person.

"Answer me one question," says Mercy when they reach the hut.

Her father's hand pauses on the door.

"If I weren't a Seeker, how would you have voted?" She glares at them. "Be honest."

Her father opens the door without answering and goes inside. But her mother grips Mercy by the hand.

"There's no point asking what if," she says. "Your dad and I can't pretend we're not your parents."

"I know you'd vote for the Seekers to go," says Mercy, seeing her mother's eyes widen just enough to know she's right. "Dad wouldn't. But you would. It's the right thing to do and you know it."

"I voted no." Her mother lets go of her hand to go into the hut.

"And you hesitated before you voted," says Mercy, going in after her. "I saw it!"

"Where's Charity?" her father asks, walking out of Mercy's room and looking around. "We asked her to wait here."

Mercy shrugs. "Maybe she went to meet Seb? I told her I was going to introduce them before I left."

The door bursts open behind Mercy and she turns to see Sam's younger brother. He's out of breath and sweating like he's run a marathon, even though it was likely only a few paces.

"Speak of the devil," says Mercy's mom. "Have you seen Charity?"

Seb nods, trying to speak but having trouble getting his words out. "Mom sent me here to tell you."

They wait for him to catch his breath so he can explain.

"I saw Charity run into the forest while you were at the vote." His words come out in a tumble now. "I tried to follow

20

her, but she was too fast. I got puffed and had to stop. So, I went home to wait for Luca. He can find her for you. He can find anyone."

"Not anyone," says Mercy, thinking of Luca's mother in the Outlands, and wishing everyone would stop giving him more credit than he deserves. The guy voted against letting them go! He of all people should understand how important it is that the Seekers be allowed to leave. His vote would've made all the difference.

"Mercy and I will go and look for her," her mom says.

"I'm coming, too." Her dad goes to the door.

"We need you here." Her mom holds up a hand and shakes her head. "In case Charity returns. There needs to be someone she trusts here so she doesn't take off again."

Mercy nods. "She's right, Dad. And no offence to Mom, but it shouldn't be her."

Mercy's mom has asked too many tough questions of Charity since she arrived.

"She can't have gone far." Mercy's mom tugs on her sleeve. "We'll be back before you know it, Dex."

"Well, if you're not back in an hour, I'm coming after you." He sighs as he plonks himself into a chair.

"I have my rocks, Uncle Dex!" Seb pulls a handful of well-worn stones from his pocket and dumps them on the table. "We can play rocks! If Charity comes back, we'll teach her how to play, too."

Mercy's dad pats the chair next to him. "Let's play rocks, my friend."

And that, right there, is exactly why Mercy loves her father so much. Playing rocks is the last thing in the world he would want to do. And yet, just look at him. At least it will keep him occupied for a while.

"Which way did you see Charity heading?" Mercy asks.

Seb points. "She disappeared behind the syrup tree."

Mercy nods. There's a large maple near their group of huts with a tap and a bucket attached that produces the most delicious syrup. According to Sam, it's not as sweet as it would be if they had a cooler climate, but Mercy still thinks it's one of the best things she's ever tasted. She should've looked if they have a maple tree in the Newlands. Not that it matters if she never gets to go back there...

"Mercy!" Her mother is already out the hut and walking away. "Come on!"

Mercy rushes to her father and kisses his cheek before chasing after her mother.

They head for the maple tree and into the forest.

"Charity!" they call over and over. "Charity!"

Mercy's mom walks slowly, studying the ground. Surely, a skinny young girl's footsteps wouldn't be visible out here?

Dread grips Mercy around the chest like a vice. "Why would she even run off in the first place?"

"Leaving your family and everything you know isn't easy." Her mom squats down and trails her fingers over a patch of dirt. "She just needs time to adjust."

"Do you think she got spooked being left at home alone?" Mercy asks.

"It probably made the situation feel more real." Her mom picks up a broken stick, looks at it like it can talk to her, then turns to the left and walks on with Mercy trailing behind. "I don't think she'll be far. It's not like she can swim home."

They walk further into the trees, eyes scanning, voices calling until Mercy's mom grips her arm, pulling her to a halt.

"The footsteps end here," she says, pointing to the ground.

Mercy frowns, not seeing anything different about this patch of dirt than any other in the forest.

"Up there," her mom whispers, tilting her face to look into the tree beside them.

Mercy follows the line of her finger, her jaw falling to see Charity perched on one of the high branches.

"Charity!" they both call at once.

Charity tilts her face down to them. There's no hint of a smile and even at this distance Mercy can see her cheeks are streaked with tears.

"I'm going to jump," says Charity. "Don't try to stop me."

The color fades from Mercy's mom's face. Nobody would be able to survive a fall from that height. But that seems to be exactly the point.

"Don't jump!" Mercy shouts. "Just climb down one branch at a time. We're right here."

But Charity shakes her head. "I can't do this anymore. It's hopeless."

"We need to go up there," says Mercy, already steeling herself for what she knows she has to do.

"I...I can't." Her mother shakes her head.

"You totally can," says Mercy, remembering how she scaled the dare tree during the Proving. If she can do it, her mom can, too.

But her mom has fallen silent, her head still shaking, her face pale with sweat beading on her forehead.

Maybe she can't do this.

But Mercy can.

"Hold on!" she calls to Charity.

Sucking in a deep breath, Mercy climbs onto the lowest branch and pulls herself up. Again and again, she moves skyward, not looking down, not allowing herself a moment for her fear to creep up. She's done this before, and she survived. She can do it again.

"Don't come near me!" Charity shouts when Mercy is only a branch below her.

Mercy concentrates on her breathing, keeping her focus on

the scared girl above her. Crouched on a thick branch, Charity is staring at Mercy with wide, scared eyes.

"What happened?" Mercy asks.

Charity shakes her head, not willing to talk.

"Did it all just get too much?" Mercy tries to keep her voice level. "Because I know exactly how that feels. I thought I was going to pass out on the boat over to the Newlands. Change is difficult. The unknown is tough. You've been through so much in the last two days."

"It was so quiet after you left for that meeting," says Charity, her voice little more than a whisper. "I've never been by myself before. Not ever."

"Oh, Charity." Mercy's own eyes fill with tears. "I'm so sorry. I didn't realize. We should have had Seb come to sit with you. We didn't think..."

"I miss my mom." Charity's shoulders shake as the emotion sweeps through her frail body. "Take me back to her. Please?"

Mercy draws in a breath, tempted to tell Charity what she wants to hear. Anything to get her out of this tree. But that wouldn't be doing her a favor. Instead of earning her trust, it would only drive her further away when she gets to safe ground and discovers the truth.

"I promised your mom I wouldn't do that," says Mercy. "If I take you back, your father will send you to the Outlands. You're safer here with us. It just takes some time to get used to."

"I'm scared," says Charity.

Mercy holds out one of her shaking hands. "Look at this, Charity. See how I'm shaking?"

Charity bites her lip as she nods.

"I'm petrified of heights. But...you know what?"

Charity tilts her head, reminding Mercy of a curious sparrow.

"I'm up in this tree with you anyway," says Mercy. "I'm scared but I'm okay. And the more I climb trees, the less afraid

I'm going to be. Sometimes our brains just take longer than our bodies to get used to something different."

Charity nods, breathes in deeply and clambers down a branch to stand beside Mercy.

"Let's climb down together," says Mercy. "And we'll never leave you by yourself again. That, I can promise. You're going to have a happy life."

"I didn't think you were scared of anything," says Charity.

"*Everyone's* scared of something." Mercy smiles at her. "Even my mom."

"I heard that!" her mom calls up to her.

Mercy giggles. Charity joins in, and just for that moment in the tree, it feels like it's the two of them conspiring against the world. Charity's a nice kid. If things were different, they might even become friends. But Mercy doesn't plan to be here for that to happen.

"Come on," says Mercy. "Let's get out of here."

Charity nods. "Okay."

Together, they climb down the tree. Mercy squints as she looks down, noticing her heartbeat isn't as rapid as it was the last time she did this. She tests every branch, determined not to make the same mistake again and go crashing down. Especially without Luca and that face of his waiting there to surprise her. At least she's fully clothed this time… Feeling heat rush to her face, she continues on. Now isn't the time for those kinds of memories.

Her feet touch solid ground and her mom looks at her, letting out a deep breath. "I'm so glad you're both okay."

"Thanks, Mercy." Charity throws her arms around Mercy's waist and grips her tightly.

As Mercy hugs her back, she notices her mom's eyes filling with tears. But strangely, they're not happy tears. There's something more going on here.

"What, Mom?" she asks.

But her mom shakes her head as she urges them to follow her out of the forest.

The sound of the ancient horn echoes across Askala.

"The re-vote," says Mercy, her stomach turning over. "That was fast."

"Don't leave me again!" says Charity, gripping Mercy's hand.

"Come with us," she says. "Anyone is allowed to watch a meeting of the leaders, even if they're not allowed to vote. We don't have any secrets."

"Could I be a leader of Askala one day?" asks Charity as they weave their way through the trees.

"I don't see why not," says Mercy. "When you turn sixteen you can do your Proving. Although, you might need to stay out of trees in the meantime."

"I'm sorry for making you do that." Charity looks so despondent. There's so much more to this girl than Mercy had first thought.

"Come on, you two." Mercy's mom is waiting at the edge of the trees. She still has that look about her, the one Mercy's having trouble reading. And she doesn't have long to figure it out.

They take the path to the ballroom, knowing Mercy's dad will meet them there. If they're late, there's a chance the vote will be cast without them.

And sure enough, there he is, pacing the entrance to the Oasis. He breaks into a smile to see them.

"You found her!"

They approach and Charity smiles shyly at Mercy's dad. "Sorry to worry you."

"You don't need to apologize," says Mercy. "No harm done."

"With thanks to you," her mom says.

"You were the one who found her," Mercy replies, not wanting to take all the credit.

They walk through the gardens of the Oasis and Mercy runs

her hands over green leaves as they pass. Would it be possible to establish something like this in the Newlands one day? Surely, it must. The soil is clearly fertile given the way the trees have flourished there.

The leaders are gathered around the table. There's tension floating in the air, mingling with the scent of the herbs and flowers that surround them.

Mercy leads Charity over to Sam and gives her cousin a hug. "Think anyone's going to change their vote?" she asks.

Sam shakes her head. "There's a low probability of that. I think that's why Dad called us back so soon. The longer we wait, the more chance someone might have a re-think."

"But what if it's a draw again?" asks Charity.

Sam's brow fills with lines. "Then the Seekers won't be allowed to go. If the leaders can't agree, then the vote always goes in favor of no change being made."

Mercy groans. She'd forgotten about that rule, not having paid too much attention to Askala's politics in the past. But, of course, Sam remembers.

"Thank you for returning to the table," says Kian, his voice filtering over the gathered crowd of leaders and people who've come to watch. "As you're aware, a re-vote has been called."

Mercy's eyes flit across the people, searching for *that face.* The one that makes her heart do a dance whenever she stares directly at it.

She finds him, surprised to see he's watching her. Has he been looking at her since she arrived?

Luca. His name silently caresses her lips as she drinks in the sight of him. Should a miracle happen and she's allowed to climb aboard the boat and head to the Newlands, she's going to need to remember every detail of that face.

Kian clears his throat and the people fall silent. "All those who believe the Seekers should stay in Askala, please raise your hand."

Mercy tears her eyes from Luca as his hand shoots into the air, joining Kian and Nova as the first to vote. More hands rise, including Mercy's father.

The scene of a few hours ago is playing out all over again.

She looks to her mother, waiting for her to cast her vote.

But her mom's hands remain planted by her side, her eyes glued to Mercy.

"All those who believe the Seekers should stay in Askala, please raise your hand," Kian says again, now looking at Mercy's mom.

"Wren!" Mercy's dad gasps. "It's time to vote."

Now, everyone's looking at Mercy's mom while her eyes remain on Mercy with that strange look she's had ever since Mercy came out of the tree.

"They can do this," her mom says. "They can make a difference. We can't stay here and do nothing. We have to let them go."

"No, Wren." Mercy watches her father's face fill with lines. "This is our daughter."

"Our amazing, fearless daughter." Mercy's mom smiles, tears streaming down her face. "Our daughter who can carry forward our legacy. It has to be her. I'm sorry, Dex."

"Mom." Mercy's jaw has fallen open as she steps toward her parents. "Mom, you don't have to do this."

Why is she trying to talk her out of this? It's madness! Her mom is making her wish come true. She should be jumping for joy. But she can't. Not unless she knows her mom truly means it.

"It's the right choice," her mom says. "I have to let you go."

Mercy swallows, nodding her head as her chest fills with pride. Her mom can see her. Like, *really* see her. She's putting her faith in her like nobody else has before.

"A decision has been reached," says Jagger when Kian fails to declare it. "The Seekers will leave immediately."

"Immediately." Mercy's dad repeats the word like it's in a foreign language.

Mercy goes to him and wraps her arms around him, but he's shaking too hard to hold her in return.

"I'm okay, Dad," Mercy says. "This is the right decision. You'll see. I'm going to make you proud."

His arms close around her and as the people file away from the table, heading in the direction of the beach, he squeezes her close to his chest.

"I can't let you go," he says.

"You can." She releases her grip on him and urges him to follow the others. "You must."

Kian and Nova are leaving the table, each with an arm wrapped around Sam's shoulders, Luca walking beside them. Hawk is following closely behind, his parents also with him, having come to watch the vote. They're managing to do what needs to be done. Her dad can do it, too.

Hawk's sister, Dove, has latched herself onto Charity and is leading her away, talking a mile a minute. Charity looks over her shoulder and smiles at Mercy, letting her know she's okay.

Mercy loops one hand in the crook of each parent's arms and they take up the rear of the procession to the beach. It's hard to believe this is actually happening. She's leaving Askala. She's leaving her parents. She's setting out to make sure that everything she's learned can be shared with the rest of the world.

She's a Seeker.

A thousand thoughts race through Mercy's mind as she tries to think of all the things she needs to say before she goes. It's hard to decide what's most important. But there's one thought that keeps pushing itself forward.

"Your mom died protecting you," she says to her dad.

"That's why we named you after her," her mom says when he doesn't reply.

Mercy tugs her father a little closer as they walk. "I want you to know I'm going to make a difference out there. I'm going to make sure her sacrifice wasn't for nothing."

"I wanted you to have children of your own," her father says, his voice breaking under the strain.

"And who says I won't?" Despite trying to keep the sunshine in her voice, her words are failing to chase away the dark clouds in her father's eyes.

"We should go with her," he says, leaning forward to look at Mercy's mom.

"Dex." Her mom sighs. "We have responsibilities here."

"What made you change your vote?" he asks, his voice lacking the normal warmth when he speaks to her.

"I saw a different side to Mercy today," her mother says. "One I couldn't ignore. She's not our baby girl anymore, Dex. She's a Seeker. Through and through."

Her father makes a noise that strangles any words he's trying to find.

They walk down to the beach where two boats await them in the shallows. Already stocked with food, clothing, seeds, and a thick cloth that can be used to make a tent, the boats look heavy, sitting lower in the water than Mercy would like.

Gust and Nikita climb aboard first, leaving their parents weeping on the beach.

"For Bryan!" Gust calls to them.

His mother smiles proudly through her tears. "For Bryan!"

Siena is next, hesitating but then joining Gust and Nikita. Mercy watches in silence as Sam tears herself out of Nova's shaking arms to give Kian a long hug. Hawk hovers nearby, waiting to help her into the boat. Luca says something to him and Hawk nods a reply before heading toward the second boat. It seems he's prepared to let Luca help Sam this one last time.

"You need to stay strong together," Mercy says to her

parents, hoping their bond is enough to see them through what's going to be a difficult time.

With a heavy heart, she hugs them both and they stand there as a solid unit of three. The way they've always been since Mercy was born. She can only hope to fulfil her father's wish and replicate that with a family of her own one day.

Tearing herself away, she has no words left. She gives them both a tearful smile and goes to the boat. Hawk is waiting for her and lifts her over the water, climbing in after her.

"Thanks," she says.

"We're going to be okay." He puts a hand on her shoulder.

She nods, even though he can't possibly know that.

Luca lifts Sam into the boat next, calling to those gathered on the beach that he'll push them out to sea. Diesel does the same with the second boat.

"Luca!" calls Mercy, leaning over the side of the boat and reaching out a hand. She can't go without saying goodbye. She can't be upset with him. This *can't* be how it ends.

He hesitates and for a moment she thinks he's going to leave her hanging. Please, let this not be the last memory she has of him.

But then he wades over to her and takes her hand.

"We could have been really great," she says, unable to stop her tears.

"I know." He draws her hand to his lips. "I know."

Mercy's heart cracks and breaks. None of this is right. How can he know how amazing what they have between them is, yet let her get away like this? He could have tried harder in the tests. He could have been a Seeker.

He *chose* not to be.

Dropping her hand, Luca pushes the boat deeper into the water. Diesel has already returned to shore. The acid must be stinging Luca by now, but he's not showing it.

"Bye, Luca!" calls Sam.

He gives Sam a long, hard stare, his expression impossible to read. Anguish? Worry? Regret?

Mercy shuffles over to Sam and holds her hand. "We're going to be okay," she says, repeating Hawk's words.

With one final shove, Luca launches the boat forward.

And...leaps aboard.

He grins at Mercy and Sam. "You didn't really think I was going to let you leave without me, did you?"

LUCA

"*L*uca!" Sam gasps in astonishment. "You're not a Seeker!"

Luca picks up an oar. "I didn't see a sign on the boat that says Seekers Only."

"But...but..." Sam splutters, her rule-driven brain trying to process her brother coming along, anyway. She glances over his shoulder at the disappearing shoreline of Askala then snaps her mouth shut.

Luca's made his decision. Passing or no passing, he's coming anyway.

Hawk nods at Luca solemnly. "Good call."

Luca hides his surprise. He wasn't expecting any sort of welcome from Hawk, but he's obviously realized that having Luca around could be useful...despite their differences of opinion.

His gaze falls on Mercy. Her eyes are alight in a way that has his heart jack-knifing.

"You came," she murmurs.

Luca swallows. It was a split-second decision. Sam was in the boat, leaving.

Mercy was in the boat, making the impossible seem possible.

As he leaped in, he'd told himself he was doing it to keep them safe. Now, as his eyes dip to Mercy's lips, he's not so sure that was his only motivation.

Her tongue flicks out, moistening them. His gaze darts up, locking with hers. Luca wonders how everyone else can't see the awareness crackling between them.

Sweet Terra, what has he done?

"Hey," Gust calls from the adjacent boat. "The boats are uneven now!"

Four in the boat Luca just jumped in, with only Gust, Siena and Nikita in the other. Luca sighs.

Now he's really wondering what he's done...

"We'll stay close together this time. It'll be a slower trip because we have the supplies, so we'll need to take turns rowing."

Luca studies the stacks of urns and packages wrapped in hemp. The water laps only a few inches below the lip of the boat. The leaders obviously wanted them to have everything they needed.

Gust turns to Siena and Nikita. "Let's share the load of rowing," he suggests. "Siena and I can start."

Sam frowns. "Why is he repeating you, Luca?"

Gust's face takes on a pleasing shade of tomato. Luca's lips twitch as he suppresses a smile. Some days, Sam says just the right things without intending to.

Luca shuffles to the middle of the boat, clambering around the piles of supplies. He picks up an oar, surprised to find Mercy settling beside him with an oar of her own. Silently, they start paddling, Askala fading behind them as the afternoon sun invites them to sail into their new future.

This isn't the first time Luca's left Askala, but this time, it feels...big. Life changing.

Life threatening.

He glances at the three others in the boat with him. They're all a little pale, all avoiding looking at everything they're leaving behind.

Yep. The trajectory of their destinies have taken a new turn. And have just become undeniably entwined.

Just as Luca predicted, it's slow going. Mercy watches Luca's paddling technique, her brow crinkling as she works on replicating it. It's not long before they've established a rhythm. Dip. Stroke. Pull. Mercy smiles at him triumphantly and Luca's returning grin leaps up before he can stop it. It's like their bodies intuitively follow the other's cadence.

Twice, Hawk offers to take over, but Mercy shakes her head. Even Sam tries once. But when they see the determined set of Mercy's chin, they face forward, shoulder touching shoulder as they talk quietly between themselves. Well, Sam talks, Hawk nods.

Mercy glances at Luca. "You don't like to be predictable, do you?"

Luca snorts. "*I* don't know what I'm about to do most of the time."

"What changed?"

The Falcon is dead.

Luca's hands tighten around the oar. Those four words changed everything.

He shrugs. "The Outlands no longer had the same hold on me."

Mercy's voice drops. "Is it because you realized we'll be... free?"

"Free?"

Mercy turns to him, her gaze intense. "We can make our own rules in the Newlands. No parents. No one thinks we're cousins..."

Luca's eyes widen. It never crossed his mind, but then again, he doesn't tend to think that far ahead. It seems Mercy has.

"But..."

His words fade away. Is there a but?

Mercy arches a brow, challenging him to find one.

Luca realizes he's stopped rowing, and he quickly resumes, matching his strokes to Mercy's. He stares straight ahead, conscious his heart is leaping like a frog in his chest. "What are you suggesting, Mercy?"

She shrugs, her shoulder brushing his. "Maybe it's time you planned for a future, Luca."

The two of them. Starting a new life in the Newlands. No longer defined by their families. Luca freezes.

Surely, they couldn't...

He turns back to Mercy. She has 'we totally can' written all over her beautiful face.

"Luca." Hawk's quiet voice intrudes on their hopeful bubble. "What's that?"

Luca squints in the direction Hawk's pointing, wondering what he's seen. It's too soon for them to be approaching the Newlands. The ocean around them is calm, sparkling as the rays of the afternoon sun glint and glimmer on the surface. At first, he doesn't see anything.

Then, he sees it.

An unmistakable mottled fin.

"Hawk! Take over the other oar!"

Gust shoots to his feet on the other boat. "What? What is it?"

It's Siena who answers the question for him, her voice little more than a horrified mutter. "Leatherskin."

Hawk's already clambering over to Luca. Without needing to be asked, Mercy quickly swaps. She moves to sit beside Sam, both their gazes focused on the approaching shark.

The leatherskin has seen them. And it probably had long

before they realized it was there. Its fin slices through the water, carving a razor sharp line toward them.

Luca turns to Gust and the others, waving his hand frantically. "Bring your boat closer!"

Nikita and Siena paddle furiously, the boat zigzagging erratically because they're so out of time. Gust has his hands on his head, his focus totally on the silent, deadly predator coming their way.

The one that's found its prey.

Mercy grips the side of the boat, only to jerk her hands back. The ocean around them has suddenly become far more dangerous than just the acid water. "Breathe, guys. You need to row together."

Nikita and Siena pause, glancing at each other. As if they've made a silent agreement, they plunge their oars into the water simultaneously.

Luca lifts his oar. "Get ready," he mutters to Hawk. "When the shark gets close, we want to make sure it regrets it."

Hawk nods once, his jaw set. "Damn right it will."

A quick glance at the other boat shows them only a few feet away. "Hurry!" Luca calls. "We need to join the two boats—it'll make us look bigger."

And less like prey-sized afternoon tea.

Gust tears at his hair. "Paddle faster!"

Siena and Nikita's faces are pale with terror, their brows low with determination. The gap closes, their boats bumping together only to bounce back before anyone can grab a hold.

The leatherskin seems to know what they're planning, because it aims for the space between the two vessels. It slices forward, unrelenting in its speed. Before they can come any closer, it spears between them.

The side of its massive body hits Luca's boat, slamming into it with the force of a battering ram. Sam screams as the boat tilts wildly, water sloshing over the side in waves. The second boat careens to the side, lurching back and forth, too.

The shark's gone before Luca can take a swing at it.

"Hurry!" screams Gust, reaching toward them desperately. The shark has pushed them further apart, meaning there's lost ground to recover.

The leatherskin continues to swim away, but Luca knows it's just getting a run up. As he expected, it spins around a few yards away. Shooting forward, it slices toward them again.

The second boat bumps against their side and Mercy scrabbles over to it. "Pass me one of your oars!"

Siena jabs the wooden paddle toward Mercy, who grabs it with both hands and digs her feet into the side, bracing herself. Sam joins her, wrapping her own hands around it. On the other side, Siena and Nikita do the same. Gust is more preoccupied with yanking out his own hair and staring at the fast approaching predator.

"Sit down!" Luca shouts.

But it's too late. The shark plows into the place where the two boats join, rocking both with the power of thousands of pounds of weight. Mercy and Sam's arms strain as they fight to keep the boats joined.

Gust is knocked sideways, his arms waving like windmills. He stumbles backward and trips on a stack of supplies. His eyes widen with terror as he realizes he's about to fall into the water.

With the bloodthirsty shark.

Siena releases the end of the oar she was holding and leaps forward, grabbing Gust by the shirt. For a split second, he seesaws, teetering between the safety of the boat and the danger of the sea.

Between life and death.

But a hard tug from Siena and Gust stumbles back into the boat. He falls onto all fours, drawing in lungfuls of breath like he's realized how precious the act itself is.

The next slam from the leatherskin rocks both boats. Nikita grimaces as her hands strain to hold her end of the oar. The boat sways violently and more water splashes over the side, sinking it even further.

"Lose some of the weight," Hawk calls.

"Are you okay with this?" Sam shouts to Mercy.

Mercy nods, her face resolute. She doesn't plan on releasing the oar if she can help it.

Sam throws back a hemp cover to find a stack of clay urns. Gust must've done the same in their boat, because he starts frantically throwing them into the ocean.

The leatherskin doesn't swim as far away this time. It twists in the water, barreling back at them. Luca braces himself, pressing his feet into the bottom of the boat as he lifts his oar.

The moment the shark hits them, he pummels it, slamming the oar over and over, Hawk doing the same beside him. Sometimes, he punches through nothing but frothing water. A few of the hits thud as they strike hard flesh.

"Their eyes and gill areas are the most sensitive," shouts Sam.

Suddenly, an urn flings past Luca's head, landing in the water with a splash.

"Yes, Sam!" calls Mercy.

Sam's throwing the urns at the shark like rocks. Luca turns back to the shark, knowing it's probably not going to do much. Especially when most of them are going wide of their mark.

This time, the shark doesn't leave. It slams into the boats again and again.

As timber creaks and splinters, Luca realizes the boats aren't going to hold up against this assault much longer. Nor are Mercy, Siena and Nikita going to be able to keep the two boats together. Once the shark separates them, it's only a matter of time before one of them tips.

On the next attack, the shark rears out of the water, its

cavernous mouth wide open and exposing rows upon rows of dagger-like teeth.

Gust screams. Nikita tumbles backward with the force and releases her end of the oar. Siena cries out as it's yanked from her hands. The boats split apart, rocking wildly and taking on more water despite some of the supplies being thrown overboard.

It's Luca's boat that the shark decides to target. Again, it thrashes as it leaps, mouth open and ready to clamp onto anything it can find.

Three things happen simultaneously.

Mercy grabs one of the urns now that she's free, throwing it at the shark. It sails into its mouth as if it was a black hole sucking it in and lodges it in the leatherskin's throat.

Hawk leaps forward and spears his oar in straight after it, jamming it between the razor sharp teeth.

And Luca's oar slams into the side of the shark's head, rupturing the beady eye that had pinned them with its hungry gaze.

The shark jerks and thrashes, but the damage has been done. It can't close its mouth. It's choking. And it's lost an eye.

It sinks, a ribbon of blood trailing after it into the depths of the ocean.

Luca looks around, shock and relief coursing through him. "Is everyone okay?"

Three mute nods answer him from Sam, Hawk, and Mercy. Gust has collapsed into a heap, his eyes wide with shock. Siena and Nikita are pale as they each whisper "yes."

Hawk slides over to Sam. "Good thinking with the urns."

She smiles shakily at him. "Nice job jamming an oar into a shark's mouth." She lifts a trembling hand but before she can touch Hawk, he's hauled her into his arms. They hold each other silently, their breathing slowly becoming one.

Luca sinks onto the bench seat, his heart rate still a rapid fire staccato in his chest. That was a close one.

There's a rustle and he finds Mercy slipping in beside him. "Are you okay?"

Luca almost tells her he's fine. That he doesn't need anyone to look out for him. But he doesn't. In fact, right now he wants to kiss Mercy. Feel her warmth, her pulse, her sweet, intoxicating energy. As if that's the only thing that could really assure him that anything's okay.

He swallows. Then nods. "I'm just glad no one was hurt."

Or killed.

Mercy slips her hand into his, clamping on tightly as she wraps her other hand around their clasped ones. "We did good."

Luca tucks a strand of glossy hair behind Mercy's ear, allowing himself a tender press of his lips on her temple. "We did."

Clearing his throat, he looks around. The boats are sitting higher in the water now that some of the supplies are gone. Luca wasn't sure what was in those urns, but it must've been heavy.

"Let's get going."

There's a murmur of assent, everyone no doubt wanting to be far away from the dying shark as possible. It's only a matter of time before others of its species arrive to cannibalize it.

Sam leans down and shuffles around in the equipment at their feet. With a small smile she holds up another oar. "They packed a spare."

She passes it to Hawk and this time Mercy doesn't object. They need to get back sooner rather than later.

Adrenaline still buzzing through his veins, Luca starts rowing again. Beside them, Gust takes one of the oars, suddenly far more interested in getting them to their destination.

The trip will be quicker now. Fewer supplies to weigh them down.

No one wanting to be in the ocean any longer than they have to.

When Luca sees the hazy slip of land that's the Newlands, he's almost relieved.

Except then he remembers there are far more dangers there than in the ocean.

This is the new life they've all chosen.

And it's already begun.

HAWK

*T*he Seekers touch sand at the Newlands and Hawk breathes a sigh.

They made it.

He leaps out of the boat and drags it up onto the beach. Luca helps with the other boat and they glance at each other, the concern in their eyes doing all the talking for them. They're by no means out of danger.

The others climb out and Gust makes a show of crouching down and kissing the sand while Nikita shakes her head.

"I can't believe we're alive," says Siena. "That was a genius idea to throw the urns at the leatherskin. Who thought of that?"

"Sam," Hawk and Luca say at once.

Sam pulls back her shoulders and smiles. "Thankfully everyone else is a better shot than me. It was teamwork."

"Did you see how I slammed that beast with my oar?" Gust stands up and stretches. "I weakened it nicely for the fatal blow."

"Whatever you say." Luca rolls his eyes, shifting the boat slightly so it sits better on the sand.

"So!" Sam claps her hands and Hawk notices how pale she is.

Although, if she's feeling unwell, she seems determined not to show it. "What do we do now?"

The Seekers all look to each other. This is the moment they dreamed of. The one they all worked so hard to make sure they were a part of. And now that it's here, nobody seems to know quite what to do with it.

"We need to build a shelter," says Gust, looking at the clouds.

"We need water first." Nikita climbs back into the boat and shuffles through the supplies. "And something to eat."

"I think we need to talk to Grace," says Mercy, squinting into the trees. "Food and shelter will be kind of useless if people start throwing spears at us."

Hawk nods and is just about to say that Mercy's right when he notices again how pale Sam is. Could she be getting dehydrated? Maybe Nikita's right. They're going to need water. And urgently. He's determined not to have a repeat performance of Sam collapsing on him. She hid how unwell she was feeling last time in the Proving. He has no doubt she'd do it again.

"Umm." Nikita stands up in the boat, hands on hips. "Guys!"

"What's happened?" Gust asks.

"No water, that's what's happened. You threw out all the urns!"

Hawk feels disappointment crawl down his spine with icy fingers. They don't have water.

"What did you want us to do?" Sam snaps at Nikita. "Leave the urns on the boat so we could all become shark food?"

"It's nobody's fault," says Mercy, putting a hand on Sam's back. "It happened. Arguing about it won't help. Anybody got any ideas?"

"We could catch rainwater?" Nikita suggests.

"Except it's not raining," Mercy points out.

"We could ask the Outlanders," says Gust.

"The less dependent we are on them, the better." Hawk doesn't like the idea of asking Corbin for anything.

"I agree." Sam touches her cheek, dropping her hand when she realizes what she's doing.

Hawk looks to Luca. He wasn't supposed to be here. But he is. So, they may as well use his knowledge. "Any suggestions?"

Luca swallows as all faces turn to him. "Hawk's right. We need to be as independent as possible. Which means we should set up camp in the forest close to here to save having to lug our supplies too far."

"That doesn't solve our water problem." Nikita plants her hands on her hips.

"We'll dig a well," says Luca. "I've seen them in the Outlands."

"A well?" Gust laughs. "If we dig one of those here, all we're likely to hit is salty water."

"Not necessarily." Sam's dark eyes are alight with possibility. "Freshwater has a lower density than seawater. Given the amount of rain the Newlands gets, the freshwater will have absorbed into the soil and formed a layer on top of the seawater. If we dig down—"

"I'm going to get started on the shelter," says Gust, clearly making a point that he's not going to be bossed around. "Let me know when your well's ready. I'm thirsty."

"Fine," Sam and Mercy say at once.

Hawk smirks. The idea of having Gust out of the way is an attractive one.

"Where do we dig?" Hawk stretches his arms as he prepares for more work. They're a little sore from the rowing but he should be fine. He can push through.

"Sam can help you find a good spot," says Luca. "While Mercy and I go to see if we can find Grace. We're the ones she trusts."

"*I'm* the one she trusts," Mercy corrects.

"Would you like to go on your own then?" Luca cocks a brow at Mercy.

Mercy looks stricken. "No! I'm good. You can come."

"Be careful, Mercy," Hawk tells his cousin, not too sure about this idea.

"Careful's my middle name." She winks at him.

"What's your last name then?" he asks, rolling his eyes.

Mercy laughs. "You're so old-fashioned, Hawk!"

"Come on." Luca takes a step away, and Mercy follows. "We'll just take a quick look around and report back here so I can give you a hand with the well."

Hawk nods, watching them leave, unable to shake a sense of unease. There's so much they need to do. And it all needs to be done first. Maybe splitting up really is the best idea for now.

"They'll be okay." Sam squeezes his hand. "Luca knows what he's doing."

"I still can't believe he came with us."

"Neither can I." Sam makes no move to release his hand and he's glad for the comfort. "But I should have guessed. It's a very Luca kind of thing to do."

"Do you think he'll stay around?" asks Siena, reminding Hawk they're not alone, no matter how much it always feels like they're the only people in the world when he's with Sam.

"Of course, he'll stay," Sam shoots back, but Hawk can't help wondering if her confidence is misplaced. There's no rule keeping Luca here. That same sense of rebellion that brought him here could just as easily see him disappearing again.

"Let's get digging!" Nikita throws a shovel from the boat onto the sand followed by a bucket.

"We need to go where there's likely to be an aquifer close to the surface." Sam drops Hawk's hand and snaps into business mode as she picks up the bucket. "It means we won't have to dig so deep."

Hawk scratches his chin. "What's an aquifer?"

"The layer of freshwater under the surface," says Sam. "Also known as a lens. If we're lucky it might only be around ten feet down."

"Ten feet!" cries Gust. "We'll die of thirst by the time you hit water."

"If you can get the shelter built before you die that would be great." Hawk picks up the shovel. "Come, on, Sam. Show me where to dig."

"I'll help Gust." Siena gives Hawk a look, which isn't too hard to interpret. The moment Gust is left alone with the supplies, he'll start helping himself. They can't let that happen.

"Why don't you stay as well, Nikita," Hawk suggests.

Nikita nods. "We'll unload the boats and find a good spot to set up camp."

Hawk's pleased with the way this has worked out. Now he gets some time alone with Sam away from the air pollution that comes out of Gust's mouth.

They walk up the beach and into the trees. Sam scans the ground, her eyes sweeping the forest floor.

"What are we looking for?" he asks.

"A bit of a clearing would be ideal." She turns left and moves around some overgrown bushes. "If we can find a section of grass that looks especially lush then that will be our best bet. We don't want to go too far. Best to stay roughly close to where the others will be setting up camp."

They make their way through the trees, pausing at a few potential sites until Sam settles on a spot she declares to be perfect.

The grass doesn't look all that lush to Hawk, but it will have to do. Sam needs water. They *all* need water. This is the single best thing they can be doing with their time right now. There's no way the Outlanders are going to spare them anything going by the welcome they gave them last time. And the worst thing Hawk can imagine would be having to row back to Askala and admit defeat. They're supposed to be the best of the best. What hope does Askala have if even they can't make a go of it here?

Sam sets down the bucket she's been carrying and points at

exactly where she wants Hawk to dig. "Hopefully it's not too far down."

He drives the tip of the shovel into the soil, pleased to find it's soft. Tossing the dirt away, he goes back for more, aware he's really going to be in need of a drink when he's done here, or he'll be the one who dehydrates this time.

"How wide do we make it?" he asks.

"Wide enough for you to fit inside as you keep digging," she says.

"We'll need a rope then," he says. "So, you can haul up the dirt when I get to the bottom."

"I'm on it!" Sam dashes away in the direction of the beach and Hawk keeps digging. It's hot, thirsty work, and before long he strips off his shirt, trying anything he can to reduce the feeling of suffocation. It's bad enough with the pendant tied around his neck.

Feeling a little better, he scoops out more dry soil. According to Sam he should start seeing some moisture in the soil when he gets about six feet down. If they're lucky. He can't be any more than two or three feet down right now at most.

"Hello."

Hawk gets such a shock at the sound of a woman's voice, he almost stabs himself in the foot with his shovel. Spinning around, he sees Grace watching him.

"I didn't mean to startle you," she says, venturing a little closer.

The sunlight breaks through the canopy and caresses on her face. Her long braid is draped over her shoulder and she smiles at Hawk with dark eyes. He has to blink at how dazzling she looks. She has a different beauty to Sam's. It's more obvious. More...dangerous somehow. It makes sense that the Commander claimed her as his own.

"What are you doing here?" she asks, stepping closer.

"Digging a—"

"I mean what are you doing here?" She sweeps her arms out wide.

"Oh." He leans on his shovel, crossing an arm over his chest, wishing he hadn't taken off his shirt. He feels so exposed. "A small group of us came back."

"Corbin won't like this." Grace shakes her head.

"We come in peace." Hawk lets his shovel fall to hold up his palms, noticing that Grace's eyes dip to his chest and hover for a few moments before being drawn back up to his face.

"How's my daughter?" she asks. "Did Charity come with you?"

He shakes his head. "She's safe. She's being well looked after."

"Are you sure?" She narrows her eyes at him.

"I'm sure! She's living with Mercy's parents. She's totally fine."

"Then why are you here?" Grace asks.

"We come in peace," he says again. "We want to make peace. With you. With Corbin. With everyone."

Grace nods as she mulls over this. "For what purpose?"

He frowns, wondering how much he should tell her. Where's Mercy when he needs her? She'd know exactly what to say.

"Did Luca and Mercy find you?" he asks, remembering that they should be here with Grace. "They were looking for you."

She shakes her head.

"We need to find them." Hawk picks up his shirt and slips it over his head, the act of dressing himself in front of this woman strangely feeling almost as intimate as if he were undressing. Her eyes never leave him. Surely, she's not checking him out?

"What were you digging?" she asks, pointing at his shovel.

"A well. We need water. We didn't think you—"

She tips back her head and laughs. "You can't dig a well here! We're surrounded by saltwater."

Hawk shakes his head. "The rainwater collects in a kind of lens thing that sits on top of the water that's..." He pauses, wishing Sam were here to explain. "If we can dig down deep enough, we should be able to access it."

Grace looks at him in astonishment, coming to stand beside him to inspect his work.

"Keep digging," she says. "We have to know if this is true."

"Of course, it's true." Sam steps out from behind a tree, a long rope snaked around her shoulders. "The aquifer should be just down here. With some luck, the soil will have acted as a filter for the rain, and it should be safe to drink. Especially if there's limestone in it."

"You remember Sam?" Hawk asks Grace.

Grace nods. "The clever one. I remember her."

There's more movement behind the trees and Hawk is surprised to see Luca and Mercy right behind Sam.

"Grace, we were looking for you!" says Luca. "I'm glad Hawk found you."

"I found him actually," says Grace smiling. "And you're lucky it was only me. If my husband found you, you'd already be back on your boats heading home."

"Not this time," says Mercy. "We're here to stay."

"So I'm told." Grace frowns. "How many of you are there? Is this it?"

"There are three more back on the beach," says Sam. "We mean you no harm."

"I've also been told that, by..." She turns her gaze to Hawk. "I'm so sorry, I forget your name."

"Hawk," says Sam before he gets a chance. "His name's Hawk."

"A name that suits." Grace smiles in a way that makes Hawk unsure if she means it as a compliment. But she's given them no reason not to trust her so far. In fact, she's the best hope they have.

Luca clears his throat. "Grace, what are the chances of the

Commander allowing us to stay here? We have trades we can make, information we can share."

"Well...a few minutes ago I would have said zero. However, Hawk tells me that you know how to dig a well."

Hawk shuffles his feet. "We don't exactly—"

"That's right," says Sam. "We can get you freshwater. Is that what you need?"

"That's very much what we need," says Grace.

"Keep digging, Hawk." Sam picks up the shovel and thrusts it at him. "Please?"

He grins, unable to help falling in love with this complicated girl all over again. Grace may be beautiful, but she's not a patch on his Sam.

He slides the shovel into the soil and continues his work with renewed focus. He's now not just digging a well, he's digging for their survival. This could be the best bargaining chip they've got. The difference between life and death out here.

In the background he can hear Mercy telling Grace about Charity, but he ignores them, focusing on his work until he's down to his chest in the hole and his hands start to blister.

"Let me take a turn," says Luca, noticing him slowing down.

Hoisting himself out, he passes the shovel to Luca with a nod.

"If you can dig it into the bucket, I'll lift it out," he suggests. "Might be easier."

Luca climbs into the hole and continues the work with impressive agility while Hawk holds the rope of the bucket and waits, trying to ignore the burning thirst in the back of his throat.

"What do you do for water at the moment?" he asks Grace, hoping there's a back-up plan on this island. Surely, they must be drinking something to have stayed alive this long.

"Rainwater," she says. "But it's not easy to purify and can get challenging in dry spells. It's a precious resource."

Hawk nods, turning his attention back to Luca, and the hauling of the bucket begins.

"They're getting heavier," he says after a few dozen buckets. "The soil must be getting damper."

"Sure is!" Luca calls up to him. He's almost completely inside the hole he's digging now. "There's a small puddle at the bottom."

Sam's face lights up at this news. "I knew it was the best spot!"

"You're a good Seeker," he tells her, smiling proudly, hoping this will chase away any doubts she had about her abilities.

A few more buckets, and now the soil is coming up wet.

"Can we drink straight from the well?" Grace asks, peering in.

"We could," says Sam. "But safer to boil it first."

"We'll take a bucket to the Round House," says Grace. "You can present it to Corbin as a peace-offering and he can boil it there."

"Round House?" asks Mercy.

"The place where you spoke to Corbin last time."

"Of course." Mercy gives Grace a tight-lipped smile and glances at Sam's still-bruised cheek. It seems she hasn't forgotten the greeting Corbin gave them, either. They can only hope this time will be different.

"Are you sure you want to go through with this?" Grace asks Mercy, her eyes filling with fear. "He can be... argumentative. It might be safer for you to go home."

Mercy shakes her head. "This is home now."

Hawk tears his gaze away to empty out another bucket onto his growing pile of dirt.

"Who's the Falcon?" Mercy asks.

Luca curses from inside the well and Hawk isn't sure who to give his attention to first.

"Are you okay?" he calls down to Luca.

"Just stabbed my toe with the shovel," he calls back. "All good."

"What do you know about the Falcon?" Grace asks Mercy in a hushed tone.

Mercy shrugs. "Nothing. Just that he's dead."

"Where did you hear that?" Hawk notices Grace leaning forward just slightly, in the way people do when they're more interested in something than they're letting on.

"There was a n—"

"I think that's it!" shouts Luca. "I'm knee-deep in water down here."

The others join Hawk at the edge of the well, and they look down to see Luca holding a bucket of water above his head.

"Pull it up carefully," he calls to Hawk. "Once we know it's safe to drink, we can come back and dig this out a little more."

Hawk brings the water back up to ground level and sets it down, his mouth aching at the sight of that delicious cool liquid sloshing around.

Sam dips her finger in the water and licks it.

Hawk frowns at her. "Is that safe?"

"Just checking if it's salty." She closes her eyes as she tastes it. "It's not."

"Thank Terra for that!" says Mercy.

"Need a hand up, Luca?" Hawk leans over the well.

"Nope. I made a couple of footholds." Luca hoists himself up and out of the well with ease.

Hawk is impressed. He's not sure he would have had that much foresight if he'd continued digging.

"We should get the others," says Sam.

But Grace shakes her head. "Leave them for now. Corbin will be less threatened if it's only the four of you. They're safer back there."

Hawk has to physically bite down on his tongue to stop himself suggesting that Sam return to wait with them. She's a

Seeker. She's got this! He has to stop hovering over her like some kind of oversized guardian angel.

Grace smiles at the bucket. "Well done, Hawk. I'm impressed."

Luca coughs loudly, but Grace doesn't move her eyes to him.

Hawk isn't sure how comfortable he is with the prolonged gazes Grace keeps sending his way. "It was Luca's idea to dig this well. And Sam found the perfect spot."

"The clever one." Grace smiles at Sam. "Now, are you ready?"

Hawk picks up the bucket and nods. "We're ready."

"I'd wish you luck," says Grace. "But I'm afraid you're going to need far more than just that. Let's hope this water is enough to please the Commander."

"It will be enough," says Sam.

"We don't know that," says Mercy, her voice faltering.

"It *will* be enough." Hawk puts a gentle hand on Mercy's back, hoping he's right. Because if he's not, they're all as good as dead.

SAM

*G*race pauses outside the Round House. She glances over her shoulder at the four Seekers, her brows pulled low. Muttered voices rumble from within as thick smoke pours out the top. "Corbin must be meeting with his men again. I'll go in first and let them know you're back."

She slips through the doorway before anyone can respond.

Sam chews on her lip. Hopefully Grace is saying a whole bunch of good things. And surely Corbin is going to see the advantage of having them here. She glances at the bucket of water beside Hawk's feet. Their peace offering.

Please let that be enough.

It's not Grace who steps back out, but a burly man, his naked tattooed chest gleaming with sweat. His expression is definitely not welcoming. "The Commander said you may enter."

A quick glance among each other and they all nod. This is what they came here for. Well, technically not Luca. But as he shifts closer to Mercy, Sam's glad he came, even if it meant completely disregarding the rules.

They've already decided it should be Mercy who'll carry the bucket of water. Luca was the one who escaped his ties, Hawk's size can be seen as a threat, and Corbin's already lost his temper with Sam.

It means Mercy will be the first to step through the doors. The first to discover what their welcome is going to be.

Luca is next. Sam follows her brother, conscious of Hawk just behind her. Everything her parents warned her about the Newlands flashes through her mind. These people are planning something. They're not open to working together.

They just want to take.

Squaring her shoulders, Sam steps through the door. This is their chance to prove there's good in these people. In everyone, no matter where they're born. The irony is that it's her parents who instilled this belief in her.

Mercy's stopped only a few feet in the door and as Sam's eyes adjust to the smoky interior, she realizes why.

Just like last time, men and women line the walls of the circular hut. But this time, they're standing. And already holding their spears.

Sam swallows, telling herself at least they're pointing at the ceiling and not them. That's progress...

Mercy clears her throat. "Thank you for agreeing to see us again, Commander."

Corbin inflates his chest. The silver statue of Ronan gleams in the firelight across from him. Grace is standing behind him, her face downcast and her hands clasped. He pins Mercy with a glare, not responding.

Luca moves to stand on Mercy's right, and Sam does the same on her left, Hawk her shadow on Sam's other side.

"We come in peace." Mercy places the bucket on the ground. "And bring you this water as a gift."

Luca nods. "We dug a well. There will be more than enough water for everyone."

There's a murmur around the room but Sam can't tell whether that's a good thing or not. Usually, she'd turn to Hawk so he could tell her, but she knows she needs to keep her gaze straight ahead. There's no room for uncertainty when you're a Seeker.

Waiting to see whether you'll be welcomed.

Corbin's gaze flickers to the bucket. "Drink it."

Mercy hesitates, and it seems to be exactly what he was expecting.

His hand tightens around his spear. "As I suspected. It's poisoned."

Sam reels back. Why would they do that? They've told Corbin they come in peace.

Mercy squats down, her hand dipping into the bucket. Except Sam is already listing all the microbial contaminants that could be floating in there. *Escherichia coli, Salmonella typhi, Legionella* species, and that's just the pathogens! Enteroviruses can persist in water supplies for long periods, along with parasites such as protozoa and helminths.

Sam leaps forward, her hand outstretched. "We need to boil it first."

Corbin's eyes blaze as he turns to her. "You." His chest inflates all over again. "You do not know when to stay silent."

Sam shakes her head. "I'm thinking of everyone's health. Boiling the water kills microorganisms that can cause disease." Sam glances at the blazing fire. They might as well use it for something useful. "It would only take a few minutes."

There's a movement beside Corbin as someone joins him. Sam recognizes Raiden from their first visit, the Commander's son. He whispers something in Corbin's ear.

Corbin nods. "You shall drink it." He lifts his spear, pointing it at Sam.

Knowing she has no choice, Sam kneels beside the bucket. She tries not to scrunch up her face as she dips her hand in. If microscopes still existed, she'd be able to show Corbin exactly what's swimming around in this water.

Hawk lands beside her, scooping up a handful and drinking it. "See? Not poisonous."

Corbin shakes his head. "I want her to drink it."

Sam throws a grateful glance toward Hawk. At least this way, if there's anything in the water, they'll be sick together. Without letting herself imagine the single-celled animals she might be ingesting, Sam scoops up a handful and drinks.

She sits back, acknowledging that the coolness sliding down her parched throat is a welcome sensation. As if to prove a point, she bends over and has another mouthful. She's already learned what happens if she becomes dehydrated, after all.

"See?" she smiles at Corbin. "Although, I'd still recommend boiling it."

Corbin glances around the room and Sam's relieved to see a few nods. He thumps the end of his spear on the ground. "My daughter is unwell in her hut. Water will help her get better, won't it, wife?"

Grace nods meekly, not looking up.

Sam has to stop her eyes from widening. Corbin thinks Charity's still here? What will it mean when he discovers she's not?

"The water is our gift to you," Luca says quietly, but in a way that seems to have the words carrying through the entire hut. "As a token of peace."

Suddenly, Corbin sneers. "Or we could kill you and take it for ourselves."

As if on cue, every spear is raised and pointed at them.

Hawk and Luca tense simultaneously. Mercy seems to shrink. Sam's heart rate spikes, each sharpened tip feeling like it's only inches away.

They have to have faith, she tells herself.

Sam steps forward. "But then you won't know where else you can dig wells."

Raiden's brows shoot up as Corbin's crash down. Grace hasn't moved.

"You can have this bucket, or we can ensure the village always has water." Sam extends her hand. "We have a lot of knowledge to share that could be very useful to you," she promises, hoping she's not lying.

Grace moves for the first time since they entered. Her hand flickers, and if everything wasn't so still and tense in the hut, Sam's not even sure she would've seen it.

But nothing happens, meaning the tension is now thicker than the smoke. Sam can feel the energy vibrating off Hawk. He's ready to defend her. She's hoping Corbin understands what an advantageous arrangement this could be...

Corbin lowers his spear, thumping the base into the ground again. "Very well. You may build a shelter at the edge of our village. We will see how useful you will be."

Sam blinks. They've done it?

Raiden steps forward. "And to celebrate your arrival, we shall have a feast tonight!"

The spears around them thump the ground in an uneven frenzy. It seems the people of the village are glad to hear that.

Sam's gaze flies to Hawk's. They've done it!

Hawk doesn't move, but his eyes smile in a way that has Sam's heart rate tripping all over again.

Stepping back, she slips her hand into his. For some reason, this moment feels...more because they were here together. As if this was the first step in the future they're building.

And it was a success.

Mercy nods. "Thank you, Commander. We're grateful for your hospitality."

"I'll give you a tour," offers Raiden.

Leaving the bucket where it is, they exit the hut, following him into the sunshine. Once they're outside, Sam pulls in a deep breath. Sweet, clean air fills her lungs and she can just imagine all the smoke particles already coating her entire respiratory system. And each of those flecks of ash were once a living fragment of a beautiful tree.

There is much these people can learn from them.

Raiden turns to them, not smiling, but not looking unfriendly either. "Are you sure you can dig more wells? Ones that will have water we can drink?"

Sam nods firmly. "Once you find the right spot, it's just a matter of digging."

"Says the one who didn't have to dig," grumbles Luca.

Sam raises a brow. "I would've been happy to dig," she says archly.

Raiden looks among them. "You are all family?"

Mercy shakes her head vehemently. "Hawk and Sam aren't related, neither are Luca and I."

Sam opens her mouth to clarify their genealogy, but Mercy has already pulled up a blinding smile. "A tour sounds lovely."

With another quick scan of their foursome, Raiden turns and walks away from the hut. They've only followed him for a few yards when he turns and extends his arms. "This is our village."

They all turn around to look out over the motley scattering of huts radiating out from the central Round House. This village is their new home. A village built from the trees that used to stand here, desecrating the ecosystem that now doesn't exist. There's nothing but beaten dust between each of the huts. The place must turn into a giant mud pool when it rains.

Raiden sweeps his arms in the direction of the small shelters. "Each family now has one of their own," he says proudly. "And they've withstood every storm since we've arrived."

Sam can already see Luca assessing the joins holding the huts together. Knowing they need to learn as much as they can about their new home, she smiles at Raiden. "And your kitchens? The dining hall?"

Raiden looks at her quizzically. "Each family cooks for themselves. And eats in their hut." He grins. "Which is why this feast is so special."

"It's very generous of you," murmurs Mercy.

Sam turns back to surveying the huts. "So, each hut has its own kitchen? And some sort of plumbing?"

Raiden frowns. "They have a cooking fire. And we have the forest to use for our...personal needs."

"There's no sanitation?" Sam tries to keep the horror out of her voice, but she knows she fails when Hawk moves closer to her.

Raiden's brows sink even deeper. "We're too busy hunting for food and collecting water."

Realizing she could be about to offend the very people they're trying to befriend, Sam places a hand on Raiden's arm. "It would've taken a lot of hard to work to build what you have here."

Raiden glances down at where Sam's touching him, then looks at her with a sudden smile. "Cutting down the trees with the few tools we had was the hardest."

Sam holds her smile with concerted effort. They've made good progress today. Next, it'll be a matter of making this village sustainable. Of caring for Earth just as much as themselves.

She turns back to Hawk to see if he's proud of her. He's the one person who understands what she's trying to do.

But Hawk's not smiling. In fact, he has that look when he's trying to suppress a frown. He glances away before Sam can get some idea of why.

A commotion on the other side of the village has them all turning toward it. Hawk's instantly by Sam's side, Luca glued to Mercy. Sam understands their caution, but surely Corbin wouldn't allow them to stay only to attack them?

Not when he's realized how useful the Seekers can be.

Several people exit the forest, spears in their hands as they shout and brandish them.

Sam's hand flies to her throat. She could tell Luca was thinking this was too good to be true. Maybe he was right.

Raiden grins. "Our hunters have returned."

Sam's breath whooshes out, feeling foolish at the conclusion they just jumped to. If they want the people of the Newlands to trust them, they need to trust them, too. "They look very pleased with themselves."

Corbin exits from the Round House, having heard the commotion..

A woman in the front holds up a bundle of dead hares. Although there doesn't look to be more than three or four flopping sacks of fur, she's smiling broadly. "Our most in a day, yet!"

Corbin throws his arms out wide. "Let's have a feast!"

His answer is more whoops and spear thrusting.

Suddenly, Raiden spins back. He steps in closer to Sam. "I'd like for you to sit with us, at the head table."

Behind him, Hawk imperceptibly shakes his head. Luca opens his mouth to object. Mercy's about to do the same.

Sam's smile grows. Don't they realize what an opportunity this is? She'd be talking with Corbin directly! "That would be wonderful. Thank you, Raiden."

Raiden's grin is blinding as he sets off to join the hunting party talking to his father. Grace must've stayed in the hut because she's nowhere to be seen.

Mercy lets out a breath through pursed lips. "I suppose that went well."

Luca frowns. "I'm not sure you should sit with them, Sam."

Sam looks at the three faces staring at her. She thought they'd be pleased! "But this is what we came here for. I could talk to Corbin."

"Aren't you a little suspicious as to why Raiden invited you?" asks Hawk quietly.

Something spears down Sam's spine. "Because his mother calls me the clever one."

Hawk's mouth settles into a thin line.

But before Sam can ask him what's going on, a cramp rips through her stomach. As her gut contracts, demanding she double over, she spins on her heel. "Someone's going to have to go get the others," she calls over her shoulder.

Clenching her teeth, Sam focuses on walking back to the Round House.

Sweet Terra, she can't afford to be sick.

Not again.

MERCY

*M*ercy's surprised when she returns to the beach with Luca to see the boats have been completely emptied. Following the trail of footsteps in the sand to the tree line, they find Gust, Siena and Nikita working on a shelter, their supplies piled up beside it in a precarious stack.

"Impressive!" Luca whistles.

"We're copying the technique you used in the Proving," says Siena proudly. "Although, we can't quite remember how you got the supports to attach to the roof."

"Let me show you." Luca goes to the shelter to inspect it and Mercy feels a familiar jolt in her stomach as she watches him. How is it even possible a guy like that could be interested in her? The way his strong arms are flexing when he reaches above his head is just too much to look at directly. It's making her want to run over there and rip the shirt from his chest so she can see more of him.

Gust comes up behind her and drapes an arm over Mercy's shoulders in an overly familiar way. Her spine stiffens.

"How did you guys get on with the well?" he asks. "Where are Sam and Hawk?"

She nods. "Pretty good actually. We dug the well and collected a bucket of water and—"

"I sure am thirsty," says Gust, practically panting.

Mercy wriggles away from him and stands beside Nikita to finish her update. "We used the water as a peace offering for the Outlanders."

Nikita's eyes widen. "Did it work? Are Sam and Hawk okay?"

"They're fine," Mercy says, hoping that's true. "Corbin made them drink some water before it was boiled and it made Sam a little queasy. She's just having a rest before the feast."

"Feast?" Gust is beside her again in a second. She really needs to stop giving him good news. "I sure am starving."

"You sure are annoying," says Mercy, stepping back again. "Give a girl some space!"

Gust holds up his hands as if to claim innocence.

"Don't get your hopes up for the feast," Mercy adds. "We're all invited, but they have about four hares to share between everyone. I'm not really sure an Outlander knows what a feast is."

"That's true," says Siena pausing her work on the shelter. "We should bring some of our supplies as a gift."

Gust is aghast. "We can't share our supplies! We barely have enough for us!"

Anger boils in Mercy's gut. She's really had enough of this guy.

"Why did you come here?" she shouts at him. "You're a Seeker, Gust! You're meant to be teaching these people there's a better way to live. One with kindness and understanding. Not selfishness and greed. That's how our planet got into this situation in the first place. It's what's destroying the Newlands."

"I was only joking," Gust says in the way people do when they realize they've made a mistake.

Given that seems like the closest Mercy's going to get to an apology, she decides to take it. She doesn't have time to hold a grudge right now.

"We'll bring the pods," says Nikita. "They're not going to last too long in that jar anyway. They need to be eaten."

"Good idea," says Luca, retying a vine at the top of a post.

Nikita points to the hot afternoon sun, now low in the sky. "It's going to start getting dark soon."

Mercy nods. "We really only came back to get you."

Luca looks across at Mercy, his dark eyes making her feel like she's the only one on the beach. "Let me just finish with this shelter so we have somewhere to sleep later, and we'll go and join them."

She nods, knowing he's working as fast as he can. He won't want to leave Sam for too long even if Hawk's there to protect her. The only reason Luca came back to the camp just now was to look out for Mercy. He couldn't exactly let her go and get the others on her own.

A flush crawls up her neck. Luca is looking after her. He really does seem to care.

Mercy takes the opportunity while they're waiting for Luca to fix the shelter to head down to the water's edge. She feels so sticky and revolting. Sweet Terra knows what she must smell like!

Letting the water lap at her toes, she contemplates diving in quickly to rinse the sweat from her body. How much damage would the acid do if she's fast?

Deciding to risk it, she draws in a deep breath and plunges into the water. As soon as it's deep enough she drops down until she's fully submerged. For a few seconds, it feels good. Then the toxic droplets find their way into her closed eyes and start to sting.

Shooting back up to the surface she gets back to shore as quickly as she can and shakes off the excess water, deciding she's okay. In fact, she feels a little better. Fresher, at least.

She drags her fingers through her hair as a comb, hoping she doesn't regret that decision.

"I like your hair."

Mercy spins around to see a blonde woman standing beside her. She has to blink to bring her into focus, wondering if the acid affected her brain somehow. She almost looks like an angel.

"Wow," says Mercy, taking in the woman's face. She's equally as beautiful as Grace, although probably a few years younger. Mercy would place her in her early twenties. But where Grace is dark and striking, this woman is fair and petite, her eyes so blue they're piercing right through Mercy.

"I'm Alyx," she says, holding out a hand.

"Mercy." Reaching out, Mercy shakes her hand, careful not to squeeze too tightly in case she breaks this delicate angel.

"I was in the Round House earlier," says Alyx. "I came down here to look for you."

"For me?" Mercy puts a hand to her chest, noticing her clothes are already rapidly drying in the sun.

"Well, not you specifically." Alyx smiles and her whole face lights up, taking her beauty to a whole new level. Mercy isn't so sure how she feels about this. She's used to being the beautiful one in Askala. It seems if she's going to be a Seeker, she's going to need to share that title. Or perhaps hand it over altogether.

"I was trying to get clean," says Mercy, feeling like she owes Alyx an explanation for the water dripping off her.

Alyx nods. "That's how we do it here. Maybe your well will change that. I hate the sting of the acid."

Mercy decides she couldn't hate it that much. Alyx looks so clean she's practically shining.

"Would you like to meet the others?" Mercy asks, nodding toward the line of trees. "You said you came down here looking for us."

"Sure." Alyx smiles. "How many of you came over?"

"Seven. There were only supposed to be six, but Luca broke

the rules and came. He does things like that. He's a bit of a rebel. In a good way, of course. He's very loyal." Mercy brings her hand to her throat, aware she's rambling. Talking about Luca does that to her.

"He's special to you?" Alyx asks, tilting her head, sending a wave of blonde hair cascading over her shoulder.

"We're sort of a thing." Mercy bites down on her lip, wondering why she just said that. Staking her claim before this gorgeous creature claps eyes on her man? Maybe.

"I see," says Alyx, looking almost disappointed, which is just flat out strange. Unless Mercy's being paranoid which is equally as likely.

"Hawk and Sam are a thing as well," says Mercy, trying to fill the air with words. "Well not officially, but they will be. It's inevitable."

"Sounds very cozy," says Alyx.

"Do you have someone?" Mercy asks.

Alyx looks stricken and Mercy reaches out to touch her arm. "I'm sorry. That was too personal. We only just met."

"I used to have someone." A sadness clouds Alyx's eyes. "But not anymore."

"Come on, then," says Mercy, trying to break the awkward-ness that she's found herself in. "Meet the others. I warn you though that Gust is going to really like you. Especially when he finds out you're unattached."

"You know, I might head back and see you at the feast if that's okay?" Alyx gives Mercy a wide smile. "I just remembered I promised Grace I'd help with the food."

Mercy frowns, hoping it wasn't something she'd said. "Okay."

"It was really lovely to meet you." Alyx smiles warmly and Mercy decides she must've imagined the awkwardness. "And I do love your hair. It's like a waterfall at midnight."

"Thanks." Mercy puts her hand to her half-dry hair, feeling

flattered that someone as beautiful as Alyx would pay her such a compliment. "I like your hair, too."

Alyx gives Mercy a small wave and walks back down the beach.

Mercy watches her, wishing she possessed that same kind of cool sophistication. Who knew the Outlands could produce someone like that! She'd been sure it was full of thugs, the way her mom had described everyone there.

Tearing herself away from the sight of Alyx's disappearing back, Mercy heads up to camp. The difference with the shelter is obvious immediately. Luca's done an amazing job. Not even a storm is going to blow that thing down now.

"Did you wash in the ocean?" Nikita is staring at her, looking slightly horrified.

"It's how they do it here." Mercy gives her a reassuring smile. "I wouldn't recommend it, but I do feel better."

"I'll wait for the next rain." Gust lifts an elbow and sniffs at his armpit.

"Hope it's soon," says Siena through gritted teeth.

Mercy has to stifle a laugh. She's given Gust a hard enough time already.

Luca finishes with the shelter and flashes Mercy a grin. "Ready to go?"

"Sure." She goes to pick up the large jar of pteropods, but Gust beats her to it.

"I'll carry this," he says.

They all know he's going to pass the pods off as his own personal gift, but Mercy couldn't be bothered arguing. In truth, Gust needs every advantage he can get given he has a personality less appealing than a leatherskin.

"How much do we trust these people?" Nikita asks, as they set off in the direction of the Round House.

"Not at all," says Luca. "Treat every single one of them as if they're a threat."

"They're not all bad," says Mercy. "You're forgetting about Charity and Grace. And I met another one of them down at the beach just now."

"This is why I told you not to go off on your own." Luca shakes his head and walks on ahead. "Take Nikita or Siena with you next time if you need a private moment."

"Private usually means alone, Luca." She pokes out her tongue at the back of his head.

"I saw that," he says.

Her jaw drops open. "You could not possibly have seen that."

"No, but you just confirmed it." He turns to grin at her and Mercy laughs. Why is it that the more frustrating he gets, the more she wants to tear off his clothes and cover his body with kisses?

"I hope we're not the feast," says Siena as they break through to the clearing. "Because I'm not smelling much food."

A cluster of tables has been set up outside the Round House. They're actually just tree trunks that have been split in half and set on the ground with large palm leaves laid beside them as seats. Mercy supposes it was too much to expect to be seated at a proper table with real chairs and a plate full of steaming food set down in front of her.

It's almost dark now, the clearing lit by a small fire at the end of each table. If they weren't in the middle of such a harsh environment, it would almost look beautiful. Romantic even. Mercy glances at Luca who's scanning the clearing, no doubt looking for Sam.

Shifting her gaze, Mercy sees if she can spot her.

Hawk's easy to find. Seated alone, his large frame is hunched over one of the logs, his legs pulled up in an uncomfortable pose. Sam is easy to locate after that. All Mercy has to do is follow Hawk's line of sight.

Sam is seated between Grace and Raiden right in front of the Round House. Corbin sits on Grace's other side. Placed behind them is the giant statue of Ronan, watching over them like some kind of evil spirit.

Sam and Raiden are chatting animatedly. Sam is telling some kind of story and Raiden is laughing at her every word.

"She looks like she's feeling better." Nikita makes her way over to Hawk.

"She really does," says Siena.

"She still looks pale," says Luca. "Don't be fooled."

Seeing them approaching, Hawk smiles and extends his hand to the rest of the tree trunk in front of him. "I saved you a seat."

Mercy positions herself on a palm leaf beside Hawk and Luca takes the leaf next to her. Nikita and Siena sit on his other side while Gust approaches the main table and sets the jar of pods down in front of Corbin, dropping into some kind of weird looking bow.

"A gift for you, Commander," he says.

Corbin screws up his face. "What the hell is this?"

"It was their idea!" Gust points in their direction and Mercy cringes.

Two of the Commander's guards leap to attention and rush to stand on either side of Gust. A hush falls over the clearing as everyone stops to see what will become of him.

"Wait!" shouts Sam. "They're pteropods! The greatest source of nutrition in Askala. Packed with vitamins, they've kept us alive for generations."

Corbin eyes her suspiciously.

"I'll eat one to prove it," says Gust, wrapping his greedy fingers around the jar.

But Corbin slams a knife into the table right beside his hand, his reflexes so fast Mercy hadn't even seen he was holding a weapon.

"Remove your hand," says Corbin, glaring at Gust. "Or next time you lose it. This is my gift. You said so yourself."

Gust attempts to take a step back. But Corbin's men grasp him and hold him in place.

Corbin unscrews the jar and sniffs at the liquid inside. "It stinks!"

"They really are very nutritious," says Sam. "One of those can keep you going for a week."

Mercy isn't so sure about Sam stepping in again, but it seems to be working. She's sure Gust would be dead by now if Sam hadn't said anything. Or at the least he'd have no hand.

Thoughts of Mercy's father race into her mind and she has to push them away. She's a Seeker! This isn't the time to be pining for her dad.

Corbin dips his large fingers into the jar and removes a pod. Dangling it in front of Grace's face, he grins at her.

"Do I dare eat this, my love?"

Grace smiles. "The clever one says it's safe."

Corbin looks from Sam to Gust then back at Mercy's table. "If I eat this and die, then every last one of you will have your throats sliced open, do you understand?"

Luca slides his hand across to Mercy's leg and squeezes it. They both know Corbin won't die from eating a pod, but his brutal threat is unsettling. Like he's looking for any excuse to kill them.

Corbin throws the pod into his mouth and chews. Closing his eyes he winces as if it's causing him pain to swallow it but he gets it down.

"Not bad," he announces, pushing the jar in Grace's direction. "Try one."

"No, thank you." Grace shakes her head.

"The Commander insists." Corbin waves the jar at her. "Eat one, wife."

Mercy puts her hand on Luca's and squeezes, hating seeing Grace being humiliated like this.

"Very well." Grace dips her hand into the jar and retrieves a pod. Putting it in her mouth she chews it for what feels like an eternity before swallowing it down.

"Did you like it?" asks Sam. "They take a while to get used to. But you'll feel terrific tomorrow."

"It was unusual." Grace gives Sam a tight-lipped smile before shooting a glare at Corbin. Mercy can only hope he doesn't punish her for that later.

"Let the feast begin!" Corbin announces, standing up and beating his tattooed chest.

Mercy cringes. These men are so animalistic. Nothing at all like Luca. It's hard to believe he was born in the Outlands.

Four women emerge from the Round House holding wooden trays with what looks like a roasted hare on each. Corbin pulls back his shoulders and smiles proudly.

"Is that the feast?" Mercy asks Luca.

He nods. "This is likely to be the most these people have eaten in a long time. Meat is rare in the Outlands."

The women move between the tables, taking a small leaf and depositing a chunk of meat on it and passing one to each person. It's impossible not to notice that those on Corbin's table get a larger serving. At least Sam will be eating well tonight. Luca's right. She *is* still pale. She needs all the sustenance she can get.

"Is Sam okay?" Mercy asks Hawk.

He shakes his head. "She's putting on a brave face again. I won't relax until she gets color back in her cheeks."

"Same here." Mercy shakes her head. "What's the deal with Raiden?"

"Might be a question for Sam." Hawk takes his portion of meat and eats it in three bites.

Mercy and Luca take their servings and chew on them quietly.

"Sam loves you," Mercy tells Hawk quietly. "I know she does. She's just doing what she thinks is best right now."

There's no way Sam would be interested in the likes of Raiden, no matter how much attention he's lavishing on her. Surely, Hawk knows that. Then she remembers how possessive she'd felt of Luca when she'd looked at Alyx, who was nowhere near him at the time, and a wave of sympathy washes over her. This must be really difficult for Hawk to watch. Raiden is clearly enamored with Sam.

She looks around, trying to find Alyx in the clearing, certain she isn't here. She'd have noticed her if she was. Perhaps she's in the Round House cleaning up from the feast? She had said she needed to help Grace with the food.

Corbin stands and claps his hands. "As a special treat tonight we have a second course to serve you!"

There's a murmur of excitement as the people speculate what it might be.

"Shark fin soup!" Corbin calls out, licking his lips. "Made with fresh water from our new well."

Two men emerge from the Round house carrying the bucket that the Seekers had used earlier to collect water. Only now it has steam rising from it and a pungent fishy smell floats across the clearing.

The people cheer, bouncing on their heels as they lick their lips.

Mercy gags. There's no way she can eat any of that foul-smelling soup.

"A leatherskin was found washed up on shore today," says Corbin. "All praise our fallen Commander, looking over us even after his death."

"All praise the fallen Commander," the people repeat. "Thank you for this blessing."

Luca looks to Mercy and Hawk and raises his eyebrows. "Wonder how the shark died."

Hawk smirks. "Yeah, I wonder."

"I didn't think leatherskins were edible?" Mercy's brows

shoot up. If they were, they'd have been eating them in Askala for years.

"They're not," says Luca. "But their fins are sometimes used to flavor soup."

Mercy blanches. "The smell is making me sick. Think we can sneak away?"

Hawk shakes his head, his eyes returning to Sam, who is even paler now that there's the smell of rotten shark in the air.

"I think it's nearly finished anyway," says Luca. "Food's almost gone, and it's not like there's any wine to fuel the festivities."

People are milling about now, moving between tables as they talk and celebrate having fallen on such good luck as to be eating two meals instead of one. A line has formed in front of the bucket of soup as they take turns to drink a cup full of steaming liquid. Clearly, they don't have enough cups to go around.

"If we stay, we're going to have to eat that soup." Mercy looks at Luca, the firelight flickering over their faces.

Luca grimaces. "Smells delicious."

Hawk leans into them. "Why don't you two head back to camp? I'll wait for Sam. We can meet you there. People are starting to leave, anyway."

"Good idea." Mercy turns to Hawk. "I need to pay a visit to one of the trees and I'm afraid to go alone. I don't like the way those men look at me."

Luca rolls his eyes as he stands. He knows full well she's saying whatever she needs in order to get him alone. "We'll see you back at camp, Hawk."

"Don't wait for us," Mercy whispers in Hawk's ear before kissing him on the cheek.

She can hardly believe her luck that Luca's agreed to this.

They leave the clearing and hit the tree line, and Mercy slips her hand into Luca's.

"So we don't get lost," she tells him.

"Mercy—"

"No, Luca. Stop it. Don't speak."

They walk further into the forest.

"That tree looks good," he says, pulling her to a stop. "You go and I'll wait right here."

"I don't need to go anymore." She grins in the dark, knowing he can't see her in the shadows. "False alarm."

"Should we head back then?"

"I was hoping we could go to the beach to talk."

"Talk?"

She nods in the dark. "Talk."

"You just told me not to speak," he says, as she pulls him in the direction of the beach.

"I never said you were going to do the talking," she laughs, having no intention of them having any kind of conversation. But he doesn't seem to be resisting her with too much effort. Maybe he's started to realize they're free to be whoever they want to be in the Newlands.

It's a warm night with only the gentlest of breeze and as they step out onto the beach and into the soft moonlight, Mercy's stomach clenches into a knot. This is the moment she's been waiting for ever since Luca climbed aboard that boat. That kiss they'd had in the forest during the Proving is *not* finished yet.

Slipping her hands around his neck, Mercy urges Luca's face down to hers.

"This isn't a good idea," he protests, making no move to remove her hands.

"You're not my cousin out here," she says. "You're just a man. And I'm just a girl desperately in love with that man. I want you, Luca."

He lets out a sigh and presses his forehead to hers, his hands tentatively resting on her hips as he seems to be deciding what to do. The chemistry between them is undeniable. Surely, she's not the only one to be feeling these waves of desire pulsing through to her core.

Mercy steps closer to Luca, closing the gap between them as she fits her curves against the firmness of his chest.

"I want you, Luca," she says again, her voice low and breathy.

His sigh becomes a moan and his lips crash toward hers and now he's kissing her like their last encounter never finished.

Stepping up on her toes, she slides her fingertips from his neck down his back to that firm butt she'd been eyeing off all day. Who's she kidding—she's been eyeing off that butt ever since he returned from the Outlands. This guy is unbelievably hot!

Luca's palms slip underneath the back of her shirt and now it's skin on skin. The sensation has Mercy groaning and their kiss ignites, merging into a blur of lips and tongues and warmth and pure bliss as she loses track of everything else around her. ·

It's only Mercy and Luca right now in this moment. Nothing else exists.

Dropping to his knees, Luca pulls her down with him until she's lying on her back, the weight of him pressed against her. She's never gone this far with a guy before. She's never wanted to take any of those clumsy kisses in Askala in this direction. But she knows where she wants this to go with Luca.

Further.

Higher.

Faster.

All. The. Damn. Way.

His hands delve underneath the hemp fabric of her shirt once more, only this time it's to tear it from her body and toss it to the side.

She wants to scream out that she loves him, yet somehow she can't. As much as she does love him—and she believes he loves her—this has little to do with love. It's white hot lust. It's a fire burning deep inside her that only Luca can put out.

Mercy reaches up and tugs on his shirt, wanting to feel more skin.

More Luca.

He obliges and slips it over his head, leaving it tossed on the sand with her own discarded clothing.

"I want you," she says once more, needing him to be clear that she consents to whatever he wants to do with her. Only this time he replies...

"I want you, too."

And as he takes things to the next level, as he turns her from the girl he grew up with to the woman who will stay by his side, tears of joy run down Mercy's face, and she acknowledges that this *is* an act of love.

She loves this man.

Wholly. Completely. With every ounce of her being.

And when he presses his cheek to hers, rakes his fingers into her hair, holding her still as he lets out a gasp filled with everything that's good in this world, she honestly believes that he loves her, too.

LUCA

*L*uca's never wanted to stay in one place. There always seemed to be something pulling him elsewhere.

But, for the first time in his life, he's found somewhere he wants to stay.

Mercy's arms.

She shifts beneath him, stretching languidly. Everywhere their bodies touch, Luca feels the fire ignite all over again. Never before has he experienced something like that.

So fast.

So hot.

So…consuming.

Mercy drifts a finger down his jaw, sending tingles racing over his skin. "Can we do that again?"

Luca's breath disintegrates. They've fed a fire that will be impossible to put out. Gently, he presses his lips against hers, tasting the lingering sweetness of their passion. He should regret this.

He should've tried to stop it.

He pulls back. "We can't. We need to get dressed before someone gets a rude shock."

Possessiveness flares within Luca. The need to protect Mercy has now become a force to be reckoned with.

Standing up, his skin instantly misses her warmth. He holds out his hand. "Do you want another quick dip in the ocean?"

"One a day is probably all my skin can take."

And probably all Luca's heart can take, too. Wet Mercy was a whole new level of distracting. Slick skin. Thick hair darker than night. Clothes clinging to her curves.

Luca turns away before he can pull her back into his arms. This was Mercy's first time. She needs time to…recover. Grabbing his clothes, he quickly gets dressed, listening to the rustle of material as Mercy does the same.

He holds out his hand only to realize she probably can't see it. "Shall we get back to the hut?"

But Mercy doesn't move. "Are you regretting this, Luca? Are you going to say we shouldn't have done it in the first place?"

From the tone in her voice, Luca can tell her hands are on her hips. There's frustration, an edge of anger. But also a hint of vulnerability.

Quickly banishing the distance between them, Luca does what he wanted to from the moment he pulled away. He draws Mercy close, pressing all of her against all of him. "I couldn't have stopped that any more than I can stop the tide, Mercy."

"Oh."

He presses his forehead against hers. "And I have no regrets."

Her breath whooshes out and he's pretty sure she's smiling. Her arms wrap around his neck, pulling his mouth down to hers. "Good," she murmurs against his lips. "Because I have an idea."

Before Luca can ask what's leaped into Mercy's sharp mind, she kisses him. Hard. Not willing to be outdone, Luca tightens his arms, lifting her so only her toes brush the ground. Her body molds to his, the desire igniting as if it was never satiated.

Luca pulls back, already panting. Their breaths mingle, their hearts only inches away from each other.

How ironic it's the Newlands that Luca can see a future in.

Mercy's fingers tangle with the hair at the nape of his neck. "Yep. Best idea ever."

Smiling, Luca loosens his arms so he can study her in the dim light. "I'm curious and terrified all at the same time."

"Well, I was thinking…"

The fact that Mercy hesitates has Luca on alert. This is a girl who knows what she wants and goes for it. Her hands on his neck withdraw, coming to rest on his chest.

"We could build our own hut," Mercy says quickly. "And live in it. Together."

Luca's arms slacken. "Just the two of us?"

Mercy nods. "Like…a couple."

A couple.

The two of them. Together.

Surely they couldn't…

"I'm in," Luca announces with a grin.

Mercy gasps. "You're in? You said yes?"

Luca lifts and spins her around, chuckling. "I'm only human, after all." Saying no to Mercy is like trying to say no to breathing. "We can start building tomorrow. First thing."

Placing her back on the ground, they stand there for long moments, smiling in the dark. Suddenly, tomorrow and every day after that, is full of delicious promise.

Luca steps back, taking her hand. "We'd better get back. We need to check on Sam." The smell of the shark fin soup hadn't helped her lack of color.

"And poor Hawk. He's worried he's going to be nursing a broken heart."

Luca sighs. He noticed Raiden's interest in his sister. It's unsettling. "We'll need to keep an eye on her. Sam will be clueless if anyone tries to manipulate her."

They've just reached the shelter when Mercy pauses. "Being here is going to be tough, isn't it?" she says quietly, the words more a statement than a question.

Because they're now living a fragile existence on a dangerous island, where the only people they can trust are the other Seekers. And Luca's not even sure he can include Gust in that category.

He squeezes her hand. "We'll get each other through it."

Each night they'll be returning to their own hut. Each night they'll reaffirm what else they've found in the Newlands—love.

Luca stills, taken aback at the word. And yet somehow not surprised at all. The way he's felt about Mercy was different from the start. He's never felt something so...unstoppable.

But Mercy deserves to be more than an impulsive emotion. Whatever they have here needs to be given time to fully blossom. To prove that it will stand the test of time.

There's nothing Luca's looking forward to more.

"We will." The smile in Mercy's voice is undeniable.

They kiss again, a soft, breathless promise full of one word. Tomorrow.

Tiptoeing, they enter the shelter. The sounds of soft snoring and gentle snuffles fill the air. Luca hears Sam's hiccupping little snorts. He thinks he can see her tucked into the side of the mountain that is Hawk. Good. Sleep is just what she needs.

Another scan and Luca sees the outline of a mat near the front door and he smiles. Sam would know he likes to sleep near an exit.

Tugging on Mercy's hand, he lies down as she nestles in his arms. As they adjust themselves, Luca marvels at how well they fit. At how comfortable this is.

With a sweet goodnight kiss, Mercy settles down. Within minutes, she's asleep and Luca can't blame her. It's been a big day. The shark attack. Learning whether they'll be welcomed here. The feast that was more like a famine.

The culmination of their explosive chemistry.

Luca tucks his spare hand behind his head, staring up at the ceiling he can barely make out. For the first time, he's content to sleep. To stay right where he is.

His eyes have just drifted shut when he hears a twig snap. He freezes, holding his breath. An attack during the night is exactly something Corbin and his tattooed men would do.

Crickets chirp, the trees rustle in the barely-there breeze, but there's nothing else.

Still, the people who mean everything to Luca are in this hut. He's not taking any chances.

Carefully extricating himself, Luca rests Mercy's head back on the mat they were lying on. She snuffles, her hand clenching reflexively as if she's reaching for him even in sleep, before her breathing settles back into a steady rhythm. Pressing a soft kiss to her temple, Luca slips out the exit.

Knowing this could be a trap, Luca swiftly blends into the trees. He stands there, breath held as he listens.

There it is. The subtle sound of air being inhaled, then slowly exhaled. Only a few feet away. To his left.

Knowing he needs to move quickly, Luca darts forward. A few strides and his arms wrap around the intruder. He slams his hand across their mouth.

A very female gasp is muffled before the body goes still.

"One move and I'll snap your neck," he whispers harshly in the woman's ear. He thinks of the females he saw in the village. Have they underestimated Grace? Was there someone else watching them with murder in their eyes?

The woman nods.

"I'm going to take my hand away. You scream and the other Seekers will be here in a flash."

Luca knows that's probably a lie. Hawk would come running, maybe Mercy, too. Sam would ask questions so she could deduce the next best step. Gust would run the other way.

The woman nods again.

He relaxes his hand.

"You always did move like a shadow, Luca."

His arms go slack. "Alyx?"

She spins around, pressing her hands to his chest. "When I saw you in the Round House—"

Luca clamps his hand back over her mouth. "You were there?" he whispers hoarsely.

Alyx nods, not bothering to remove Luca's fingers.

Releasing her, Luca grab's Alyx's hand. "We can't talk here."

He holds it for the short walk to the beach. The sound of the waves will cover the few words they have to say to each other.

He doesn't let go until their feet are sinking into soft sand. Just to make sure, he continues for a few more yards. Far away enough that they can't be heard, but not close enough for the toxic waves to touch them.

Spinning around, Luca grabs her upper arms. "What are you doing here, Alyx?"

He feels her shoulders sag. "You know what the Outlands are like, Luca." But then they tense with the steel that Luca knows is at the core of this woman. Alyx has seen her fair share of hardships. "I did what I had to do to escape."

There's a note of challenge in her voice.

Luca releases her with a sigh. He gets it. Alyx grabbed a chance at a better life.

In some ways, he did the same when Nova and Kian entered his life.

Alyx's arms move, from memory they're probably crossing over her chest. "I could ask you the same question."

Luca clamps his mouth shut, knowing he can't say the first answer that comes to his mind. *I came here because my sister is naïve enough to believe that the people of the Outlands can be saved.*

Or the second. *And because of Mercy…*

"I'm here as a Seeker. We want to help the people here. Show them that the Newlands don't have to turn into the wasteland the Outlands are."

There's silence from Alyx as she digests this. Luca wonders what she's thinking. Despite their history, this is her village now. Her people.

Corbin is her Commander.

"And you and Mercy..." Alyx leaves the question unfinished, as if she's not sure she wants the answer.

Luca wipes his hand down his face. Just when he thought he had it all figured out, the world is turned upside down again. "We grew up together. There's a lot of... We thought that we could..." Luca huffs harshly. "It's complicated."

"Does she know that—"

"No," Luca grinds out through gritted teeth. "And she won't either."

Alyx's silhouette nods. "I understand."

They both descend into silence, the rhythmic breaking of the waves filling the air. With each muted splash, memories of Alyx roll over Luca.

She sighs. "It's going to be different this time, isn't it? We'll be different."

There's an inevitability in Alyx's tone that has Luca wincing. "What happened in the Outlands, Alyx, was a different time. We were both lonely..."

Her hand settles on his arm and Luca instinctively tenses. Alyx's sweet looks conceal one of the toughest women he knows. "It's okay, Luca." She chuckles. "You're right. Away from all that"—she waves her arm as if to indicate everything they shared in the Outlands— "we're better off as friends."

Luca's shoulders sag with relief. "Damn good friends."

They've both saved each other's lives more than once.

A breeze gusts and Alyx tenses. Luca had forgotten how finely tuned senses become when you live with the constant threat of danger. He stills, listening, but doesn't hear anything.

"I'd better go," Alyx says. "We're not supposed to leave the village without permission."

With a quick, fierce hug, Alyx blends into the night. The next time they see each other, it'll be as if they never met.

Luca's only taken a few steps before he stops. The draw to return to Mercy is like a magnetic pull.

But everything that just happened crashes around him. His legs give out and he sits on the sand, feeling like he's suddenly made of stone.

He should've known.

You can't escape your past. You can't run from the truth of who you really are.

He stays there, listening to the ocean, knowing the hut isn't far away. That everything he wanted is in there.

Now knowing he can never have it.

The sun eventually joins him, no matter how much Luca would prefer to remain in the limbo of night. He doesn't want to say goodbye to the time where Mercy was his, no matter how fleeting it was.

But fingers of light crawl over the red ocean, reaching out to him. Telling him that what will come is as unavoidable as what has been.

With a sigh, Luca stands. Mercy's safety will always come first. Which means she can never know his past.

His secret.

It means that as Mercy comes out of the shelter, her face flushed with morning joy, Luca does what he's spent his life doing.

He runs.

HAWK

*W*hen Hawk had imagined being a Seeker, he'd seem himself traveling and negotiating, protecting the weak and standing up to the rogue. He hadn't quite pictured himself on his hands and knees in the dirt planting so many seeds. But it's a job that needs to be done, so he continues his work, reminding himself there are worse tasks.

The sound of Gust grunting is proof enough of that. Over to one side of the vegetable patch that Hawk is creating with Mercy and Siena, he can hear Gust and Nikita working on digging a new well. Gust had wanted to take the glory, and Hawk's aching arms from all the digging he'd done the day before hadn't had the energy to argue with him.

Luca was nowhere to be found this morning, which has got to have something to do with Mercy's bad mood. She's raking back the dirt with such aggression it's like the sandy grains of soil have offended her somehow. Hawk can only guess they've had a fight.

Is that what he and Sam are having?

Because despite the fact she spent the night curled up beside him, he can't help but feel a distance has opened up between them. A distance roughly the size of a guy with stringy brown hair and a smile Hawk doesn't trust.

Raiden.

Even his name is irritating.

Hawk crawls along the section of earth that Mercy's just turned over and carefully places some of the seeds they brought with them from Askala. He's not even sure what kind these are. He hopes they're carrots. He could really devour a carrot right now. Or a tomato. He'd even consider a cockroach given the way his stomach is contracting and groaning.

That feast last night had been pathetic. Made worse by the fact that Sam wasn't sitting with him. Just like today is being made worse given she's headed out with Raiden again so he can show her some amazing thing he wants her opinion on.

It's obvious the guy likes her. She might think it's her brains he's interested in, but she doesn't know how guys think! Hawk does. Because anything Raiden's thinking, he's likely already thought himself.

He'd better not lay a finger on Sam, though. Or Hawk will—

"Hawk!" Siena scolds. "Don't push the seeds so far down. They'll never reach the surface if they're down that far."

"Sorry," he mumbles, snapping to attention and drawing his concentration back to the task at hand. "You're right."

They'd spent all morning breaking up the section of hard earth that Corbin had allowed them to turn into a vegetable patch. It had to be here in the clearing. The rest of the island is either too sandy or too shady to be of much use. Once the soil had been turned over, they'd raked it into neat rows ready for planting. If they can manage to get anything to grow here, they should be able to provide enough food to one day be able to have a feast like these Outlanders have never seen before.

"Dammit!" Mercy curses, hopping about on one foot.

Hawk rushes to her. "Are you okay?"

"Stabbed my toe!" she howls.

Hawk's not entirely surprised after the aggressive way she's been working on the garden. It was an accident waiting to happen.

He bends down to look at the damage while Mercy puts an arm around his shoulders to steady herself.

"It's not so bad," he says. "But you'll need to put some sap on it."

"Did you bring it with you?" she sniffs.

"I left it at camp." He straightens up and hugs his cousin. "Sorry, Mercy. I'll get it for you."

Mercy buries her face in Hawk's chest and dissolves into tears that he suspects have nothing to do with her sore toe.

"Do you want to tell me what's wrong?" he asks, rubbing her back.

She shakes her head, making no move to dislodge herself from his chest, so he holds her a little tighter.

Siena's stopped working and is watching, a concerned look plastered on her exhausted face. Hawk raises his eyebrows to see if she understands what this is all about, but Siena only shrugs.

"Why don't you two head back to camp and take a rest?" Hawk suggests. "I can finish up here. You've done enough."

Maybe Mercy needs to talk to another female. And given Sam is nowhere to be seen, Siena's the next best thing at this moment.

"Good idea." Siena goes to Mercy and touches her on the arm. "Come on, Mercy. You're tired. You need a rest. I do, too."

Mercy pulls away from Hawk and blinks up at him with sad eyes. She has the imprint of the pendant he's still wearing pressed into her cheek, but she doesn't seem to care. Her whole world is being consumed by something far greater right now.

Anger bubbles deep inside Hawk. Just when he'd started to respect Luca, he goes and does this. How dare he upset Mercy! Next time he shows his face, Hawk's going to give him a piece of his mind. This was why he wanted Luca to stay the hell away from Mercy! She's too innocent for the likes of him.

He puts his hand to Mercy's face and drags his thumb down her cheek. There are so many things he'd like to tell her right now, but the words aren't coming. He has to hope she knows him well enough to realize how much he cares.

"Thanks, Hawk."

She takes Siena's outstretched hand and they disappear into the trees.

Hawk glances at Gust and Nikita, still busy with the well, and returns to his task, grateful for a moment alone. His anger at Luca floods back as he imagines what he might be getting up to right now. Walking along a deserted beach? Climbing a tree and resting in the crook of a branch? Running through what remains of the forest? All things that Hawk wouldn't mind doing right now but isn't. Because there's work to be done. People are counting on them. That's what being a Seeker is about. Luca may not be a true Seeker, but he still has a responsibility to do the right thing.

Finishing the row, he goes to the small pile of supplies they'd brought to the clearing and picks up the next small jar, certain these are pumpkin seeds.

His stomach growls. This soil had better be as fertile as it looks! He can't live on three bites of roasted meat for long. Corbin and his men must be eating something more substantial, looking at the size of them. He just needs to figure out what.

As he crouches down, ready to start on this next row of seeds, he notices Grace approaching. Her long hair is down today, draping over one side of her face and she's moving slowly with the hint of a limp.

"Grace." He stands and wipes his dirt stained hands on his pants.

"Hawk." She smiles shyly at him through her hair, her face partially turned away. But not enough that he can't see what she's trying to hide. The right side of her face is badly bruised, reminding him of his grandmother, Avis, although Grace's injuries are a dark storm of colors rather than Avis's puckered burns.

He doesn't ask Grace about her face though. If she wanted to talk about it, she wouldn't be trying so hard to cover it. Besides, he's got a pretty good idea of exactly how the bruises happened.

And who was the one to give them to her.

Thoughts of his mother come racing to him with force, his longing for her punching him in the gut. She always said the world needs more good men like him. It's only now that he's outside the safety of Askala that he's starting to see what she means. In the short time his mom had spent in the Outlands, she must've seen some terrible things.

"Do you like the new garden?" he asks, giving Grace some time to get to the point of whatever she came here to talk to him about.

"It's wonderful," she gushes. "We're all so very grateful."

Hawk smiles. He hadn't gotten that impression at all from the suspicious glances he's been getting from the Newlanders.

"I brought you something." Grace holds out her hand, turning her back to where Gust and Siena are digging the well so they can't see. "You must be hungry."

It's a piece of flatbread and Hawk's heart tears in half to look at it.

"I can't," he says. "It wouldn't be fair."

"Fair?" she asks, still holding out her hand. "You've done most of the work here from what I've seen. And you're twice the size of the others. You need it more than them. Just eat it. Quickly."

"I..." Hawk's mouth fills with saliva and his hands start to shake. He really is very hungry.

"Take it, Hawk. Please? It would be rude of you to refuse

me." Grace smiles at him and before he knows what he's doing, he's taken the bread and demolished it in two bites.

The effect is instant. Despite the fact he could eat twenty more of those portions, he feels better than he has all day.

"Thank you." He goes to wipe his mouth with the back of his hand but stops when he sees how filthy he is. He's going to need a dip in the ocean later, unless they can spare enough water from the well.

"You look like your grandfather," says Grace, staring at him. "The real life version, not just the statue."

"Did you know him?" Hawk asks. "He died before I was born. You couldn't have been all that old yourself."

She nods. "I saw him once when I was a young girl. But he was the kind of person you never forget. He had a presence. Like you do."

Hawk squats down and opens the jar of seeds, wanting to distract from the fire that's burning his cheeks. He has a presence?

"How did he die?" Grace asks. "I've heard so many rumors about it."

Hawk concentrates on the seeds as he decides how to answer this.

"There was a fire," he eventually says. "A lot of people died in it."

"And what became of his men?" She readjusts her hair to ensure it's covering her cheek. "Did they die in the fire, too?"

"Some did." Hawk moves down the row of soil to continue the planting. "The rest joined Askala after the battle to live in peace."

Grace shakes her head. "You must have some serious weapons over there to have won a battle like that."

Hawk pauses. Why does it feel like this was the exact question she came over here to ask? What is Corbin up to, sending Grace to do his dirty work?

"Tell Corbin Askala is full of weapons." Hawk stands to make sure she gets the message, even if it's a lie. "Tell him if he sets one foot there, he'll meet the same fate as the Commander before him."

"I...I didn't..." Grace's hand flutters to her face. "He didn't...I was just curious."

Hawk reaches out and gently lifts her hair from her face. "You can't let him hurt you like this, Grace."

Tears fall from her dark eyes and trail down her cheeks, her fear unmistakable. "He didn't hurt me. I tripped in the dark. It was nothing."

"The next time he raises a hand to you, I want you to come and find me." Hawk's protective instinct is a fireball of rage inside him now. He has to do something to help this poor woman! "I'll take you to Askala myself if I have to."

"I need to keep Charity safe," she whispers. "If I join her, he'll know. I must stay here."

Hawk lets his hand fall as he returns to his seeds. It won't do Grace any good if Corbin sees him talking with her like this. He wants to help her, but he has to be smart about it if he's going to be of any genuine assistance.

Blinking in surprise, he pauses his work when a large raven lands in front of him.

His hand flies to his pendant. Surely, not a message from his father already? The bird had better not be after any of these seeds he's just planted.

But before he can check if the raven's holding a note, Grace gets to it with surprising speed and unties something from its leg.

"I'm pretty sure that's for me," says Hawk, standing up and putting out his hand.

"You don't know that," says Grace. "It could be for anyone here. We get ravens from the Outlands when they're sending supplies."

The bird takes off into the sky, leaving them to sort out the dilemma it just delivered.

"Oh." Hawk withdraws his hand, not wanting a fight. "Shall we look at it together then?"

Grace unravels the note, tilting it so only she can see the contents. He leans over and catches a glimpse, recognizing the same code as the note he and Wren intercepted in Askala. He fights a wave of disappointment, realizing he'd have liked some news from home.

"Looks like it's for you," he says. "I can't read that code."

Grace shoves it in her pocket. "It's just letting us know that a supply boat will be on its way at the next opportunity."

"I didn't think the Outlands had supplies to spare," says Hawk. "Things are pretty barren over there."

"Oh, it won't be much," says Grace. "Just fresh water mainly, which of course we won't need anymore, and some hares. Maybe a bag of flour if we're lucky."

"What do you send them back in return?" Hawk asks, the sheer size of the clearing around him suddenly making a whole lot more sense. "I'm guessing timber."

Grace gives him a tight-lipped smile, her lack of response her answer.

"You do realize if you keep doing that you won't have any timber left to give, don't you?" Hawk shakes his head, unable to believe what he's just discovered.

"It's a temporary arrangement." Grace waves her hand like he's worried about nothing "As soon as we're self-sufficient here, the trade will stop. And thanks to you and the Seekers, that might be sooner rather than later."

Hawk squats back down and finishes up with the jar of seeds. Sam would see that as progress—less wood being cut down to be shipped to the Outlands.

"I'd better get back to Corbin," she says. "Thanks again for what you're doing here."

"If you see Sam, could you please ask her to come and find me?" he asks, feeling desperate but not especially caring. His need for Sam trumps any other emotion right now.

"Sure." Grace smiles warmly at him. "He's a good son, my Raiden. He'll take good care of her. You don't need to worry."

Hawk grimaces. He can't exactly tell Grace that this is precisely what he's worried about.

"Can I ask you a question?" Hawk keeps his distance, studying her face for a reaction to what he's about to ask.

"Ask me anything," she says.

"Who's the Falcon? And how did he die?"

Grace drops her smile for only a heartbeat but it's enough to tell Hawk she knows exactly who he's talking about.

"I have no idea." Grace shrugs as she takes a few steps backward. Then, giving him a wave, she turns and walks away at a much faster pace than when she'd arrived.

Now Hawk doesn't know what to think. On the surface, everything is going so unbelievably well. They've been accepted and allowed to stay. And they're slowly sharing their knowledge with the Newlanders. So, why is every one of his senses on high alert?

Grace knows who the Falcon is and she's not prepared to tell him. And Corbin had clearly sent her here to find out how well-equipped Askala is to defend itself.

Which reminds him of the stage one mentioned in the note found in Askala. These things all must be connected.

If only Sam were here, maybe they could figure it out.

SAM

Sam doesn't like being in the Round House. The smoke is cloying. The light is terrible. And the people smell.

None of those help her lingering nausea after drinking the water. Thankfully, one vomit and she was relatively fine. Although, after spending almost an hour in here, her stomach has joined her lungs' demand to leave.

But sacrifices need to be made, so Sam remains where she is, nodding as Corbin continues to talk.

"We came here with nothing," he booms. "And look at what we've built."

Destroyed, thinks Sam.

There's a round of grunts from the others here. From what Sam can tell, that's their role—agree with Corbin.

"We have enough timber to build hundreds of huts." He points his spear at the fire in the center of the hut. "To stoke the fires of our Commander's legacy."

Sam has to cover her wince as she avoids glancing at the statue of Ronan. Corbin's talking of creating more scars that will have to be healed. The world is still trying to recover from the previous generation's devastation.

Corbin's unwashed chest expands. "No one has died of starvation."

Possibly malnutrition.

"And no one has taken it from us."

This has Sam frowning. "Others have tried to take it?"

Corbin frowns at Sam as if she's not supposed to talk. But that doesn't make sense. Why would he have invited her here if he didn't want to hear what she had to say?

"Of course they have," he grunts. "We have what they want."

"Food," someone calls from the other side of the hut.

"Enough timber to build all the shelters and fires and weapons we want," says another.

"Water," says Raiden, who's sitting beside Corbin.

Sam smiles at him. "You're welcome."

Big and strapping, Raiden already has the promise of his father's physique and presence. Sitting on his father's right hand side, he's undoubtedly being groomed as Corbin's successor. Making friends with him was a lucky stroke of fate.

Corbin scowls. "As you and your friends found out—if you come to take what is ours, you will be met with our spears."

There's a round of thumping feet and said spears. The protectiveness of what the Newlanders have is apparent.

"It's a good thing we came to give then, isn't it?" Sam says cheerfully.

She doesn't point out that Corbin and his village don't *own* the Newlands. Mother Nature is everyone's and no one's at the same time.

His understanding of that will come later.

Right now, they need to build connections. Common ground. Sam needs to find the spark of goodness that's buried under Corbin's smelly, hostile exterior.

"I could tell you all about the *Pinus rhizophoras* species you're using to build your huts, if you like?"

The same timber that's burning only a few feet away, making

Sam sweat and probably start to smell as much as the others around her.

Corbin acts as if she hasn't even spoken, staring intensely at the statue of Ronan.

Sam reassesses. Maybe biology isn't Corbin's personal area of interest. That's too bad. If he understood the fascinating species he's destroying, it's possible he'd think twice about doing it.

She leans forward. "You'll be glad to hear we brought soap-wort seeds, Corbin. When the leaves are chopped and boiled, the liquid can be used for cleaning all manner of things."

Like bodies.

And the few clothes these people wear, neglecting to protect their skin from the harsh sun.

This time, Corbin turns to Sam slowly. His gaze, hard and angry, settles on her. She almost flinches but doesn't back down. Maybe hygiene isn't a priority for him either, but she's determined to find something they can connect over.

Raiden clears his throat, and Sam glances at him. He shakes his head imperceptibly. Sam leans back a little, the memory of Corbin's hand slamming across her face flashing through her mind.

But that was back when Corbin saw the Seekers as a threat. Now, they've brought them water. Hawk and the others were starting the garden this morning. And they've planted soapwort.

Grace slips through the door in that moment, silently sitting behind Corbin, her hair hiding much of her face. There are a few grunts of welcome from the people around her. She takes Raiden's hand and squeezes it and he nods, understanding whatever silent communication his mother just conveyed.

It reminds Sam of her mother doing that with her—a squeeze of encouragement, a gesture of affection...a reminder for Sam to stay quiet.

She turns back to Corbin, smiling again. The Commander

has established what Askala was founded on. Family. Fierce loyalty. Determination.

Sam leans forward again. "You've built far more than a village, Corbin. I can understand your pride."

He turns to her in surprise. "This is only the beginning of Cy's legacy," he growls.

Knowing she needs to meet Corbin halfway, Sam keeps her smile in place. "I'm sure, deep down, he wanted a sustainable legacy, too."

Corbin blinks, and Sam's not entirely sure what that means. He hadn't considered that? He's not sure what sustainable means?

Raiden shoots to his feet. "I'm going to take Sam for a walk," he announces.

Grabbing her hand, he hauls her to her feet and drags her out of the hut before anyone can say anything else.

Outside, Sam drags in lungfuls of fresh air. As much as she doesn't want to go back in there, she stops, pulling Raiden to a halt. "Will your father think that was rude? We left rather abruptly."

"This is the time that...ah...Dad likes to be alone. His thinking time."

Sam glances over her shoulder, noting no one else is leaving the hut. But before she can ask, Raiden is already pulling her away.

"I want to show you something."

Sam's about to object when she sees he's pulling her toward the forest. Something inside her smiles. She misses the forest as much as she misses Askala.

Still holding her hand, Raiden leads her through the village. On the other side, she sees Hawk still working on the garden. He straightens as he sees them pass, wiping the sweat from his brow.

Sam waves, hoping to see his smile. She's only recently

noticed how the lighting up of his face sparks sunshine in her chest.

But Hawk gives a small wave back before returning to his planting. Even at this distance, Sam can see the frown on his handsome face. Something in her tightens. She can't be happy if Hawk's not happy.

But there's no time to talk, because they're at the tree line. The mangrove pines aren't as big or thick as the ones in Askala, but they're living, breathing tranquility, nonetheless. Raiden releases her hand, turning to Sam with a look of pride. Instinctively, she smiles at him. She knew someone else would realize what a wonder this place can be.

She's about to point out the understory species that would've been one of the first ones to colonize the island when Raiden throws his arms out wide.

"This is where we'll expand the village to, next."

Snapping her mouth shut, Sam works hard not to frown. "You'll clear this area, too?"

"Of course. How else will we have the timber to build more huts? And for our fires?"

And for their spears.

"But...you don't need any more huts."

And they certainly don't need spears.

Raiden's smile dies. "Is Askala larger than our village?"

"Well, yes, of course it is. Our colony has been there for generations."

"So, you've cleared more land than we have?" Before Sam can answer, Raiden arches a brow. "How many people are there in your colony?"

Sam blinks. "You're right, Raiden. Many more than you have here. And we did clear land to build our dwellings."

Raiden nods, placated. He looks like he's about to say something else, but Sam presses her hand on his arm as she leans forward. She wants him to understand. "But we've also planted far more than we've taken."

Raiden glances down at where she's touching him before looking back up. "You were never hungry in Askala, were you?" Raiden covers her hand with his. "Or scared."

Sam shakes her head, noting the softness in his tone despite his harsh words. "Askala is a beautiful place, Raiden. There's plenty for everyone. No one needs to fight for anything."

Raiden's hand tightens and Sam's suddenly conscious of how close they're standing. A part of her is excited that they're connecting. A part of her suddenly wishes Hawk were with her, that it is his hand holding hers.

Raiden smiles. "Are all the girls there smart like you?"

"Intelligence is valued in Askala, yes. As is kindness."

"And as beautiful as you?"

Sam flushes, unsure what that has to do with anything, but she's spared from replying because a primal squeal comes from deeper in the forest. Raiden's eyes light up as he spins around. "Another hare!"

The high-pitched scream certainly sounds like a trapped animal. Raiden rushes off and Sam follows him, reaching him as he untangles the thrashing animal from the snare tied beneath a bush.

Raiden's just grasped its neck and is ready to twist when Sam shoots forward. "Wait!"

"What? Now you don't want the bunny to die?"

Sam shakes her head. "Protein is a necessary part of our diet. I was going to ask whether you've considered breeding them."

Raiden glances at the hare still struggling as it hangs from his hand. "Breed them?"

"Well, yes. That's what we do in Askala with pteropods and cockroaches. All you need is a male and female. In a few months, your village will have ten times as many hares, ones you won't have to catch."

Raiden hesitates and Sam holds her breath. This could be another small step forward.

But he shakes his head, lifting the hare again. "We're hungry now."

Sam reaches out to stop him before he can kill it. "But imagine the feast you could have if you just waited."

A real feast. Not one where everyone leaves hungry.

Raiden frowns, not releasing the hare, but also not tightening his grip.

"Then there's all the feasts after that. Your people would become stronger and stronger."

He releases the squirming animal and it dangles by his side. "I'll think about it."

Sam has to stop herself from grinning. Another win!

They make their way to the village, but the sight of Hawk still working in the garden has Sam stopping. There's no one else she wants to share the good news with. Except she can't leave Raiden. Not so close to a breakthrough...

Nikita materializes beside them, dirt streaked across her arms. "The well's almost finished. Even more water coming through than the last one."

Sam beams. "That's great."

Nikita's eyes travel to the hare Raiden is holding. "Nice work." Her gaze roves to his other hand. "That's the only one today?"

She keeps her voice neutral, but Sam suspects all that digging has worked up quite an appetite. She nods sympathetically. No one is going to be eating well for a while, from the looks of things.

Raiden grins. "So far, but imagine how many we could have if we bred them."

"Great idea!" Nikita gasps.

Sam opens her mouth only to close it again. It doesn't matter whose idea it was, just that it helps the village and Mother Nature.

Nikita angles her head. "I could help you build a cage, if you like." She angles a hip. "A few hours in the forest and we could build quite the little love nest."

Sam blinks, wondering if Nikita's aware of the double meaning her words had.

But then she beams as she flaps her hands towards the tree line she and Raiden just left. "Another wonderful idea!"

This could give Sam a chance to talk to Hawk.

Raiden hesitates but then he grins. "Let's go build a love nest."

Nikita giggles as they head off, commenting that he's certainly got the muscles for that.

"Just remember, no more than two branches from a tree." Sam calls out after them.

"Hey, Nikita!" Gust shouts. "Where are you going?"

But Nikita ignores him, smiling up at Raiden as they continue to walk away. Gust throws his hands up in the air as he stomps off.

Sam realizes she's alone for the first time since they arrived in the Newlands. She looks across to the other lone body still on the outskirts of the village.

Alone with Hawk.

Excitement tingles across her skin. She's spent half her life with Hawk, and yet, suddenly, time with him has taken on another dimension.

Everything is...heightened.

Except, Hawk seems to be ignoring everything that just happened, which has Sam hesitating. In fact, he's working that soil with such ferocity, Sam wonders if he's considering carving out another well. Hawk's focus can be very single-minded when there's something he wants done. It's one of the reasons he's such a great Seeker.

Sam takes a half-step toward the village. She doesn't want to interrupt him if he's busy.

Hawk stops and looks up. His gaze zeros on Sam, as if he knew exactly where she was. They hold there for long seconds in suspended animation, and Sam has no idea what that means. Hawk doesn't ask her to come closer, but at the same time, his gaze never lets her go.

She realizes things were much simpler when she knew where they stood. When she saw Hawk as her best friend. There was far less second-guessing. Far less...uncertainty.

But there also wasn't this *feeling*. As if she was asleep before. As if her heart was dormant. Waiting to come alive.

Without conscious awareness, Sam drifts toward him. With every step, she realizes it's not just her heart that's coming alive.

Everything's alive.

She stops when she's in front of him, and for the first time, Sam's at a loss for words. Hawk's beauty is always the most mesmerizing out in the sun. His hair glints with earthy fire, his skin's caressed by the shadows created by the valleys and rises of his corded muscles. And his eyes...

They're clear as the sky. And yet hold depths of emotion Sam is only just discovering.

Hawk clears his throat. "You shouldn't have gone into the forest with him like that."

Sam's brow crinkles. "With Raiden?"

"Yes. With Raiden."

There's a hardness in Hawk's tone. Almost as if he's angry. "Why not? They caught another hare in the trap."

And Sam was the one who suggested they breed them. Despite her excitement that Raiden listened to her idea, she doesn't say any more. Hawk's upset about something, but she isn't sure what.

"Raiden...could be dangerous, Sam. Especially if you're alone with him."

Sam looks back at the tree line where Raiden and Nikita have disappeared into. "But it's okay for Nikita to go with him?"

Hawk's jaw tenses. "Raiden hasn't shown the same level of interest in her."

Confused, Sam shakes her head. "But that's because I know where to dig for a well. Because I can tell them about all the variables they'll have to take into account to successfully breed a food source."

For a moment, Hawk looks confused, too. But then his arms explode out wide. "He likes you, Sam! You can't leave yourself vulnerable like that!"

Sam reels back. "Are you saying that's why he's spending time with me? That's why he's listening to my ideas?"

Hawk's hands clench. "Yes, that's exactly what I'm saying."

For a moment, Sam wonders whether he's right. But then she remembers the invite in Nikita's eyes. And it seems Raiden's considering taking her up on the offer. It's not exactly the assimilation Sam thought they were here to do, but connections are connections.

She shakes her head with a smile. "Raiden isn't interested in me. He's off building love nests with Nikita."

Hawk glances over her shoulder. "He is?"

"Yes." Sam hesitates. "It meant I could come and talk to you."

Although, this isn't how she imagined the conversation was going to go.

Hawk's frown doesn't dissolve. "I still don't like it."

"But we're making progress, Hawk. I'm learning so much. Connecting. This is how we'll show them there's another way."

"Connecting, huh?" If anything, Hawk's frown seems to deepen.

Not sure what she's saying wrong, Sam shrugs helplessly. "Isn't that what we're here to do?"

Hawk's shoulders slump. "So you're going to spend more time with him? So you can *connect* with Raiden?"

Sam frowns. "Probably." So far, it's been their only opportunity to get close to Corbin. "I thought you wanted this, too."

How could she have read this so wrong? She thought Hawk would be happy with what she's achieved.

"You think I want you falling for Raiden?"

Sam's eyes spear open with surprise. "Why in the world would I do that? Raiden isn't..." You. She shakes her head, even more unsure of where things stand between them. "I just want to be a good Seeker, Hawk."

With you.

"Can you stop touching him, then?" Hawk chokes out.

Everything stills. Hawk's...jealous?

Sam doesn't smile, although she wants to. Hawk's jealous!

Instead, she does what she's been imagining since the day of their Announcement. When Hawk said those words.

"Sam, I really want you to come with me. And not because you're my best friend. Because you're so much more than that. You have been for such a long time now."

So many questions had followed. How much more? And for how long? And why didn't he say something?

She reaches out and grasps his hand. Instinctively, their fingers weave together like threads of fabric.

"I didn't even know I was." Sam draws in a breath, hoping for once, she's reading this right. "But when I touch you, Hawk, it's...unforgettable."

Even the slightest brush has become a brand.

"Sam," Hawk breathes.

Suddenly, that contact isn't enough. They move simultaneously, shrinking the distance between them.

For once, Sam's mind isn't thinking. Guessing. Questioning.

It's full of one word.

Hawk.

His gaze flickers to her lips and a new word appears.

Yes.

The inevitable begins to happen. They lean forward, the magnetic pull contracting.

"Hawk." His name pierces the emotions that had become their new center of gravity. "Can you help me with this?"

It's Grace. She puts a bucket down, obviously struggling with the weight. She rubs her arm across her forehead only to stop, wincing.

Drawing apart is hard, like Sam's fighting a tide, but that's exactly what they do. They hold gazes for long moments, disappointed but strangely elated. The understanding that they both wanted this now rests between them.

"I'd better go," Hawk says quietly.

Sam suppresses a sigh. Grace needs help. She can't begrudge her that. "Of course."

Hawk's only taken a couple of steps when he turns back to her. "Sam..."

Her breath held, Sam waits. "Yes?"

But no words slip past Hawk's lips. Instead, he smiles.

His Sam-smile. Realizing that's what she'd been wanting from the moment she saw him, Sam's own smile blazes back.

As he walks away, she sighs, telling herself that's enough for now.

They have time.

They're Seekers.

And right now, their future feels as bright as the sun.

MERCY

*M*ercy lies on her back, her chest aching from the heaving sobs escaping as if her tears are trying to drag out her despair against her will.

Siena is sitting beside her in the shelter, holding her hand, seeming to want to do more but not sure what. There's nothing she can do. Except, maybe row Mercy back to Askala.

She doesn't want to be here anymore. Not now. Why did Luca have to insist on joining them if this is how he planned to treat her? Take what he wanted and then cast her aside. Mercy's mom had warned her there were guys like that in the Outlands and it seems that Luca's Outlander blood runs thick in his veins.

The bastard! He's got to be the most selfish human who ever lived in the history of mankind.

And she's got to be the most stupid.

To think that she'd given herself to him like that only for him to run off in the middle of the night and never come back.

Yep. Bastard!

The sobs come harder now, and Siena squeezes her hand. "It's going to be okay," she soothes.

A noise in the bushes has Mercy sitting bolt upright, her eyes wide. Is that Gust trying to be funny?

Siena holds a finger to her lips as she scans the trees. "I think it's a child."

Mercy lets go of Siena's hand to wipe her tear-stained face with her sleeve. She hasn't seen many children here in the Newlands. And she certainly hasn't seen one alone.

A holler comes from behind the largest of the bushes and a small child comes running out. They're moving so fast it's hard to tell if it's a boy or a girl, not helped by the fact they seem to have a collection of leaves tied around their head like a mask.

If this were a fully-grown human, Mercy would be scared. But instead, she looks at Siena and they both suppress a smile.

The child launches into a series of tumble turns, then leaps to their feet and Mercy sees that underneath all those leaves, is a little girl. Her dark hair is wild, poking out from underneath her mask, and her eyes are alight with curiosity and fun. She's wearing a jumpsuit made from a tough brown fabric and her arms and legs are covered in dirt. This is exactly how Mercy imagines her mom would have looked as a child.

The girl stalks forward and removes a short spear from her belt, trying desperately to hold her mask together with her other hand.

Mercy puts her hands in the air, more than willing to play along with this game. Anything's got to be better than sitting here weeping over a guy who clearly couldn't care less about her.

"Please, don't hurt us," says Siena, unable to keep the smile from her face.

The sight of this tiny warrior has got to be the cutest thing Mercy has seen in a very long time.

The girl stops, her dark eyes peering out from a slit in her mask and she locks her gaze on Mercy. Letting her hand fall, she presses her palm to her chest.

"I am the Falcon," she says in a tone far too deep to be her natural voice. "I heard crying. I'm here to rescue you."

Mercy looks to Siena. Neither of them are smiling now, seeing this as the opportunity they've been waiting for. Instead of quizzing Corbin or Grace about this mysterious Falcon, *this* is who they need to talk to.

"Thank you, Falcon," says Mercy. "I'm feeling better already just to have you here."

A large leaf breaks away from the mask and flutters to the ground. The girl picks it up, tries to stick it back on, then realizing it's too difficult she throws it away.

"Is the Falcon thirsty?" asks Siena, holding out a cup of water.

The girl snatches the cup and downs the liquid in a few short gulps, then thrusts the cup back at Siena.

"The Falcon thanks you," she says. Then realizing she forgot to use her Falcon voice, she lowers her tone and tries again. "He thanks you very much."

"Tell us more about yourself, brave Falcon," says Mercy, trying to figure out how old this girl is. Seven? Maybe younger? She looks so malnourished it's hard to tell.

"My story is long," says the girl. "As is the list of my good deeds. Although, not everyone thinks my deeds are good."

"Tell us about your deeds," prompts Siena when the girl falls silent.

"I steal!" The girl beats her chest and another leaf falls from her mask, leaving it barely covering half of her forehead. "I lie! I take! But I'm not bad, like they say I am. Because I also give. I save! I rescue!"

"And you came to rescue me just now?" asks Mercy, wanting to do nothing more than take this skinny child in her arms and keep her safe from the very world she claims to be protecting.

The girl nods, and the last of the leaves fall from her mask, leaving her blinking at them with a dirty face and disappointment in her eyes.

"My name is Mercy. And this is Siena." Mercy rises to her knees, not wanting to stand in case she scares the girl away. "What's your real name?"

The girl hesitates, blinking at Mercy as she seems to decide if she can trust her.

"Tarquin," she says, dropping the deep tone. "I'm not really the Falcon."

Mercy does her best to look shocked, seeing that Siena is doing the same.

"Why don't you sit with us for a bit?" Mercy suggests. "You really did make me feel better."

Tarquin doesn't move. "I'm not supposed to talk to you."

"Who told you that?" Mercy asks.

Tarquin shrugs, not willing to elaborate.

"We have food." Siena jumps up and rifles around in their supplies. The truth is that they don't have much left to eat, and they're not supposed to touch their supplies without all Seekers present, but this is important. Tarquin could provide them with some valuable information. If only they can convince her to stay.

Siena holds up a bag of walnuts. "Have you ever eaten one of these?"

"No." Tarquin licks her lips, betraying her hunger.

"Well, you're in for a treat, then." Mercy pats the ground next to her and Tarquin scrambles over. This poor girl looks so neglected.

Siena cracks open a walnut and hands the contents to Tarquin who shoves it into her mouth without even looking at it.

"Can I have another one?" she asks.

"Did you even chew that one?" Siena laughs as she cracks open another walnut.

"You make a good Falcon," says Mercy, trying to steer Tarquin back on course.

Tarquin's eyes light up and she nods. "I've been practicing, ever since that night in the Outlands."

"Would you tell us about it?" asks Siena, handing over another walnut. "I like hearing stories."

"So do I," says Tarquin, getting herself comfortable.

"We're listening." Mercy gives her a reassuring smile.

"It was a full moon, so the sky was bright with stars," says Tarquin, crossing her legs and shifting just a little closer to Mercy. "I was in the hut pretending to sleep but I wasn't really. Grown-ups say lots of interesting things when they think the kids are sleeping."

Mercy laughs gently, remembering doing the same when she was young.

"My dad was talking about a village that was starving. He said they were too stupid to find food, but mom was saying we should share with them. Dad told her not to be ingorent."

Siena looks puzzled.

"Ignorant," says Mercy.

Tarquin nods. "Yep. Ingorent. But then there was a noise outside, and Dad grabbed his spear and went out to see what was happening. He told us to wait inside but Mom never listened, so she followed him and stood just outside the door in a shadow. She was watching Dad so hard she didn't even notice I was behind her. I'm good at sneaking."

"We saw that just now." Siena hands her one last walnut then puts the jar away. "You're an expert."

"Ex-pert," says Tarquin, trying out the word like it's a new treasure.

"What did you see?" asks Mercy. "Who was out there?"

"It was the Falcon." Tarquin chews the walnut, her face lighting with excitement at the memory. "I'd never seen the Falcon before although I'd heard plenty about him."

"Like what?"

"Dad said he helped people too stupid to help themselves. Mom called him a heron."

"Do you mean a hero?" Mercy asks, not sure how a heron bird makes sense here.

Tarquin shrugs. "Maybe."

"Your father didn't like him helping people?" asks Siena, settling herself beside them.

"He didn't like the way he did it," corrects Tarquin. "He took from the smart to help the stupid."

"Oh." Mercy shakes her head as she realizes what Tarquin's saying. This Falcon really does sound like a hero if he was taking from those who had more, to give to those who need it most. "And what did he look like when you saw him that night?"

Tarquin tucks her short legs underneath herself and bobs up and down at the memory. "He looked like a Falcon, of course! He had a mask just like the one you saw me wearing. Except, his mask was stronger so it didn't' fall apart. And it was made from feathers. That's why they called him the Falcon."

Mercy notices her use of the past tense, realizing the note they found in Askala must be true. It seems the Falcon really is dead. "And what was the Falcon doing in your village at night?"

"He was trying to steal from us to give to the village who needed the food." Tarquin looks at Mercy like she might be a little dim. "But he got caught and my dad and the other men of our village surrounded him. He was a good fighter, though. He kicked and he punched, and he did somersaults, and he nearly got away but then Corbin caught him by his ankle and dragged him right into the middle of our village."

She pauses. This memory clearly isn't as pleasant for this small girl as the earlier one.

"You can tell us what happened next," says Mercy as gently as she can. "We'd like to know."

"They ripped off his mask and tossed it into the fire. It

smelled bad when it burned." Tarquin waves her hand in front of her nose.

"And what did he look like underneath the mask?" Siena asks.

"He had lots and lots of white hair," says Tarquin. "It went right down to his waist. He didn't have any tattoos either. His skin was clean. He looked a bit like a ghost the way the moonlight lit up his face all yellow."

"What did your father do next?" Mercy asks even though she's dreading the answer.

"He put his spear right though the Falcon's guts," says Tarquin. "So far that it came out the other side and Vitron grabbed the other end and then they held him up in the air until he turned up the other way with his feet pointing at the stars and his hair hanging down. Everyone started cheering as the blood dripped to the ground. Then the Falcon's white hair turned red and his screaming went quiet. So, they put him on the fire with his mask. That smelled even worse..."

Mercy gasps. Her hand claps to her mouth to hear such a young girl describe an act so violent. Although, in truth, this story would be shocking no matter who told it.

Siena, more used to this kind of thing having grown up in the Outlands, seems to recover much faster. "And you want to continue the Falcon's work?"

Tarquin nods. "But don't tell anyone. Dad caught me once and threatened to put me on the fire. He said that's what happens to Falcons."

Gust chooses that moment to break through the trees and lope toward the shelter. Siena motions for him to stay back but he either doesn't understand or pretends not to.

"I don't like him," whispers Tarquin, scrambling to her feet.

"You don't have to go!" says Mercy, realizing she's about to flee.

But short of physically restraining the girl, there's not a lot she can do to keep her here. Tarquin darts away, disappearing back into the bushes.

"Who was that?" asks Gust, plonking himself down in the shade of the shelter.

Siena hands him a cup of water which he devours. "Maybe you should go and clean yourself up? You're getting mud in the shelter."

"Yes, Mom." He hauls himself to his feet and walks off toward the ocean. "I'll let you two decide which one of you is going to give me a massage when I get back."

"Sure thing," says Siena, poking her tongue out at his back.

"What do you think that all meant?" asks Mercy, the moment Gust is out of ear shot. "I can't figure out what in sweet Terra the Falcon has to do with all of this? Why would anyone in Askala need to know that he's dead?"

"I've got no idea." Siena shakes her head. "But it's making me feel uneasy. What do you think is happening back home? Do you think they've worked out who that note was for yet?"

Mercy's stomach contracts as she thinks about how vulnerable her peace-loving people are. The murderous act that Tarquin had described isn't like anything she's ever heard of before. She knew people in the Outlands had murdered, but it's inconceivable that anyone would take joy in such a brutal act.

Have they underestimated what they've come up against here? And had it taken the innocence of a child to point it out? Maybe none of this is connected at all!

But just when she decides that maybe she's being as dramatic as everyone always says she is, the trees around them vibrate with the unmistakable sound of Tarquin's scream.

LUCA

"Sh." Luca grips the wriggling mass of child harder, grimacing when a heel connects with his shin. "It's okay. I won't hurt you."

He's about to tell her that he'll take off the hand he has clamped across her mouth if she promises to be quiet when she opens it wide and bites him. Hard.

Luca releases her, gripping his throbbing fingers. "Dammit, Tarquin!"

Already several paces away, she stops and spins around. "Luca?"

Luca grins, holding his arms out wide. "Although you weren't trying to eat me the last time you saw me."

Tarquin's face explodes into a smile as she runs and leaps, slamming straight back into his arms.

They hug, her small body clasped tightly against his. This time, willingly.

Tarquin pulls back, her white teeth a stark contrast against her grubby face as she smiles broadly. "I didn't know you were one of *them*."

She half-whispers the last word, like she does when she curses.

Luca releases her, not sure how to answer that. He's not.

For a little while, he wanted to be.

Then he learned he can never be...one of them.

Instead, he grins. "I just came along for the ride."

Tarquin's smile fades, the eyes that always seemed too large for her face filling with loss. "The Falcon. He's dead."

Luca nods. That's why he's here, trying to talk to her.

After he ran this morning, Luca hasn't been far from Mercy. Not that she knows it, because he's deliberately kept himself hidden.

It's meant every tear she's cried has carved its way across his heart, but he's welcomed the pain. It's what he deserves.

Following her meant he was high in a tree when the little bullet streaked out of the bushes toward Mercy and Siena. His hands slackened around the trunk when he recognized Tarquin. He almost fell out when he heard her story.

Luca grips her thin shoulders. "The Falcon was a fool who was lucky to survive as long as he did."

Tarquin frowns fiercely. "No, he wasn't—"

"And now that he's dead, he needs to stay that way. No more stories. No more games."

Impossibly, Tarquin's brows sink deeper into the layers of dirt on her face. "He saved—"

"No, Tarquin!" Luca has to modulate his tone. "Or you'll end up as dead as he is."

The powerful people of the Outlands hated the Falcon. He stole from them, sharing their wealth whether they liked it or not. Every one of them would have danced to hear that the thief in their midst had finally been captured and killed.

A young girl hero worshipping him is dangerous. A young girl trying to keep his memory alive is deadly.

The sound of people running through the forest has Luca cursing.

"Tarquin! Are you okay?"

Hastily, Luca grabs Tarquin again. "We don't know each other," he whispers urgently.

"Yes, we do—"

"Ouch!" he calls out loudly. "I said I'm not going to hurt you."

Tarquin's already struggling when Mercy and Siena burst through the trees. She screams, her heel connecting with the same place as last time, yanking a curse out of him.

Releasing her, Luca reaches down to rub it. He doesn't bruise easily, but he's willing to bet the unerring accuracy of Tarquin's foot is going to leave a purple mark.

She runs to Mercy's side. "He grabbed me!"

Mercy wraps a protective arm around Tarquin's shoulders. "It's okay. He's a..." Her gaze shutters. "He's with us."

Tarquin frowns at Luca. "Then why did he grab me?"

Mercy arches a brow at him and Luca grits his teeth. He should've known Tarquin was a great actress. "She was running so fast, I thought someone or something was chasing her." Knowing how lame that sounds, Luca frowns. "I was trying to make sure she was okay."

Tarquin crosses her arms. "I'm fine."

Unlike Luca's shin. He works to soften his face. "I'm glad to hear that."

Silence creeps through the trees. Mercy crosses her arms. Siena shifts uncomfortably. Tarquin looks between them all, trying to figure out why the adults have all run out of words.

But every muscle in Luca's body is wound too tightly. He can't speak. He can barely breathe.

Mercy's only a few yards away.

Siena holds out her hand to Tarquin. "How about I take you back to the village? Your mother's probably wondering where you are."

"Oh, my mother's dead."

Tarquin says the words in the matter of fact way of the Outlanders. Death is just as much a part of their life as hunger.

Siena blinks. "I'm sorry to hear that. Let's get you back to your, er, family, then." She smiles. "We'll stop off for a drink of water at the well."

Tarquin was looking like she was about to object, but the mention of water has her grabbing Siena's hand in a flash. The concept of more water than you can drink isn't something she's seen in her lifetime.

They're gone and Luca finds he's still rooted to the spot. This is the last place he wants to be.

And yet, being with Mercy is the only place he wants to be.

Even when she's glaring at him like that.

Mercy's arms twist even tighter across her chest. She angles her chin, the picture of haughty anger.

But they grew up together. What's more, Luca's held her, touched her, kissed her. He knows her more intimately than he should've allowed himself to.

Mercy's skin is too pale for anger. Her lashes are still dark with moisture. Tears.

Tears he caused.

"Mercy, I'm sorr—"

"I don't want apologies, Luca. I want an explanation." Her eyes flash, finding the anger to cover the hurt. "I deserve one."

She's right. It's what she deserves.

It's also the one thing he can't give her.

Luca looks away. "I thought we could escape who we are. But we can't."

Mercy shakes her head. "We were past this. The Newlands was going to be a fresh start. We were talking of a future."

Her voice cracks on the last word, and the fracture in Luca's heart grows wider. "I never meant to hurt you, Mercy."

Her arms spear to her sides, her fists clenched. "Well, you did! You used me, Luca! And now you're walking away!"

Mercy throws each word at him, waiting for him to deflect them. Wanting him to deny them.

But he can't.

No matter how much he wants to.

"I tried to warn you." Luca takes a step back, hating himself. "You thought I'd be someone who would stay still long enough so we could have a tomorrow." Another step, and he can no longer see her lip trembling. "I told you over and over. I'm not that kind of guy."

Spinning on his heel, Luca turns away. He strides through the forest toward the village, not looking back.

Knowing he's destroying the one beautiful thing he thought he could have.

He doesn't stop until he's reached the first hut. He comes to a halt, wondering how he's going to find Alyx.

They need to talk.

Except they're not supposed to know each other.

When he sees Sam and Hawk walking back from the well, Luca takes a quick turn. The last people he wants to be with right now are the two lovebirds who are slowly coming into each other's orbits. It's only a matter of time before his sister and her childhood best-friend find out what it feels like to go supernova.

Just like Luca has.

Shaking his head, he circles a hut, trying to come up with a reason he can ask Grace where Alyx might be.

"Hey!"

Luca rears back, having almost collided with a burly brick of man. Luca instantly recognizes him as one of Corbin's right hand goons. There are about four of them, each taking it in turns to shadow him, adding to the bad smell.

Luca lifts his hands, palms up. "Sorry."

The man scowls when he realizes who Luca is—one of the outsiders—his shoulders flexing back an inch. "What do you want?"

Luca keeps his posture casual. He dealt with plenty of thugs like this in the Outlands, but he's pretty sure knocking this guy unconscious isn't what Sam would call assimilating. "I was hoping you could help me," Luca says lightly, figuring he'll start with the truth and go from there. "I'm looking for Alyx."

The man's face relaxes into a grin as his eyes develop a knowing glint. "Her name's already making the rounds, huh?"

Luca grins, although his gut knots at the way the man is practically salivating. "It seems so."

The man inclines his head toward a hut not far away. "Although, she doesn't usually see customers during the day."

Customers...

Feeling a little ill, Luca winks at the guy. "Challenge accepted."

The man chuckles as he thumps Luca on the shoulder. "She prefers real men. Not skinny pretty boys."

Laughing at his own words, the man strolls away, scratching his chest. Luca wonders how many lice have established themselves amongst the dirty hair.

Alyx's hut is set slightly apart from the others, even for those along the edge of the village like this one. It only clenches Luca's gut tighter. These huts are always reserved for the sick, or... women who have one thing left to trade.

His feet feeling heavy, Luca approaches it. Like most of the other huts, a length of leather hangs over the entry, acting as a door. He's about to call out when it pulls back, Alyx freezing when she finds Luca only a few feet away.

Luca opens his mouth, but then he glances behind her. Not far from the firepit in the center of the room, is a thin sheet of tattered material spread over a bed of leaves. A mattress of sorts. Big enough for two.

"What have you done, Alyx?"

Shoving past him, she lets the flap drop. Spinning around, she crosses her arms. "What I had to."

Out here, in the sun, Alyx's pale hair is a golden blaze around her shoulders. Her beautiful face is tight and defensive, but beautiful nonetheless. Many a man had sought her back in the Outlands.

Her father knew it and was waiting for the highest bidder.

Luca shakes his head, his gut churning. "No. Not...this."

Alyx strides up to him, fury making her movements sharp and stilted. "What was I supposed to do? Coming here was my one ticket out of the Outlands."

He never considered how Alyx became a part of this colony. Why they'd bring a young female when brawn is what builds huts and protects what little they have.

Luca's fingers jam through his hair. "And you brought Tarquin? What the hell were you thinking?"

Alyx stabs her finger into his chest. "The alternative was to leave my little sister in the Outlands."

Where food is more scarce than here.

"With our father."

The very man who has Alyx believing women can be bought. A violent, greedy man.

Luca engulfs Alyx in a hug, his chest aching all over again. Instantly, she sags against him. "It's not that bad," she murmurs into his chest. "I've never had so much food in my life. Some days I'm barely hungry."

Because the men would be willing to pay quite the sum to spend time with Alyx in her hut.

Luca sighs. "I overheard Tarquin. Is it true about what happened? To...the Falcon?"

Alyx stills. "Yes. It was horrible."

"But..." He shakes his head, not sure what this is going to mean.

"He didn't deserve what happened to him," whispers Alyx, tucking herself deeper into his arms.

Luca's eyes slam closed, grief ripping through his chest. He knew that white hair, before it was streaked in blood. He knew Aspen well enough to be able to imagine his screams of agony, his pale blue eyes becoming glassy and blank, his white skin turning black as his body burned.

No. He didn't deserve that.

And his family are going to be devastated.

There's a gasp, and they both pull away, suddenly remembering where they are.

Luca spins around, then freezes.

Mercy is standing at the edge of the trees, her hand over her mouth. Above, her eyes are wide and luminous. Shining with betrayal.

Luca stands there, unmoving. Knowing there's no point.

He can't deny the conclusion that's stamped across Mercy's face. He can't call her back as she turns and runs back into the forest.

"Luca..." Alyx's voice is full of apology. "Maybe you should—"

"No. It's okay," Luca says, although every shred of his being denies it.

Maybe it's better this way.

Now, Mercy has a reason why he ran.

HAWK

*H*awk wades out into the harsh ocean, washing both the sweat from his body and the grime from his clothes in a series of quick movements. Their hemp clothing isn't going to last long if they keep this up. They really need to focus on digging more wells and getting enough freshwater to sustain the colony here.

Emerging from the sea, he takes off his shirt and squeezes the water out of it. Looking down, he considers the broadness of his chest. He'd never really thought of his size as a good thing before, but he's starting to notice the effect it has on women. Mercy teases him about it. Nikita singled him out because of it long ago. Even Grace seems to have trouble concentrating on anything else when his torso is bare.

Most importantly, it seems Sam may finally have noticed him, too. Hopefully for more than the size of his chest, though.

That almost kiss had been both the most blissful and torturous moment of his life. He'd waited years to break out of the friend zone and just when he'd thought it was about to happen, Grace had interrupted. If only she knew what her timing had cost him! But judging by the bruises on her face, she has more important things to think about right now.

Putting his shirt back on, being sure to tuck his pendant into the neckline, he heads up to camp. Nikita is still out making traps with Raiden, but the rest of the Seekers are here. Even Luca has returned, although there's a tension that's pulling between him and Mercy. It contracts and expands as they move around the camp, but it never disappears.

The feeling of wanting to punch Luca in the nose envelops him, but Hawk pushes it down. Mercy is capable of handling this. She knows he's there for her if she needs it.

Darkness is falling, the sky turning shades of pink and gray as another day draws to a close. But the heat in the air is still stifling. Hopefully Hawk's clothes stay damp for a while longer to keep him cool, but he can feel the thin fabric drying already.

"We're doing a good job, Seekers," says Sam, clapping her hands together as Hawk sits down in the shelter. "So far, we've made a start on two wells, we have a vegetable garden planted, we're making progress toward breeding hares and we've managed to keep our interactions with the Outlanders civil. Some strong connections are being forged that are going to serve us well."

Hawk smiles, finding Sam's enthusiasm infectious as always. And she's right. They've come a long way in the short time they've been here. The leaders of Askala would be proud. It seems the right people were sent to do the job.

Siena opens the bag of walnuts and hands them around. There's enough for two each.

"What about Nikita?" Mercy asks.

"I already put two aside for her." Siena sets down the bag. "But our food's almost out now. Do we have a plan for what we're going to eat moving forward?"

"The vegetables will take ages until harvest," says Gust.

"Nikita and Raiden's hares will take a while to breed as well," adds Sam.

"We can't keep asking the Outlanders for food." Luca paces the camp while Mercy crosses her arms and glares at him.

"Maybe Alyx can spare you some food," snaps Mercy.

"Who?" Hawk is certain he hasn't heard that name around here.

"Nobody," says Luca. "I'll go out tomorrow and see what I can find for us to eat."

"I'll come too!" Sam's eyes light up. "It will be like the test in the Proving. Mercy and I are good at finding bugs. We can eat sushi!"

Hawk blanches, not having missed eating grubs and bugs since arriving in the Newlands. Then he remembers something from earlier in the day that he'd forgotten to share.

"Grace got a raven from the Outlands," he tells them. "It said a supply boat will be coming soon. It will bring food in exchange for timber."

"Great!" says Mercy, her voice full of sarcasm. "More trees to chop down."

"We still need to be self-sufficient," says Sam. "No matter how many supplies they get. We can't convince these Outlanders that we know a better way to live if we keep taking their food. It's important to teach by example."

"Can we figure out how to be self-sufficient tomorrow?" Gust yawns widely. He really had worked hard on that well today. Hawk can't blame him for being tired.

With the sun having now set, Hawk decides that maybe Gust is onto something. They're too tired to make decisions right now.

"Let's get some rest and tomorrow when Nikita's back we'll make a plan for how to source some food." He yawns even more widely than Gust. "We can make an early start."

There are nods all round and Mercy claims a spare bit of floor next to Hawk which just so happens to be the opposite side to where Luca has stretched out in front of the entrance to the shelter. Sam nestles in on Hawk's other side and Siena and Gust lie down somewhere near his feet. The oppressive heat coupled with the lack of food and hard physical work has taken a toll on all of them. They really do need to get some kind of plan sorted out in the morning.

Hawk pulls Sam a little closer, wishing they were alone so he could find her lips in the dark and turn that spark they found in the vegetable patch into a roaring flame. But it's clear that after only a few minutes, she's fallen asleep.

Closing his eyes, Hawk fights his fatigue, wanting to lie still for a moment so he can appreciate Sam's closeness. He matches his breathing to hers, drawing in breath at the same time and letting it slowly out. With all the uncertainty in the world, Sam is his constant. Which makes moments like these all the more precious.

But before long, he feels himself matching Sam in more ways than one and he drifts off.

When he's dragged from sleep in the dead of night, he's filled with confusion.

Confusion about how much time has passed.

Confusion about the source of all the noise.

Confusion about why it feels like there are a hundred people in the shelter when there should only be six.

Shaking his head, Hawk leaps to his feet, pulling Sam up with him and tucking her behind him. But there are people behind him, too.

"What's going on?" he cries into the darkness.

There's a strange rumbling noise, then a bright flame as the roof of the shelter catches alight.

Hawk hauls Sam toward the exit, just as a blistering scream pierces the air. Was that Mercy or Siena? He's lost track of where everyone is now. Everyone except Sam. He should've kept hold of Mercy, too. Where is she?

The flames are casting an eerie light across the shelter and in the chaos he sees familiar faces as well as those of strangers. Smoke quickly fills the air and as Hawk and Sam stumble out into the cool night air, he turns to see the shelter's fully on fire now. Which means he can also see exactly what's happening around him.

Everywhere he looks, there are Outlanders. Not the people he's grown used to over the last few days, but men and women he's never seen before. And they have the Seekers surrounded.

Luca darts toward Mercy who ducks away, planting herself beside Gust, a move that reveals the depths of the anger she's feeling toward Luca right now. If they survive this, Hawk really is going to have to deck that guy.

The Outlanders are holding flamethrowers which explains the strange noise he'd been hearing. Hawk's seen these weapons before, leftover from the failed invasion of Askala, but he's never seen them with fuel. It doesn't seem right that fire can pour from a weapon like that.

"Get 'em!" one of the men shouts. "Round 'em up!"

Several of the men send bursts of flame shooting into the sky as they hustle the Seekers. Putting their backs together, the Seekers form a circle, eyes in every direction, determined not to be taken by surprise again. The only one missing is Nikita, and Hawk hopes she can somehow alert the Newlanders and get some help. But would Corbin and his goons come to their aid? It's about their only hope right now. Which is a worry in itself.

"Which one of you lot is Siena?" a man with a beard asks, rage pouring from his eyes.

"Don't answer," says Luca under his breath.

"Come on. Now!" The man circles them, studying the faces of the females.

Hawk tries to position himself to shadow Sam's face. What

could this man possibly want from Siena? She may have been born in the Outlands, but she's lived in Askala most of her life.

"If you don't tell me which one of you bitches is Gritt's daughter, I'm going to toast the whole lot of you!" The man sends out another burst of flames over their heads. "We have a debt to settle."

Siena steps forward. "I'm Gritt's daughter. I'm Siena. Leave the others alone."

Hawk reaches out to grab Siena by the back of her shirt and pull her back, but she's already been gripped firmly by the arms of one of the other men.

Making the most of this distraction, Sam slips from Hawk's side and takes a few steps away. "She's lying! I'm Siena."

A weight crushes Hawk's chest as he tries to go after her but is forced back by a flame. Then trying to pre-empt what he's certain is inevitable, he reaches in the dim light for Mercy's wrist.

But he's too late.

"I'm Siena," Mercy says as she slips out from the group. "Leave those two imposters alone. I'm Gritt's daughter."

"Don't believe her," shouts the real Siena. "Don't believe either of them. It's me."

"Oh, you want to play a game, do you?" the bearded man snarls. "It's called *Let's find the thief's daughter.* Okay, I'll play. Line 'em up!"

The men force Siena, Sam and Mercy to stand in a line. Hawk pulls forward but this time Luca holds him back.

"Careful," he hisses in Hawk's ear. "Pick our time."

He's right. One false move and they're all dead. This is no time to be rash.

Gust is shaking beside them. He's not going to be much use when the time comes, but the Outlanders don't know that. Not yet.

The bearded man calls on a woman with wild dark hair and

eyes that don't seem to be able to stay still. "Prew! Get over here and figure this out."

The woman paces in front of the girls, then stops and glares at them.

"What color hair does Gritt have?" She jabs a finger into Sam's chest. "You answer first."

Sam nods. "Brown."

Hawk knows that right now she's biting down on her tongue to stop herself from pointing out that statistically more people in the world have brown hair than any other color so it's the best guess. He really wished she'd said red so they'd get her out of that dangerous line.

"Correct." Prew looks at the bearded man. "Do we take her now?"

"No!" Hawk cries unable to stand still. He lurches forward. "Her name is Sam!"

Two men grab him by the arms while a third brings his flamethrower down on his head, sending Hawk crashing to the ground, his skull swirling with fear and agony. These Outlanders aren't here to play any games. They want Siena and it's clear they don't care who they have to kill to get their hands on her.

Hawk gets himself to his feet, pain radiating across his skull and blood dripping into his eyes, but he's unable to clear his vision as his arms are still clamped in the clammy Outlanders' hands.

Prew turns on Mercy next. "Don't really need to talk to this one, do we? No way Gritt could spawn a daughter this pretty."

"Maybe we take her anyway." The bearded man licks his lips and grabs hold of one of Mercy's breasts. Hard. She yelps and this time it's Luca who's unable to stay in place. He comes flying forward, only to be hit on the head by a flamethrower in the same way Hawk was.

Except, when Luca falls to the ground, he doesn't get up.

Hawk struggles against the men holding him. "Let me go! You've killed him! Let me check him."

"Askalan scum." The man who'd hit Luca spits on him. "Nothing to check here."

"Gust!" Hawk shouts. "Do something! Help Luca!"

Despite having wanted to take his fist to Luca earlier, when it's come down to it, Hawk is horrified at the thought of someone having killed him. He's a Seeker! He's one of them. There's no way he can watch him die.

Gust drops to his knees and crawls toward Luca.

"Look at the little rat!" The Outlanders laugh, nudging each other as Gust reaches Luca and puts his fingers to his neck.

"He's dead!" Gust screeches, pressing his face to Luca's chest. "What have you done?"

Hawk blinks away the blood from his eyes as he looks at Luca lying motionless on the ground. This can't be happening. Someone so full of life can't possibly be dead! It's unfathomable.

"Luca! No!" Sam is sobbing, finding it hard to stand in the line she's been forced into. "No, Luca!"

But the bearded man quickly draws all their attention back to Siena when he shoves her roughly in the chest. "I reckon it's this one. She has those same beady eyes at Gritt."

"I'm telling you, it's me!" Sam pushes forward, trying to position herself in front of Siena. "You've killed my brother, now kill me, too!"

"Sam! Don't!" Hawk shouts. Doesn't she realize there's nothing she can do right now to protect Siena.

"Your brother?" The bearded man tips his head back and cackles. "Funny that. Gritt never had himself a son. Much as he wanted one."

Sam's shoulders crumple as she realizes what she's said. Hawk struggles once more, wanting to go to her, needing to comfort her just as much as he needs the comfort himself. Will he ever get to hold her again?

Now that the man has Siena firmly in his grasp, the rest of the men shove Sam and Mercy over to Gust and Luca. Sam immediately throws herself on Luca, sobbing uncontrollably now. Gust says something to Sam that Hawk can't hear. He can only hope they're words of reassurance.

Hawk is marched over to them and thrown on the ground beside Gust.

"Sit down and don't move or this time I'll do a proper job of you!" sneers the man whose flamethrower is still covered in Luca's blood.

Pressing his hands to Sam's back, Hawk tries to draw her away from Luca's body. Then realizing it's an impossible task, he lets her grieve for her brother.

He wipes the blood from his eyes with his sleeve and turns back to see the Outlanders seize Siena. She has a wild look on her face as if she's summoning the courage to fight. But surely, she knows it's useless. They're outnumbered. They have no weapons. And these savages have a thirst for blood that the Seekers had only heard about in stories they'd hoped weren't true.

"What are you going to do with her?" Mercy shouts.

The bearded man snorts. "Trade her! Her good for nothing father might refuse to pay his debt, but the traders will be only too glad to have a fresh piece of flesh like this. Fair is fair, and all that."

"You're not punishing my father by trading me!" Siena cries out. "He was going to trade me himself. Why else do you think I ran away?"

Mercy leaps to her feet, trying to pry Siena from the bearded man's hands.

"I said sit down!" he roars at Mercy.

Siena takes this as her chance, lifting the flamethrower from the man's back and sending flame shooting at his legs.

He howls, spinning around, the strap of his weapon still around his shoulders, tearing it from Siena's hands.

Two of his men step forward, pressing their hands to their triggers and shooting white hot flames at Siena.

Hawk looks away as Siena's screams echo around the forest. Her final moments are built from the kind of agony nobody wants to witness. And a sadness grips Hawk as her screams fall abruptly silent. Siena was a good person. She didn't deserve to have her life snuffed out like that.

Which means now two Seekers are dead. And something tells him, these thugs aren't finished with them yet.

"You idiots!" screams the bearded man. "She's worth nothing to us dead!"

Glancing back, Hawk gags at Siena's charred remains. Sam is throwing up beside him, the stench of burning flesh the final straw for her sensitive stomach.

"It's okay," says Prew, touching the man on the arm. "The traders don't know the difference. We'll just take that one instead."

She points a bony finger in Sam's direction and the bearded man smiles. Hawk's heart rate spikes as he realizes what's being suggested.

"You were so keen to be Siena earlier." The man marches toward Sam. "Looks like you just got your chance."

SAM

a few steps and the man grabs Sam roughly, yanking her back and slamming her body against his. His hot breath gusts across her cheek. "I think Siena got an upgrade, to be honest."

Sam knows she should try to escape. At least jerk against the hands holding her upper arms so tight it makes her eyes water.

But there's no use. She doesn't need to do the math.

Luca's dead. Whatever Gust tried to whisper wouldn't have made that news any easier to bear. Now Siena's gone, too. Burned alive.

They're outnumbered. They have no weapons.

They have no idea how to fight.

Her gaze connects with Hawk's, her bruised heart feeling like it's cracking. Maybe if she goes quietly, no one else will get hurt.

She mouths two words to him. "I'm sorry."

"Let's get out of here," growls the man, his filthy beard scraping her temple.

Sam consciously relaxes her body, going limp, hating the

man's grunt of satisfaction. If this is what her role as a Seeker is, then so be it.

She only wishes… Her gaze lifts again, wanting Hawk to be the last thing she sees.

Except Hawk's no longer standing still, bloodied and helpless. He's a boulder of movement, running straight toward Sam and the man holding her captive.

Sam's heart catapults up her throat. "No, Hawk!"

But the fury powering him is unstoppable. His determination to get to her stamped in his ferocious frown.

The moment he moves, the men around them leap into action. One man raises his flamethrower as he dives for Hawk. But this time, Hawk's expecting it. He ducks, then slams his shoulder into the Outlander. The man grunts as he bounces off Hawk like he was just shoved by a battering ram.

"Get him!" screams the man holding Sam.

The Outlanders jump into action, this time two launching themselves at Hawk. Hawk sees the one coming at him from the front.

But he never realizes there's another behind.

He drops his head, intent on barging this one like he did the last.

"Hawk, look ou—"

Even though her captor slams a calloused hand over her mouth, Sam's shout is too late.

The Outlander behind Hawk leaps, launching himself at him. He tackles Hawk around the waist and they crash to the ground. In the moving light of the flames, Sam watches as another man joins the fray, his fists already primed as he pummels over and over.

Mercy runs at them only to be shoved back. She stumbles, landing on the ground beside Luca. Gust is rooted to the spot, fear dancing across his face.

The first man stands up, the second joining him. Their lips

curl as they watch Hawk roll onto his side, spitting out a mouthful of blood. Sam's chest aches but she's glad it's over. Hawk has to have realized this is futile.

She can't lose him, too.

The men glance at each other, nodding as they grin. Sam cries out, horrified, as they simultaneously draw their legs back, then viciously kick Hawk. Again. And again.

And again.

At first, Hawk groans each time a boot slams into his ribs or stomach or face. But after several blows, he goes silent.

"Please, you're killing him!" Sam begs.

Her only response are the words sneered close to her ear. "That's the idea."

The flurry of movement that happens next has Sam blinking in disbelief. A fist slams into one of the men's faces, knocking him out cold. Before the second man can respond, Luca's elbow smashes into his nose. The Outlander howls as blood explodes across his face.

Luca!

Joy soars in Sam's chest at the sight of her brother as he spins around, fists already primed for the next opponent.

Luca's alive!

"Now, Gust!" shouts Mercy.

They launch into action, Mercy grabbing the flamethrower from the man nearest to her as Gust shoves him. Gust tries to land a punch on the man only for the Outlander's fist to slam in his gut. He doubles over, but Mercy's already struck the butt of her newly acquired flamethrower into the side of the man's head. He howls with pain and fury, stumbling, but not out.

Luca's by their side in an instant. Two punches, and the man's down. Mercy slips around, pressing her back against his. No one's going to sneak up on Luca like they did Hawk.

Eyes wide above the smelly hand half suffocating her, Sam watches as the Seekers fight with everything they have.

Courage.

Determination.

The knowledge that this is life or death.

Luca downs the next Outlander with his fists. Mercy kicks out at another as he barrels towards Luca's back. Gust crawls over to Hawk to check he's okay.

For breathless moments, Sam wonders if it's possible. Could they overpower the Outlanders?

The flames of their burning hut leap higher, spewing smoke into the night sky. The flickering light illuminates the fight. Luca's elbow rams into an Outlander's throat. Mercy lands a punch on a man's jaw. Gust is now standing above Hawk, ready to protect him.

Except the Outlanders have focused totally on Luca. Because he looks like he could do this all night. And like his fists are made of steel.

Maybe they stand a chance...

Her captor's hand slips from her mouth and Sam draws in a gasping breath. His hand scrabbles at her waist, but she ignores it. She focuses on the fight, determined to tell any of her friends if there's an attack they don't see coming.

There's a blast of heat and noise from beside her and flames surge in front of Sam, the heat making her instinctively turn her head to the side. For long seconds, her tightly shut eyes see nothing but roaring reds and ravenous orange.

The moment it stops, there's silence.

As the haze of smoke lifts, her captor chuckles. "Flamethrowers trump everything, don't they?"

Luca, Mercy, Nikita and Gust are standing in the center, the three remaining men surrounding them. But three is all they need. Each of them holds the very weapon that has Sam's stomach recoiling.

Hawk's still lying motionless only a few feet away. The

stilted rise and fall of his chest is the only reason Sam's still standing.

He's alive. And so are the others.

"Burn them," growls her captor.

"No!" Sam screams the denial.

Luca, Mercy and Gust contract together, Luca pushing them behind them. His scowl tells her he won't go down without a fight.

His mouth, little more than a flat line, tells her he knows there's no escape.

Sweet Terra. She's going to have to watch them all get slaughtered. Burned alive like Siena.

Sam groans, and if the man wasn't holding her, she'd crumple to her knees. "No, please," she whispers.

But the man's chuckling. As if he's taking pleasure in what he sees.

This time, Sam fights. She turns into a screaming, twisting mass of tears and anger. She bites the arms holding her, stomps on the man's feet.

She has nothing to lose.

"Bitch."

The man throws her to the ground, lifting the butt of his flamethrower. "The traders won't care if you ain't got no teeth."

He lifts it high, his face full of anticipation. Sam refuses to cower. It's possible a part of her is welcoming the prospect of losing consciousness.

She won't smell the burning flesh.

She won't see what's about to happen.

Won't hear the screams.

But the man's there one moment, gone the next. Sam blinks, trying to understand what just happened. There's a loud grunt as he lands on the ground, a body on top of him.

Sam glances around, finding Luca where he's still standing. Hawk still on the ground.

There's another groan, but this one is more drawn out. More...filled with pain. One of the Outlanders collapses, gripping the spear that's now skewered through his chest.

Scrabbling to her knees, Sam watches as bodies materialize, stepping into the light of the flames.

The Newlanders.

Corbin's chest expands and contracts as his arm drops, his face shadowed and twisted. It was his spear that killed the first man.

The other two drop in quick succession, one screaming in agony. It's Prew. She writhes in the sand as her hideous screams fill the air. Bile sears the back of Sam's throat. Her death won't be a quick or painless one.

Turning, she sees it was Raiden who saved her. He's on top of the man who held her captive, holding his own spear aloft.

"No!" Sam runs toward them, shoving him. Raiden doesn't move from his position straddling the Outlander, but the push is enough to change the trajectory of his spear. It impales the sand next to the man's head.

Raiden glares furiously at her. "What did you do that for?"

Sam can't lift herself from the sand. She shakes her head wearily, the motion heavy with sorrow. "No more death."

Raiden's hands grip the man's throat. "He was going to hurt you, Sam. Sell you. He ordered his men to kill the others!"

Sam drags herself over to him, putting her hands over his. "But he doesn't deserve to die. Don't take his life, Raiden."

Astonished, Raiden's gaze lifts to hers. Tears prick Sam's eyes. "Desperate people do desperate things."

Raiden's hands release the man's throat and he climbs off him. "Seems it's your lucky day, scum."

Sam stands unsteadily, her knees still weak. Raiden reaches out and she holds his hand gratefully. "What's your name?" she asks the man.

The man shuffles back, dragging himself over the sand. "Bohr."

"Bohr. Go back to the Outlands. Tell them Askala brings only compassion. And a future for all."

Bohr creeps backward some more, his eyes wide with disbelief. When no one moves, he turns and runs.

Stumbling across the sand, he looks over his shoulder several times.

But no one follows him. The Seekers wouldn't.

The Newlanders probably think Sam's gone mad.

The remaining Outlanders are dead. Along with Siena.

Before Bohr's out of sight, Sam spins back. Hawk. She needs to check if he's okay.

Two steps and she realizes Grace is already by his side, his head in her lap. His bruised and bloodied head.

Sam falls to her knees, her hands fluttering, wanting to touch him, but not knowing where. Every inch of Hawk seems to be battered. "Hawk…"

His eyelids flutter open. "Sam." He lifts a hand and Sam takes it. "The Outlanders?"

"All dead but one. Corbin and his men saved us."

His hand tenses around hers. "There's one more?"

"He won't be bothering us."

Hawk's lips twitch. "I saw you. You let him go, didn't you?"

"We need to show them humanity, even if they don't show the same to us." She shuffles closer, wrapping his hands in both of hers. "We can talk about that later. Right now, we need to get you better."

Grace's hand comes into Sam's view, pushing back a lock of hair glistening with blood. "Some men have gone back to get a stretcher."

"I can walk," mumbles Hawk through swollen lips.

Grace smiles. "I'm sure you could. But this way you can save your strength."

Looking around, Sam sees the Newlanders dragging away the dead bodies of the Outlanders. Luca's draping a cloth over Siena's body. Mercy's hands are fists by her side as she stands, tearstained and shocked, beside the charred remains. Gust is standing on the edge, his face pale and eyes wide.

A movement and Sam sees Nikita by the tree line, silent and pale.

They've never experienced violence. Greed so powerful someone would kill for it.

They've never seen a murder, knowing they were next.

The flames of the hut have died down, sinking the world into shades of black. As Sam turns back to Hawk, she's struck by how much they've lost. "We no longer have a hut."

"I'll take him to mine," says Grace. "I have sap, and I'm familiar with many of the herbs that will help him heal."

Sam nods even though a part of her doesn't like that idea. She doesn't want to leave Hawk's side. She doesn't want to let his hand go.

But she doesn't have a choice. The stretcher arrives, and two large men heave Hawk's body onto it. He grits his teeth, but a strangled moan still escapes his lips. His head flops to the side as he falls unconscious. Sam's chest constricts, but she stays where she is.

These people saved their lives.

No matter what her heart says, Grace is the best person to care for Hawk right now.

Once the dark has swallowed Hawk, Sam turns away. She'll see him first thing in the morning.

She almost collides with Raiden, who's standing right beside her.

He grabs Sam's shoulders, studying her closely. "Are you okay?"

No. Hawk's hurt and she's not with him. He's looked after

her their whole lives, and now she wants to do the same for him.

Sam swallows. "I'll be fine."

Raiden shakes his head. "I don't get you, Sam. One minute you're the smartest person I've ever met, and then you go and do something like that!"

Releasing Bohr. Not wanting to see him dead.

Sam shrugs and Raiden's hands fall away. For some reason, Hawk's request to stop touching Raiden floats through her mind. "I told you, we do things differently in Askala."

Corbin comes to stand beside his son, his face unreadable in the dying light.

Sam tries to process everything that's just happened.

They've lost all their possessions. Hawk's injured. Siena's dead.

And it's these people who came to their rescue.

"Thank you."

If it weren't for the Commander, none of them would've survived.

Corbin grunts. "No one takes anything from this island without the Commander's permission. The man can take that message back to the Outlands."

Without waiting for a reply, he spins on his heel and strides back toward the tree line. His men follow him, barely glancing at the Seekers.

Raiden grasps Sam's hand before she can pull away. "I'll come and see you in the morning," he says quietly before following his father.

Turning back, Sam finds the others scattered amongst the light and shadows. Luca walks toward her, and she nods, already knowing he's checking up on her. "I'm fine. For once, I have the least bruises out of anyone."

Luca nods, coming to stand beside her. Finally, silence

descends, punctured by the crackling of flames and the steady pounding of waves not far away.

Suddenly, it's stifling. The air feels too full. Laden with everything they've lost.

And yet...

"The Newlanders saved us," Sam says quietly. "We're making progress with them."

Luca sighs, a sound Sam's heard many times in her life. Usually, it's followed by "You don't see it, do you Sammy?"

Luca shakes his head, walking away as if the shadows are calling him.

"Except, now we owe them."

MERCY

*M*ercy groans.

Everything hurts. And everything that hurts is hurting the thing next to it. Her muscles, her skin, her tendons, her joints, and all the other bits that Sam would know the name of, but Mercy's never bothered to learn.

She's one giant, pulsating mass of pain. Her knuckles are raw from the punches she'd thrown, and her arms are bruised from being grabbed and thrown.

"What's wrong?" Sam asks on the sand beside her. With no Hawk to cuddle up to Sam had slept beside Mercy. Her elbow is pressed into Mercy's back and it feels like a thousand daggers.

"I'm not built for fighting," says Mercy.

"You didn't even really do that much," says Gust.

Mercy rolls onto her back and winces. "Nobody asked for your opinion."

"Mercy did quite a lot, actually," Luca points out. "I didn't know she had that much fight in her."

Mercy huffs. "Nobody asked you, either."

Surely, Luca doesn't think he can throw a compliment her

way and she's going to forget everything that's happened between them? Although, she has to admit she's glad to hear his voice after thinking he'd been killed during the attack. Those had been some of the worst moments of her life.

"How's your head, Luca?" Sam asks, sitting up.

"I'm fine," he replies.

Mercy knows he can't possibly be fine. He may have played dead to give himself the element of surprise, but that blow must have hurt. He almost certainly had been genuinely knocked out to begin with.

"I really did think you were dead," says Sam. "It was awful."

"I didn't," says Gust. "Did you like my acting skills? I fooled you all. Genius!"

Mercy isn't sure if he's calling himself the genius or Luca. Knowing Gust, he's talking about himself.

"You did well, Gust," says Sam. "They'd have killed him for sure if they hadn't already thought he was dead. I'm very grateful."

Mercy rolls her eyes in the early morning light. There's only one thing worse than Gust complimenting himself. And that's someone else doing it for him.

"So, seven Seekers becomes four," says Gust.

"Hawk is still a Seeker," snaps Sam.

Mercy smiles, far preferring it when Sam uses this tone for Gust. "And Nikita will come back when Raiden moves on to the next shiny thing."

"Can you believe she went back with Raiden last night?" Gust shakes his head.

"Beats sleeping out here on the sand," says Mercy. "I'm not sure I'd have turned down the offer of a bed last night."

"Even if it had Raiden sleeping in it?" asks Gust.

Mercy grimaces. The guy seems nice enough, but she doesn't trust the way he was all over Sam then ditched her for Nikita the moment she showed interest. Not all that different to the way Luca ditched Mercy for Alyx, really.

Anyway, it's not like Sam was interested in Raiden so it's for the best that he's moved on.

"Poor Siena." Sam lets out a sigh. "I can't stop thinking about her."

Mercy tries to sit up, then deciding it hurts too much she lies back down. "Siena didn't deserve that, no matter what debt her father might have owed."

Before they'd collapsed on the sand, Luca had carried what was left of Siena's body to the ocean to be swallowed up by its acidic depths. Mercy had held Sam's hand as they'd watched from the shoreline, salty tears splashing down their cheeks.

"I can't believe she's gone," says Sam.

Luca huffs as he pushes to his feet. "Now do you understand why I didn't want you to come here? This isn't a game."

"I never thought it was!" Sam also gets to her feet and pulls back her shoulders.

"What you did last night was stupid." Luca scowls at his sister. "You almost got yourself killed. Or worse."

Personally, Mercy had thought Sam's idea to pretend to be Siena had merit. It had bought them some time that they'd very much needed. Even if it had failed to save the one person they'd been trying to protect.

Sam reels back at Luca's comment. Being called stupid is possibly the worst thing anyone can call her. She prides herself on her brains. And rightly so.

"It's too dangerous here," says Luca. "Especially for you girls. I'm going to prepare a boat this morning and take you back to Askala. And Mercy. It was a mistake for you to come here."

Now Mercy is on her feet, her anger at Luca's words surpassing the aches in her body.

"How dare you!" she shouts. "Women are just as capable as men around here. We haven't exactly been sitting around weaving baskets since we got here, have we? We might lack some of the physical strength you have but all the negotiating has been done by us! Corbin would never have come to our rescue like that if it weren't for all the hard work we've put in. Sam especially."

Luca opens his mouth as if he's about to reply, but then changes his mind. In typical Luca style, he turns and stalks away.

"Where are you going?" Sam asks.

"To find us some food!" he calls back over his shoulder.

Sam shoots Mercy an apologetic look and takes off after him. He might have finished arguing with them, but it seems Sam isn't done yet.

Good for her!

Mercy returns to the flattened-out section of sand she'd slept on and stretches out.

"And then there were two," says Gust.

"I'm really thirsty." Mercy looks up at Gust standing over her, hoping he might feel sorry for her. "Any chance you could please bring me some water from the well?"

"What happened to your independent woman speech?" Gust puts his hands on his hips. "Can't you get it yourself?"

Mercy smiles. He's got a point.

"Please, Gust." She shades her eyes with her arm. "I'm really thirsty."

"Fine," he huffs. "I'm thirsty, too. Good thing we left the bucket over there or it'd have burned to a crisp last night."

Mercy winces, hating that Siena is the first thing she thinks of when she hears that expression. But Gust hadn't meant that, so she lets it go.

"Thanks, Gust. I'll get it next time."

He nods like he doesn't believe her, even though it's true. She doesn't want to owe that guy anything.

Mercy closes her eyes as Gust walks away, pleased to find

herself alone for a few moments. Siena had been so kind to her when she'd been upset about Luca. Holding her hand and trying to find nice things to say. If Mercy had known that was going to be Siena's last day alive, she'd have been the one holding her hand instead. Making sure she had the best day ever and knew just how valued she was, not only as a Seeker but a person.

Mercy's hair falls across her forehead and she brushes it aside, only for it to tickle her again.

Fluttering her eyes open, she wonders if it might have been an insect. Hopefully, not a spider.

But instead, she sees the tip of a palm frond above her forehead. It lowers and tickles her again.

"What the—" Mercy sits up to see who's holding the other end of the frond.

It's a cheeky girl with dark eyes and a dirty face.

"Tarquin!" Mercy bats the frond away. "You gave me a fright!"

Tarquin seems to find that hilarious and plonks herself down on the sand next to Mercy and grins. "Sorry."

"You are not, you little scamp!" Mercy reaches over to tickle her, but Tarquin pulls back like she's afraid she's going to be hurt.

"I'm sorry!" she says a little more urgently this time.

Mercy draws back. "No, I'm sorry, Tarquin. I wasn't going to hurt you. I'd never do that."

Tarquin nods as her fear shrinks away and Mercy's heart breaks for her. What would a child have to go through to react to a simple touch like that?

"Where's your father?" Mercy asks, remembering she'd said her mother had died. "Does he know you're running all over the island like this?"

Tarquin shrugs. "We left Dad in the Outlands. But Alyx says Mom watches me from the clouds. So, she must know what I'm doing."

"Alyx?" Mercy asks, wondering what their connection is.

"She's my big sister," says Tarquin. "She takes care of me now."

Mercy sighs. It seems there's no getting away from Alyx in a colony this small. "Won't Alyx be worried about where you are?"

Tarquin shakes her head. "She's busy having a conversation. I have to go for walks when she has conversations."

"Who does she talk to?" Mercy tilts her head, wondering what talks Alyx is having that are so top secret.

"Just men." Tarquin shrugs. "They bring her food so they can talk to her. Once a man brought her a blanket and she talked to him for a whole night."

"Oh." Mercy claps her hand to her mouth as what Tarquin's saying sinks in.

"You want to know something funny?" asks Tarquin.

Mercy nods, grateful to change the topic and what this could possibly mean for the *conversation* she'd seen Luca going to Alyx's hut to have.

"Once, back in the Outlands, I listened into Alyx talking to a man and they weren't even talking at all!" Tarquin laughs and Mercy feels the color drain out of her face. "He was making grunting noises like he was trying to say something but forgot all his words. And instead of Alyx being nice about it, she told him he was very bad. And he didn't even get mad!"

Tarquin rolls around on the sand laughing, and Mercy dreads the day Tarquin grows up and realizes exactly what she'd overheard.

Tarquin pulls herself together and bobs up onto her feet. "But that's not why I'm here. Corbin asked me to tell you he's made a space for you in the village. For your new hut. He says it's too dangerous here and he doesn't want to have to save your sorry asses again."

"Tarquin!" Mercy gasps. "Watch your language!"

"What?" Tarquin seems genuinely perplexed. "I was just saying what he said! That's not the same as saying it myself."

Mercy decides given the kind of childhood Tarquin's experiencing, perhaps that wasn't such a great crime. It's going to be a miracle if this girl grows up unscathed. Bad language is the least of her problems.

"Are you happy to come to the village?" asks Tarquin. "We'll be able to play together."

"I'm happy." Mercy smiles at this sweet girl, wondering if she has any friends her own age. "I'm just surprised the Commander would allow that."

Tarquin drops her voice into a low whisper. "Corbin's not a nice person."

"Don't say that," Mercy warns. "It's not safe to say things like that."

"Come back with me and I'll show you where your new hut is going to be." Tarquin reaches for Mercy's hand and tries to haul her to her feet. "It's right next to the hut Alyx and I live in. It's behind the other huts but it's a good spot."

Mercy lets out a long groan, both at the physical pain she's still feeling and the ache that's settled deep in her heart. Had Alyx organized the location of their new hut? It seems a little convenient. Although, Luca had mentioned once that the outcasts are forced to live on the outskirts of the villages in the Outlands, so it does make some kind of sense.

"You're like an old lady, today!" Tarquin laughs. "You have bruises everywhere."

"I *am* an old lady, today." Mercy gets to her feet, trying to decide which of her injuries hurts the most. "Those Outlanders were vicious."

"That's why we came here," says Tarquin proudly. "Alyx said it was the first stage to our new life stuffed full of happiness."

Mercy turns these words over in her head. *The first stage.*

That sounds awfully like the note they'd received in Askala about Stage One being complete.

"What's the next stage?" she asks.

"Dunno." Tarquin shrugs dramatically. "Nobody tells me anything. Maybe one day when I'm all grown up, people will come to our hut and pay to talk to me, too. Then I'll know everything like Alyx."

A sick feeling winds its way through Mercy's core, and she squeezes this precious girl's hand. There has to be something she can do to save Tarquin from the inevitable path her future's been set on. Alyx is a terrible role model.

Then another sick feeling rolls over Mercy as she accepts it's not Alyx's fault. She's doing what she has to do to keep herself alive and provide for her sister. If anything, what she's doing is noble. Mercy can't say for sure that in the same situation she wouldn't do the same. Desperation is a persuasive beast.

But what's Luca's excuse for his actions?

"Hey, Tarquin, do you remember meeting Luca yesterday?" she asks.

Tarquin kicks at the sand. "Uh-hum. Yes."

"He had a talk with your sister." Mercy feels guilty bringing Tarquin into this, but she has to know the truth. "I saw him there."

But Tarquin shakes her head. "That was just talking. He didn't bring her a gift and she didn't tell me to go for a walk. It wasn't a trade."

"Did you hear what they spoke about?" Mercy squats down to get on eye level with her.

"Not really. Well, I mean, I did. But I didn't understand it." Tarquin chews her lip. "They talked about the Falcon. Luca said he didn't deserve to die like that. He seemed upset."

Mercy gets back up to her feet. *Interesting.* So, Luca knew all along who the Falcon was, yet claimed he didn't. Why would he be protecting a masked man like that? That information could have been useful for them. Although, she's not sure why.

It's time she had a talk with Luca, instead of avoiding him the way she has. She has some questions for him.

And this time, she's going to make sure she gets her answers.

LUCA

"*L*uca, wait!" Sam calls out. "Where are you going?"

Luca doesn't slow his stride as he stalks along the beach. "I told you," he calls over his shoulder. "To get us some food."

"But we need food for everyone."

That stops Luca in his tracks. He spins around, stomping back to his sister. "For the whole village?"

Sam frowns. "Of course, for the whole village."

Luca's hands grip his head, pressing the heels into his temples. "You want me to go find food for the whole village?"

"Well, how does it look if we just feed ourselves? After they saved us?"

"Don't remind me," growls Luca.

Watching Sam about to be dragged away was like being in a waking nightmare. One where his biggest fear was coming true. Sam, taken to the Outlands. Traded.

How would he explain that to Kian and Nova?

He takes hold of Sam's shoulders. "Please, Sammy. Go back to Askala. You saw what happened to Siena."

A death Luca was unable to stop.

Sam's face softens and hardens all at once. "I love you, too, Luca, but I'm not going anywhere. I'm…I'm making a difference here."

Because all Sam can see is the good that's happening. She doesn't see the barely contained violence that these people carry like armor. She doesn't see what Alyx has to do to be able to feed herself and her sister. It never occurs to her to wonder why Raiden was instantly interested in her…in a society that values brawn over brains.

Which is a mystery Luca has yet to solve, only adding to the uneasiness.

Sam crosses her arms as she lifts her chin. Luca's hands drop to his sides. Short of dragging her and Mercy to the boat, they won't be leaving the Newlands.

He sighs. "If there was something that could feed the whole village, they would've thought of it by now. I doubt there are any hazelnut trees around."

"Unlikely. Their preferred habitat are the edges of forests, and this one hasn't been around long enough."

Thinking of their Proving, Luca's lips twist. "I could try and find a nest of snakes."

Sam's eyes widen with horror. "That's a terrible idea."

Especially considering how sick the snake made her. Luca turns to face the ocean, seeing the boats they arrived in tucked up above the water line. In Askala, at least they have pods.

He sucks in a sharp breath, staring out over the red ocean. "Pods…"

Sam grips his arm, her gaze following his. Pteropods are Askala's foundation. They're what allowed their people to flourish.

"They are highly nutritious," Sam says quietly. "I shudder to think what vitamin deficiencies these people have." But she shakes her head. "It's too dangerous, Luca."

Luca grins. "Less dangerous than a nest of snakes." He scans the horizon, noting it's clear of clouds. "The weather's good. One trip to see if we can find some won't take long."

Sam stills. "We could keep a proportion to breed."

Of course, his little sister would think along those lines.

Luca strides to the boat closest to them, having made his decision. "All I'll need are two buckets. Preferably one of them bigger than the other."

Sam comes to stand next to him. "I'd like to come."

"No," Luca barks. With a sigh, he modulates his tone. "Why don't you go check up on Hawk?"

Sam hesitates, biting her lip. Luca could see how hard it was for her to watch Hawk be carried away. Every cell of Sam's being wanted to be with him.

"He'll probably be sleeping. And I'm sure Grace is taking good care of him." She blinks, her face tightening with pain. "They really hurt him, Luca."

Because Hawk wasn't going to sit by and let them take Sam. It seems he loves her more than life itself. The knowledge comforts Luca. If anything happened to him, there's someone else looking out for Sam.

"Still, you can't go alone," Sam continues. "If you find pods, you'll need to change their water frequently on the return trip to keep them alive. They need warmth and oxygen."

Luca grits his teeth. "I know what they need."

But Sam's not coming with him.

"You could take Mercy?"

His jaw tightens even further. The fact Sam suggested that shows exactly how clueless she is. Another reason she should return home.

"Maybe," he says, having no intention of doing that.

"Then you could sort out whatever's happening between you two," she says quietly.

Luca frowns. So she has noticed... And if it's got on Sam's radar, then that's saying something.

"Look, I know you grew up as cousins—I thought it was weird at first, too—but you're not actually blood related. You can't allow that to keep you apart."

Luca bites his tongue. That stopped being an issue the moment they set foot in the Newlands. "It's not that simple, Sammy."

"Well, you're going to have to figure out a solution, because as Seekers, we need to work as a team. We can't afford to have the Newlanders more united than we are."

Luca blinks at the truth in those words. He's managed to do anything but that.

Sam squeezes his arm. "You're a natural leader, Luca. People are drawn to you. You just need to let them in."

Luca looks away with a sigh. He's not just protecting himself.

"You stay here. I'll take Nikita or Gust." He even manages to say the second name without a shudder.

"I suppose so…" Sam says, clearly unconvinced.

"Plus, you'll want to consider what you're going to need to set up a breeding system for the pods." An idea strikes him. "And after that, I want you to find Alyx. Get her to help you. I'm thinking we could put her in charge."

"Wonderful idea!" Sam says excitedly. "Education is the best thing we can give these people."

It's a freaking fabulous idea. If Alyx can breed pods, she can trade them, generating herself an income. One she can be proud of.

Sam presses a quick kiss to Luca's cheek. "I'll do that after I check on Hawk."

She's gone before Luca can reply. Although the pod breeding is what finally convinced her to stay, she's already running back to Hawk as if everything can't be right in her world until she knows he's okay.

Luca loads up the boat as quickly as he can, not willing to

admit why he's in such a hurry. As he puts in the buckets and some rope, covering it with a sheet of canvas, he looks over his shoulder repeatedly. It's only a matter of time before Mercy comes looking for him.

Before she figures out the half-answers he's given her aren't enough.

Going back to the ashes of their hut, Luca grabs the oar that was sitting beneath a tree nearby. Sam had insisted that they keep at least some of their supplies away from the hut. "It shows trust," she said.

As much as Luca disagreed at the time, those few tools are all they have left.

Ahead, Luca sees Mercy stand, turning until her gaze zeroes in on him. His pulse spikes as he looks away. He has everything he needs to collect some pods and he fully intends on going out there solo.

But a quick glance over his shoulder shows Mercy's now walking, her shoulders set in a determined hunch.

Luca picks up the pace. He needs to get in the boat and get out of here. Half-jogging, he grabs it the moment he reaches it, shoving it down the sand. Every muscle strains as he takes on the two-person job, but with a few grunting shoves, the bow reaches the water. Once the front end is lifted, Luca gives another great push, and the boat is afloat.

"Luca!"

He doesn't turn to see how far away Mercy is. If he can hear her, it's too close. Picking up the oar, Luca paddles hard. Never before has he been so keen to be out in the deadly ocean. In fact, he'd prefer to face a leatherskin rather than the woman now standing at the edge of the waves.

He waves, the motion supposed to be cheery, but it feels too heavy with regret. Mercy doesn't reciprocate, her fisted hands jammed firmly on her hips.

Turning back to face the ocean, Luca ignores the twinge in

his chest. He can't run forever, but right now, being around Mercy is too hard. Too painful. Acting like he doesn't care about her is impossible.

No matter how much he does.

So instead, Luca rows with all his might. Behind him, the Newlands quickly become a blur on the horizon. But Luca can still feel Mercy's gaze. Angry.

Betrayed.

Disappointed.

"You know, Mercy's a nice person. You should've let her come."

Luca spins around in disbelief. For a split second he's ready to fight, but then he recognizes the voice.

He frowns ferociously. "What are you doing here, Tarquin?"

She scrunches up her dirt-smeared nose as she crawls out from beneath the canvas. "Helping you, of course. Like I did in the Outlands."

Luca raises a brow. "Like that time we fixed your hut?"

Tarquin settles herself on the bench across from him. "Exactly."

Luca's thumb ached for days because he was foolish enough to give Tarquin a hammer.

"Or the time I went hunting for rabbits in Fairbanks."

The crumbling city held together with nothing but decay. Although, that time Tarquin was able to squeeze her arm into a burrow a rabbit had scurried into. It was the only food they ate that night.

"And you tried to leave without me," Tarquin scoffs.

Luca hesitates. Out on the ocean is no place for a child. The best thing he can do is take Tarquin back.

Except Mercy's there. Which means he's stuck between an angry woman who wants answers and a dirty urchin who won't leave this boat unless he carries her. In both situations, there's likely to be screaming. And kicking.

With a groan, Luca starts rowing again. "You do exactly as I tell you."

Tarquin grins. "Of course."

Unless she disagrees. Or something else catches her attention. Or she just plain doesn't want to.

"Keep your eye out for sections of water that are brighter than the others. We're looking for pteropods."

Tarquin peers over the edge of the boat as if there might be some right there. "Terra-whats?"

"We call them pods for short. They're like little jellyfish. Just let me know if you see anything."

Tarquin continues to stare fiercely into the water. Luca knows he was drawn to this girl because she reminds him so much of himself. Full of energy and curiosity. Eager to please. Born into a world too harsh and desperate to care.

And now her sister is selling herself to survive. What sort of future is that for Tarquin?

Luca slows down his rowing so they can scan more effectively. "What do you want to be when you grow up, Tarquin?"

She frowns as if Luca just asked a question she's never considered. But then she shrugs, returning her gaze to the water. "I'll probably be like Alyx. I'll probably trade for conversations."

Luca's gut clenches. That's what he thought.

"Or I'll be the Falcon."

"What?" Luca's hands almost fly off the oar. "The Falcon's dead. That's not a future."

"But he saved Alyx's life, even though she's a girl."

If only Tarquin knew why the Falcon started doing what he was doing. It was far from altruistic.

Tarquin straightens as she points. "Hey, do you mean a bright patch like that?"

Luca's about to tell her that it's unlikely because they need to go out further when he sees what caught her eye. A gently glowing area of water only a few yards away.

Rowing over, his eyes pop open when he sees the little blobs of light swimming below the surface.

"Yes, that's exactly what I mean," Luca breathes.

Tarquin grips the side of the boat as she watches the pulsing orbs flit beneath them. Their opaque wings flutter like underwater butterflies, their center a gentle, throbbing glow. "They're cool."

"And they're dinner."

Tarquin looks at him in horror. "I'm not going in there! I don't want to get wet!"

Which possibly explains the countless layers of dirt on her.

Luca's about to pull off his shirt, never intending for Tarquin to go into the acidic ocean, when he pauses. If he could teach Tarquin how to get the pods without getting in the water, then he's given her a chance at survival.

Grabbing the small bucket, he quickly scoops some sea water into the larger bucket. "Pass me the rope."

Tarquin has the rope in his hand in a flash, and once he's tied it to the smaller bucket, Luca drops it into the water. The pods scatter like little comets as it sinks down. Once he's holding the end of the rope, Luca waits as the pods contract back into a pulsing mass, obscuring the bucket.

"Now," he says to Tarquin. "We need to pull that bucket up as fast as we can."

She nods, her face pinched with intensity.

"Go!"

They scrabble, hand over hand, as they haul the bucket back up to the boat. The pods scatter, but some are invariably scooped up as the bucket returns to the surface. Tarquin gasps as they drag it into the boat.

"There's hundreds."

More like dozens, but Luca doubts Tarquin can count that high.

"They'll swim down to the bottom," he says. "When that happens, tip some of the water out. Then pour them into the bigger bucket."

"On it," Tarquin says, focused and intense.

She returns with the empty bucket and Luca drops it again, waiting for the pods to recover from the unexpected invasion barreling through them.

The second time, it becomes a game. They both grin as their hands stumble over the other's, seeing who can reach the furthest down the rope. The third time, it's a race to see if they can do it faster. They're both laughing as the fullest bucket so far lands in the boat.

They only have to repeat the process five times before Tarquin announces that the big bucket is full. Luca joins her as she stares at the shifting constellations revolving in their new home. "You eat these?" she asks in wonder.

Luca reaches in and scoops one up, holding it out to her. "They're really good for you."

Tarquin lifts her hand up and Luca slips it onto her palm. Before he can say anything else, she tosses it in her mouth and chews. Just as he expected, her face instantly screws up.

"Just swallow, Tarquin. They taste terrible, but they'll give you so much energy you'll be able to outrun anyone you want."

With a grimace, she swallows. Luca grabs another. "Here, have two."

Tarquin's skinny little body can't have too many. And when they get back, the ones Sam doesn't take to breed will be shared among everyone else. Equality in the Outlands isn't about who needs it more.

Tarquin's lived with hunger long enough to know not to turn down anything edible, no matter how bad it tastes. In a blink, the second pod is gone. "Are you going to have one?" she asks, her face still squeezed tight as she tries to get the bitterness out of her mouth.

Luca shakes his head, ignoring the pangs in his stomach. "I'm fine."

If he were going to have one, it would've been the one Tarquin just ate.

Tarquin's gaze slides to the bucket. "Maybe one more?"

Luca doesn't hesitate. "Last one."

And neither does Tarquin. The next pod is swallowed in a flash.

Picking up the oars, Luca starts rowing. "We need to get back. Your job is to keep taking water out, and then adding some more."

Shuffling over to sit beside the large bucket, Tarquin doesn't even notice she's getting wet as she scoops up some fresh water, already taking her role seriously.

His chest warming, Luca smiles. "You did good, Tarquin."

Instead of her usual smart aleck responses, Tarquin smiles, beaming beneath the dirt.

As he rows, Luca thinks of the haul they'll be bringing back. A bucket of pods in Askala is something they could harvest a day. A bucket of pods in the Newlands is unheard of.

Sam is going to be so excited to see them. The first thing she'll do is rush some to Hawk, knowing the vitamin-packed little pods will aid his recovery.

The Newlanders will be even more grateful.

Tarquin trails a finger over the edge of the bucket, lost in thought. "Maybe the Commander won't hate you so much, now," she murmurs quietly.

Luca's hands tense around the oars.

Maybe they're doing little more than strengthening their enemy.

HAWK

*H*awk blinks, trying to adjust to the dim light in Grace's hut. He's uncertain how long he's been here but it has to be at least a couple of days. He thinks he's seen the sun rise and set at least twice, but it's hard to be sure. Maybe it's been three times or maybe it hasn't moved at all. Sleep has had him in its grip and each time he's tried to claw his way back to consciousness it's dragged him under again.

Memories assault him like one of Thea's patchwork quilts expertly stitched together from scraps – the pieces all fit together yet, somehow, they're distorted with each fragment telling a story of its own.

Grace holding a cup to his lips and encouraging him to drink.

Grace wiping his brow with a cool cloth.

Grace cleaning his wounds to stave off infection.

Grace sleeping beside him to make sure he continued to breathe.

Grace covering his naked body with a blanket in the cool of night.

Hang on a minute…

Naked body?

Hawk's hand moves down from his stomach and he discovers he has, indeed, been stripped of his clothes. If he had enough blood to spare, he'd have the decency to blush. But he's too weak to do anything except close his eyes again. Dignity is the least of his concerns right now.

"Hawk," Grace whispers. "Are you awake?"

Peeling his eyes open again, he sees her leaning over him, her long dark hair trailing over her shoulders. "Are you in a lot of pain?"

He shakes his head. It's only a slight movement but she sees.

"That will be the hemp seed oil." She smiles. "You're lucky I had some. Don't worry. You're in good hands."

Unable to stay awake another moment, Hawk lets his eyes close, wishing it were his mother caring for him instead of this strange, beautiful woman who looks at him like he's spun from gold. He wouldn't feel embarrassed for his mother to see him naked. Or maybe he would. He's not really sure what he thinks anymore. It's like his mind belongs to someone else.

Drifting off to sleep, he's aware of Grace rubbing oil into his temples.

"Rest now," she soothes.

Doing as he's told, he lets himself slide into a world of broken sleep and strange dreams.

His mother is smiling at him. They're in Askala outside his family's hut. His mom holds out her hand and tells him he was born to do great things. It's so good to see her again. He smiles back and opens his mouth to reply, but then everything blurs and he's torn from her. Now he's back in the Newlands and Sam is running toward him. She's so beautiful. She's always so beautiful. His heart lurches and he opens his arms. But before Sam can reach him, he's surrounded by men. He looks around, desperate to find her, but she's gone. Instead, he sees large fists and hard boots closing in on him. They slam into his face, his ribs, his back... except this time he feels no pain. He's watching it happen like it's happening to someone else. The men force him to the ground and he spots Sam. She's struggling against a man who's dragging her away. He tries to shout, but no voice comes out and all he hears is Mercy scream. Now the men are gone and it's just Hawk and Mercy. She's crying as she reaches out to touch his face, but the moment she makes contact, he wakes.

He's panting. His heart is racing. Sweat has beaded on his forehead.

Trying to swing his legs over the side of the bed, pain forces him back. He groans and tries again. He has to help Sam! She needs him! The Outlanders have taken her!

A large hand pushes him down to the bed and holds him still.

He struggles against it, but the hand is strong and Hawk's unsure if he's asleep or awake.

"Hawk!" shouts a deep voice. "Pull yourself together."

"Commander!" Hawk gasps when he sees who has him pinned to the bed. What is the Commander doing in here?

Corbin lightens the pressure on his chest as he squats beside him. "Don't be a fool, boy. Lie still. You must have six broken ribs at least."

"I need to find Sam," he protests, trying again to sit up only to be pushed back down.

"Your woman is fine," Corbin grunts. "We killed the men who tried to take her. All but one of them, anyway. But he won't be bothering you again."

Hawk lets out a slow and painful breath. Sam's okay. Although, why hasn't she visited him? He'd remember if she'd come to check on him.

"They beat you up real good." Corbin stands as he moves his gaze down Hawk's battered body. "Impressive specimen, aren't you?"

Hawk reaches for a blanket, trying to cover himself. But there's no blanket to be found.

"We need to teach you how to fight," says Corbin. "We could put you to good use if we taught you the right skills. It's a waste for a brute like you to fight like such a girl."

Hawk decides perhaps that's not such a bad idea. Then he can teach the girls to fight back. Grace still has that bruise, courtesy of Corbin, and in the right light he can see a faint shadow on Sam's cheek that refuses to fade.

"I think I might give you a present." Corbin chuckles. "Do you want to become a real man?"

Hawk doesn't answer. Not one part of him trusts Corbin, even though this man could have killed him ten times over if he'd wanted to. Hawk wants no part of whatever he has in mind to turn him into a man. Especially, if being a man means being like Corbin.

"Corbin?" Grace appears at the door. "What are you doing in here?"

"I'm going to make this little birdie into a man." Corbin cocks a brow and Grace scurries to pick up a blanket and cover Hawk's lower half with it. "If you can tear yourself away from him for a moment."

"He would have died without my care." Grace crosses her arms. "You said yourself that we need him alive."

"Maybe if you took better care of our daughter she wouldn't have run back to the Outlands," Corbin snaps.

So, it seems he's finally figured out Charity is no longer with them here. But as long as he hasn't realized her true location then she's safe.

For now.

The daughter of the Commander will never be able to hide for long. Especially if Askala has a spy…

"I'll be back in a minute." Corbin slides his fingers into the back of Grace's hair and drags her face to his, placing a possessive kiss on her mouth that seems more for Hawk's benefit than his own.

Hawk lets his eyes close. Corbin doesn't need to think of him as competition. Hawk can see that Grace is beautiful. Any man can see that! But apart from being older than him she has one other major flaw.

She's not Sam.

And it doesn't matter how stunning a woman is, she'll never come close to the girl he loves with every cell in his battered body. He just needs to get well so he can return to her. He has an interrupted kiss to continue. Not the showy sort that Corbin gave Grace just now, but one filled with years of love and yearning.

The thought of that kiss is the only thing keeping Hawk alive right now.

"What are you going to do to him?" Grace asks Corbin.

Hawk peels his eyes open.

"I'm just going to get my jar of ash," says Corbin. "That pasty white chest is blinding me."

That makes even less sense. Corbin is going to rub ash into his chest? How in sweet Terra will that make him into a man?

"That's not such a good idea," says Grace. "He's still in a lot of pain."

"Then take care of the pain, wife!" Corbin growls. "I thought you knew how to do that?"

He stomps out of the room and Grace lets out a long sigh.

"What?" Hawk asks, wishing he had the strength to form a full sentence so he could ask what exactly is happening here.

"It's okay." Grace smiles before going to the corner of the room to fuss with something. It doesn't seem like she's any more keen to elaborate than Corbin was.

Grace seems to finish whatever she was doing and seats herself beside Hawk, bringing a cup to his cracked lips.

"Drink," she says. "The water's from the well you dug. Which is lucky as those supplies from the Outlands haven't come yet."

"Where's my pendant?" asks Hawk, remembering the raven and realizing he's been stripped of more than just his clothes.

"It's okay." Grace presses the cup more firmly to his lips. "I'm looking after it for you. Drink now."

Hawk lifts his head and draws in some of the liquid.

"That's right," she says. "Drink it all up."

As he drains the liquid, he wonders if he should be trusting her like this. But what choice does he have? And Grace has been a big support to the Seekers. They'd never have made it this far without her on their side. And like she'd pointed out to Corbin, he'd have died if she hadn't nursed him back to health. She's his friend, not his enemy.

"I'm sorry about Corbin." Grace sets the empty cup down beside her. "He gets jealous sometimes, but he's a good man."

Hawk nods, having no energy to argue. Any man who uses his strength against a woman is a long way off from being a good man. Which makes Corbin an extremely dangerous Commander.

"I never imagined my life to turn out like this," says Grace, sighing. "When I was your age, I was in love, just like you are with Sam. I thought we were going to be together forever."

"What happened?" he asks, intrigued.

"We grew up together. He was my protector. My best friend…" Grace's voice breaks from the strain of the memory and Hawk holds out his hand, wanting her to continue the story. She slips her hand into his and lets out a gentle sigh. "But my father had other ideas. He sold me. I was dragged from my bed in the middle of the night when I was sixteen and taken so far away I couldn't have found my way back even if I'd been able to cut my chains to try."

A sharp pain radiates through Hawk's heart. He and Sam had

come so close to experiencing the exact same fate. He can't afford to let Sam out of his sight ever again.

"He was so much like you." Grace lifts Hawk's hand and presses the back of it to her cheek and he feels the dampness of her tears. "He was strong and kind. I see him when I look at you."

"But..." He wants to tell Grace that he's not the guy she loved, no matter how much she might want him to be. If her feelings extend in any way beyond friendship, then he's not going to be able to reciprocate.

His heart belongs to Sam.

"It's okay," she soothes, even though he should be the one doing the soothing. "You don't have to say anything. I just want you to understand."

He nods, wondering what any of this has to do with him.

"Corbin's father was a wealthy man in the Outlands," Grace continues. "He bought me with plans to keep me for his own. But... but when Corbin saw me, he decided I belonged to him. His father was weak, and Corbin manipulated him into gifting me to him."

Hawk swallows, hoping that water isn't going to come back up. He can't stand this talk of treating women like they're property that can be traded. Grace shouldn't belong to anyone! Not to Corbin, his father or even to her one true love. People belong to themselves.

"That's why I sent Charity away," she says. "I had to spare her from the same fate. I couldn't watch my own daughter being sold to the highest bidder. I'd rather die."

"You're a good mom." Fatigue is gripping Hawk now, but he knows it would be unforgivable to fall asleep while Grace is pouring her heart out to him like this.

"It's Raiden I'm worried about now," she says. "Corbin wants to buy him a wife but what kind of a person would I be if I

169

allowed that to happen? I can't watch some poor frightened girl be brought here against her will."

"Of course not." Hawk's eyes blink closed but he hauls his eyelids back up.

"That's why I've told him he has to find his own wife," Grace continues, some hesitation slipping into her words. "And I know this isn't what you want to hear, but I think he already has his heart set on someone."

"Nikita," says Hawk on a breath, an uneasy feeling creeping up his spine.

But Grace shakes her head. "No, Raiden needs someone better than that. Someone who comes from a family of leaders herself. Someone who can do what a true Seeker should do... unite the Newlands and Askala."

"No!" Hawk's scream comes out as a whisper as whatever it was that Grace put in his water starts to take effect.

Corbin strides back into the room and Grace scurries aside.

Hawk is fighting against the drug now, but it's no use. His arms are lying limply by his side as Corbin positions himself next to Hawk.

There's the sting of something sharp jabbing him in the chest over and over. It's not a pain exactly, more like an insect bite. Whatever it is that Corbin's doing to him can't compare to the panic that's gripping him.

Grace wants Raiden to marry Sam. And with Hawk out of the picture, that will be even easier than before. He needs to fight whatever's happening here. He has to get out of this bed and tell Sam exactly how he feels in a way she'll understand. He'd been a fool to wait so long.

Corbin continues stinging him on the chest, moving across his skin in a series of swift but precise movements.

A realization hits Hawk.

He's being tattooed, just like his own father before he came to Askala. Just like Corbin and all his thugs. A series of thick black lines are going to twine their way around his body and there's nothing he can do about it. This isn't what makes a man.

"You'll be one of us when I'm done," says Corbin. "I've got big plans for you."

He doesn't want to be one of them! He just wants to be Hawk.

The guy who walked this world alone until he realized he couldn't take another step without Sam by his side.

He tries one last time to lift his hands to push Corbin away but the darkness calls to him and he's dragged under.

SAM

Sam clutches the clay jar to her chest. Three days. She hasn't seen Hawk in three days.

She doesn't think they've ever been apart that long in her entire life.

There wasn't a day that went by in Askala where they didn't see each other. If one of them missed breakfast for some reason—Seb was sick, or Hawk was helping with one of his younger sisters—they'd wait by the large *Picea* tree. It was their agreed meeting place. Once, Mercy had arrived with a message that Hawk had been dragged away by his dad to cut down a tree so they could build another boat. Mercy had rolled her eyes as Sam had tucked up against the trunk and opened her book.

Now Sam realizes she would've waited for as long as it took. Even forever.

Because she was waiting for Hawk.

She shakes her head, bemused. How did she not see that what she felt for Hawk was so much more than friendship? There's the undeniable sensation of lighting up when she's with him. Hawk being the first person she wants to share anything with—big ideas, fleeting thoughts, finding the first mangrove pine pod of the season, her cockroach dip just to tease him.

The want to be with him when they're apart.

Which has now been three days.

Stopping outside the Commander's hut, Sam raps on the edge of the doorway. She's determined not to be sent away this time. Even if Hawk's sleeping, she'd feel better if she could just see him.

But it's not Grace who comes out like all the times before, always smiling, but each time shaking her head as she tells Sam that Hawk's sleeping. Sam's eyes climb up Corbin's chest as she absent-mindedly wonders why he even bothers with tattoos. They're barely visible under all the grime. Eventually, her gaze connects with his.

His frown is instantaneous, but Sam was expecting it. She's determined there will come a day when Corbin greets her cordially. There's good in him, she knows it.

Sam smiles, holding out the clay jar. "I brought Hawk a couple of pods. They'll help him heal."

"He's asleep."

Corbin reaches out a hand but Sam swiftly tucks the jar back against her chest, ignoring the look of surprise on his face. "I'd like to give them to him myself."

"My wife is taking good care of him."

"Oh, I have no doubt she is. It's just that I haven't seen him since the attack."

Corbin crosses his arms. "My wife is taking good care of him."

Sam doesn't point out that he just said that. Her hands tighten around the jar. She's not leaving until she's seen Hawk.

"It won't take long. I won't even talk to him."

Corbin's eyes narrow as his arms tighten. "You don't trust us?"

"Oh, my goodness no!" Sam rushes to assure. "I just said I'm sure Grace is taking wonderful care of Hawk." She pushes the jar toward Corbin. "Here, you can give him the pods. I just wanted to see how he's going."

Corbin grabs the jar and hope sparks in Sam's chest.

"His wounds are healing well," he grunts. "What he needs is rest. Come back tomorrow."

Corbin turns away and slips past the material hanging over the doorway. Sam blinks, knowing she was just dismissed.

Her brows slam down. She should be glad they're taking Hawk's recovery so seriously, but surely she can just see him for a moment. Maybe Corbin doesn't realize how important this is to her.

She knocks again, this time with enough force that her knuckles smart.

When Corbin comes out, Sam almost instinctively steps back. The hard lines of his face look like they've been calcified... by fury.

"Obviously you don't understand who I am, girl."

Sam holds her ground. Corbin respects strength, not weakness. "Of course I do, Commander. And I don't mean any disrespect."

Corbin's only response is for his hands to flex by his sides, one still wrapped around the clay jar with the pods.

Nervousness winds through Sam's ribs, but the thought of another day without Hawk keeps her where she is. "I'd really like to see Hawk. I promise it won't take long."

The flexing stops, Corbin's hands contracting in and staying that way. Surely Corbin wouldn't hit her. Not now. Not after everything the Seekers have done for them.

Just for good measure, Sam steps in closer, gazing up at him as she implores. "Please? I miss him."

Anyone with a heart couldn't say no to that.

Corbin's nostrils flare as his chest expands. "Go. Now."

He bites out the order, his eyes hot in his cold, hard face.

Sam knows she has a choice to make.

Comply or refuse.

Walk away or demand to see Hawk.

Show the Seekers are willing to compromise or show they expect to be treated as equals.

Sam's own hands clench, having made her decision. She's a Seeker. She's not afraid to stand up for what she believes in.

"Sam, there you are!"

Raiden strides around the hut, his gaze flicking between Sam and his father. "I thought you could show me the pods."

Slipping an arm around her shoulder, he tugs her back hard enough that she stumbles a little. "I was just—"

"About to show me the pods."

Before Sam can say another word, Raiden spins them around and starts walking. Sam has no choice but to keep up or fall over. She glances over her shoulder, not liking that the decision has been made for her.

Corbin's already turned away and her eyes widen as Sam watches him as he lashes out, slamming the clay pot into the wall of the hut. Water explodes as the pods are crushed, the crack of wood splintering the air as the timber caves in. Without glancing at the damage he just wrought, Corbin stalks away.

Raiden's slight wince says he heard it, but he keeps walking, acting as if he didn't. Suddenly feeling nauseous, Sam allows him to lead her away. Those pods were meant for Hawk.

And it seems that strike was meant for her.

"Would he have hit me, Raiden?" she asks quietly.

With a sigh, his arm around her loosens, but still doesn't release her. "If you weren't so worried about your friend, you would've known when to back off."

Sam stares at the dusty ground as they continue walking. Is it possible her feelings for Hawk clouded her judgment? Was she asking too much of Corbin, too soon?

Raiden squeezes her shoulder. "My mother's taking Hawk's welfare very seriously. Isn't that what you want?"

"Well, of course."

"In fact, I was stabbed back in the Outlands. My mother's the one who made sure I'm still here to tell the story."

Sam gasps. "Why would someone do that?"

Raiden shrugs. "The guy was trying to steal from us. I disagreed." Before Sam can ask any more questions, he grins as he arches a brow. "Want to see the scar?"

Sam blinks. Why would she want to do that?

A gasp has Sam looking around, relieved she's saved from having to answer the question. It's Nikita, several yards away, standing stock still as she stares at them. Suddenly, Sam realizes how this must look. She shrugs Raiden's arm off, intending to walk over to clarify that she and Raiden are just friends.

But Nikita spins on her heel and strides away.

Sam glances at Raiden. "It's okay if you need to go talk to her."

"What for?" Raiden scowls. "I wasn't doing anything wrong."

Technically, that's true. But judging from the way Nikita's spine looks as straight as a spear, she's reached a different conclusion.

Raiden takes a sharp right, heading toward the beach. "She needs to learn I can spend time with whoever I want."

Sam follows him, chewing her lip. Is this another one of those times she should back off? Even though Raiden hasn't treated Nikita with respect? If only Mercy were here, or Luca.

Her heart clenches. Or Hawk.

The trees fall away, revealing the stretch of sandy beach at the edge of the Newlands. The lone barrel with the pods is sitting in the sun just beyond the tree line. Having the pods closer to the village would've been better, but pteropod biology required it where it is. For one, having them there is the only way Sam could think to keep them warm.

As they reach the barrel, Sam finds Alyx is just returning with another bucket of seawater. Carefully, she tips the water in, her face tight with concentration.

Sam smiles warmly. "Thanks, Alyx." She glances at Raiden. Maybe she can rolemodel treating women with respect. "She's been a wonderful help."

Which is the truth. Sam's been impressed with Alyx's dedication to the pods. What's more, Alyx is also the cleanest of all the Newlanders. Her hair is always untangled and shiny, her skin scrubbed of any dirt. She would have to bathe at least every day, even though it means having to do it in the ocean.

Alyx flushes as she puts the bucket back down. "You said they need a regular supply of fresh water."

"Yes, until we find a better way to aerate the water and filter it, this is going to have to do."

"I don't mind," Alyx shrugs. "I like doing it."

"Thank you, Alyx," Sam says loudly and clearly. "Your people will appreciate your hard work."

Raiden's lips climb up. "They already do."

He says the words lightly, as if they're a joke, but Sam notices that Alyx doesn't laugh. In fact, she looks away, her golden hair falling over her face.

Suddenly, Alyx stills. Sam follows her line of sight, her muscles locking, too. Corbin's standing at the edge of the trees, his usual scowl in place.

Has he come to finish their talk? Was smashing the jar of pods not enough?

But he crooks a finger in Alyx's direction before turning away and disappearing amongst the trees again.

"Seems my dad wants to have a chat," Raiden muses, his voice seeming to drop on the last word.

Alyx smiles apologetically at Sam. "I'll be back later this afternoon to do another water change."

With that, she scurries after Corbin.

Sam stares at where Alyx was just swallowed by the shadows. "Everyone obeys your father without question, don't they?"

"Don't your people do the same with your father?"

Sam turns back to Raiden, surprised at his question. "Why would they?"

"Isn't he the leader?"

"No one person is the leader of Askala. It's governed by many minds."

"Yeah, but the great Kian is the one who established your new order, isn't he?"

Sam pauses. How does he know who her father is?

Raiden must realize because he shrugs, turning to peer into the barrel. "Nikita's been filling me in." He looks back at Sam. "Your society is fascinating."

Relaxing a little, Sam feels a wistful smile tug at her lips. "It's amazing."

"And yet, you're here."

"Because Askala has so much to share. It would be selfish to keep everything we know to ourselves."

Raiden takes a step forward. "Well, I'm sure glad the daughter of Askala's leader is here."

Sam's not sure what makes her more uncomfortable. Her father being called the sole leader of Askala. Raiden's proximity.

Or the way his voice just dipped.

She turns to look in the barrel, stepping a little to the side as she does. "Sharing what we know about pods is a great start." She shades her eyes so she can get a better look at what's happening at the bottom, thinking that putting out the fire in the Round House would be a wonderful next step.

But as her eyes focus on the glowing orbs at the bottom of the barrel, Sam gasps. She scans frantically, hoping she's wrong.

Knowing she's not.

Sam counts how many pods she sees in one quadrant, quickly calculating how many that multiplies out to over the remaining area. The number she comes up with has her heart sinking. There are half as many pods as there were yesterday, maybe less.

Stepping back, Sam grips the edge of the barrel. "Did someone stay with the pods last night?"

Raiden shrugs. "I doubt it. Alyx couldn't have, and she's the one who knows what to do."

Sam doesn't ask why. She's still trying to process what's happened. "People have been stealing them."

The image of Corbin smashing the clay jar, killing the two lives inside, flashes through her mind. How can she justify two pods for Hawk now?

Raiden looks at Sam in bewilderment. "What did you think was going to happen? Our people are hungry."

"But, if they just wait a little, there'll be even more to be had."

"Or they'll have died of starvation," snaps Raiden.

Sam frowns at the truth in Raiden's words. Desperation is driving these people. It's what they're up against.

"This is the only way we can show them there's another way," she whispers.

Raiden's face softens. "What do we need to do, then?"

"Keep doing what we were, but it's going to take much longer to get their numbers up." Sam rubs her forehead. "And that assumes no one else takes any more."

Raiden straightens, puffing his chest out in the same way his father does. "I'll order them to stop."

Sam wonders why he didn't do that in the first place. "Will they listen?"

He grins. "Have the hares we've captured for breeding been eaten?"

No, they haven't. It's been wonderful to watch Raiden and Nikita work so hard to get everything right—the cages, the supply of food, the water. For the first time, Sam relaxes a little. "That's a good point. Well, if you could do that, I'd appreciate it."

She mentally starts doing the calculations, knowing the pods are likely to have a slower breeding cycle seeing as their conditions aren't ideal. A new batch of pods will probably be a few months away.

Raiden moves forward again. "We make a good team, Sam."

There's that dip in his voice. The uneasiness crawling over her skin.

Sam takes a step back. "Do you think I'll be able to see Hawk soon?"

Raiden's face tightens, once again reminding her of Corbin. "Staying on the Commander's good side is your best bet of that."

With a sharp movement, Raiden turns and stalks away. Sam chews her lip, knowing she's not only upset Corbin, but now his son. What sort of Seeker is she? But at the same time, how much does she need to compromise? To give just so they can succeed?

Wandering further toward the ocean, Sam's never felt more alone. Mercy is on a mission to corner Luca. Luca is determined to not be in one place longer than a nanosecond. And Hawk is… fast becoming an absent ache in her chest.

She scans the horizon, thinking of Askala. Her home. She believed she could make the Newlands home, that she could bring everything that's good about Askala here.

Straightening her shoulders, Sam tries to find her resolve. The determination that brought her here.

Askala was built on hope.

The Newlands will have to be the same.

Right now, it's all she's got.

Her eyes narrow as she spots something on the horizon. Nothing more than a dot, it still has Sam leaning forward.

The dot doesn't disappear. It grows. Gains substance.

Within minutes, she recognizes it for what it is. A boat. Heading to the Newlands.

Sam stands frozen and uncertain. If she calls for help, the Newlanders will come running with their spears. That's no welcome for a boatload of refugees. But she's under no illusion that she'd be able to defend herself if there are desperate Outlanders heading toward the shore she's standing on.

For a moment, Sam considers calling Raiden back, but something stops her. She doesn't want him to think they're any more of a team than he already does.

Hawk already owns Sam's heart, even before she knew it.

The boat gains substance, enough to have Sam squinting. The shape of it...it's familiar. Breath held, Sam waits for long minutes as it comes closer. It couldn't be...

But the bright sunlight reflecting off the blood ocean means it's unmistakable. The boat is from Askala.

Sam runs to the edge of the water, now registering there's only one person rowing. She quickly makes out the size, the glistening ebony skin, the white teeth flashing in the dark face.

Ekon.

It feels like forever, but the boat reaches land. Sam runs into the shallows, ignoring the instant stinging of her skin. Ekon grins widely at her as he leaps out, and together, they drag the boat out of the water.

Sam stumbles twice, and both times the boat continues to drag up the sand. Although Ekon's doing all the work, Sam's determined to do what she can.

They straighten, smiling at each other.

Ekon isn't much for physical shows of emotion, which Sam can respect. She's not even sure if she could reach her arms around his shoulders.

"What a surprise," Sam says. "Welcome."

Ekon looks around, probably noting everything the Seekers did when they first arrived. The virgin forest. The knowledge the people here probably aren't glad to see you. The plumes of smoke rising to the sky.

Sam finally asks the question that's waiting to be asked. "What are you doing here?"

Ekon turns toward the boat, pointing toward the stack of packages. "I brought some supplies."

Askala sent them supplies? Sam startles as her first thought is to hide them. That maybe she could get some to Hawk. Sweet Terra, she's just thought like a Newlander! Raiden was right. Hunger and desperation are powerful motivators.

Sam smiles in thanks. "We'll take them to the Commander. We can share what there is amongst everyone."

Maybe this will have the Seekers in good favor again.

Ekon nods but doesn't move. "I also come with a message."

Although the words should be good news, Ekon says them levelly...slowly. As if there's nothing good about them.

"Askala is okay?"

"Yes, Askala continues to thrive. There has been no sign of a threat."

The tension is Sam's chest unwinds. "That's...good then."

She must've read it wrong. Again.

"But it was your parents who sent me. They wanted you to know."

The knot constricts all over again, making it feel like her lungs no longer have room. Sam waits, wondering what her father and mother thought Ekon should brave the waters to convey.

"It's Seb. He's sick." Ekon's dark eyes are pools of empathy. "Really sick."

But Sam's already shaking her head. "Seb's always catching something or the other."

"This illness began not long after you left, and nothing has worked. He's become weaker and weaker." Ekon's shoulders droop. "He's asking for you."

Sam takes a step back, the soft sand beneath her feet feeling like her whole world does. Shifting and unstable.

"My parents sent you to bring me home, didn't they?"

They never wanted her to come here. In fact, they could be

exaggerating, just to get her back. One thing Sam's learned out here is that desperate people do desperate things.

Ekon nods solemnly. "They fear Seb is dying."

The words hit Sam so hard she almost doubles over. Ekon steps forward, but she raises her hand for him to stop.

She doesn't want to be touched.

No, that's not true. She wants Hawk to hold her. To help her from falling apart.

To tell her what she should do.

MERCY

*M*ercy sits on the edge of the clearing watching Luca construct the new shelter for the Seekers. Nikita is nowhere to be found. Sam is also missing this morning after being turned away by Corbin for trying to see Hawk. But Gust is there to help Luca.

Mercy would help, too, if Luca asked her. Which is pretty unlikely given he's avoiding her. So, she continues to sit here, glaring at him like some kind of dare he's not willing to accept. So much for the hut he was going to build for the two of them to live in. It feels like a hundred years ago that he ever promised her that.

The vegetable patch is beside her, the soil damp with the water she'd sprinkled on it earlier. She stares at the grains of dirt, willing tiny green shoots to burst through the surface. With fertile soil, plenty of sun and a daily dose of water, it shouldn't take too much longer. Soon, they'll have a crop to harvest and their empty bellies can be filled.

Alyx emerges from her hut and smiles at Luca, who returns the gesture with the kind of warmth he used to direct at Mercy.

Jealousy winds its way through Mercy's gut. She wants to be

better than that. To be the kind of girl who can walk away with her head held high. To rise above the way Luca's treated her and not care how he looks at Alyx. Or anyone.

But she can't.

That small wordless exchange she just witnessed is enough to tear her in half.

Alyx doesn't stop to talk to Luca. Instead, she heads over to Mercy.

Mercy leaps to her feet and fusses over the vegetable patch, doing her best to look busy. This is the last person on the planet she wants to talk to right now.

"Hi," says Alyx. "Have you got a moment?"

Mercy smooths down her shirt and finds herself nodding against her will. Has politeness really been drilled into her that much that she can't even find her voice to say no? Her mom wouldn't stand here bobbing her head like this. She'd have grabbed Alyx by the collar and told her to back off.

"Tarquin tells me she's been bothering you," says Alyx. "I wanted to make sure that's not a problem."

"She's not a bother." Mercy gives Alyx a tight-lipped smile. "She's a good kid."

Despite the way her sister is raising her.

"Here." Alyx holds out her hand, offering Mercy some raisins. "A thank you for being nice to Tarquin."

"Where did you get those?" Mercy gasps. "I haven't seen any grapevines here."

"They were a gift," says Alyx. "Have some."

"Give them to Tarquin." Mercy's stomach groans at the sight of them, her mouth watering against her will.

Alyx laughs. "Don't worry, she's had plenty! Too many, in fact."

Mercy holds out her hand and Alyx pours some raisins into her palm. Is it right for her to accept these given she's almost certain under what circumstances they were gifted to Alyx? It feels somehow like this makes her complicit in something she really doesn't agree with.

But before she can analyze this too deeply, she's tipped the sweet morsels of food into her mouth and bites down.

"They're amazing," she says with her mouth still full.

"They were found on that boat that came from the Outlands," says Alyx. "It's only right they were shared given the trouble those guys caused."

"What happened to that man?" Mercy asks. "The one who tried to take Sam."

"Corbin sent him back as a warning." Alyx shrugs like this is normal behavior. If this were Askala, they'd have spent time trying to assimilate him. To bring out the goodness that resides in each and every soul if only you take the time to look.

Mercy swallows the last of the raisins, feeling the sugar going directly to her veins. She sighs in satisfaction, even though she's sure she could've eaten a hundred more.

"Tarquin told me you ran away from your father," says Mercy, filling the silence with the first words that come to mind.

Alyx nods as she sits down, patting the ground beside her. "Nobody needs their father."

Mercy's brows pull together as she sits beside her. "I do. My father's amazing. Probably my favorite person of all time."

Alyx lets out a loud laugh, tipping her head, her blonde hair shimmering.

"I wasn't actually joking," says Mercy. "My dad's the best person. I miss him."

Alyx's face pulls into a serious expression, seeming genuinely confused. "What do you mean?"

Mercy's the one who's confused now. "What's so difficult here? My dad is a great person. That's it. I'm not sure what you don't understand."

"Wow." Alyx blinks at Mercy as if deciding if she's joking.

"No girl feels like that about her father in the Outlands. Usually they're the ones trying to sell us or beat us or use us as some kind of bargaining chip. It's our mothers who take care of us."

A sadness creeps over Mercy. She can't imagine having grown up without her father's love. What is wrong with the men in the Outlands?

"What was your life like over there?" Mercy asks with a new feeling of sympathy for this woman who stirs up so many emotions inside her. Is it possible Luca's just been kind to Alyx because he knows that nobody else has been?

"Difficult," says Alyx, a hardness creeping into her voice. "But I'm a survivor. I do what I have to do to keep my sister safe. Including bringing her here."

Alyx looks at Mercy without blinking and Mercy swallows, ashamed at having judged Alyx so harshly. It's not like she had too many other options. Especially with a sister to look after.

"Why did you come here?" Mercy asks, trying to understand. It doesn't seem like Alyx's life is any easier here than it was in the Outlands.

"The Falcon." Something lights in Alyx's face that shows how much this masked savior meant to her. It's no wonder Tarquin thinks of him as her hero. "Or rather, our lack of the Falcon. Everything changed without him."

"Why does everyone keep talking about him?" asks Mercy.

"Because he was the only good thing out there." Alyx points in the direction of the Outlands and lowers her voice. "He was our last shred of hope. There was talk of more people joining him. Of a rebellion against the Commander. That's why they killed him. You can't rule over the desperate masses when they still have hope in their hearts. The Commander wanted him gone."

"Did you ever meet him?" Mercy wonders if he could be linked to some of the people her grandmother, Avis, talks about. The ones she used to live with in Fairbanks. They sounded like good people. Not at all like the Outlanders she's met so far.

"Two men came into my hut one night," Alyx says. "They wanted what all men who come to me want. Except, these two had no intention of trading with me. We got into a fight. I managed to get myself out of my hut but one of them grabbed me by the hair and pinned me to the ground."

"And nobody from your village came to help you?" Mercy claps her hand to her mouth horrified. Nothing like this would ever happen in Askala but if it did, she can't imagine being left alone to fend for herself.

Alyx shakes her head. "They thought I deserved what came to me."

"And the Falcon saved you?" Mercy reaches out and touches Alyx on the arm, hoping she's guessing right.

"He came out of nowhere," says Alyx. "He grabbed the man and threw him off me. Then the other one came at him, but the Falcon was too fast. He pummeled both of them until they were left panting on the ground, swearing they'd never touch me again."

"And did they?" Mercy asks.

"Not until after they heard the Falcon was dead." Alyx shrugs off Mercy's hand. "Then they came back for me, only that time they got what they wanted and there was nobody there to stop them."

"Oh, Alyx." Mercy feels tears sliding down her cheeks.

"I had a chance to come here and I took it," says Alyx. "It was either that or sell the Falcon out."

"What do you mean?"

"There was a reward. For his identity. Enough money that I could have bought myself protection. Those idiots might have killed him but none of them have a clue who he really was. The Commander was prepared to reward anyone who had information."

"And you know who he was?" Mercy finds herself leaning forward, hanging on Alyx's every word.

"I do," she whispers. "I recognized him by his eyes. But I'll deny saying that if you ever repeat it."

"Then why are you telling me?" asks Mercy, folding her arms.

"I've seen the way you look at me since you figured out what I do." Alyx pulls back her shoulders. "Nobody has looked at me like that since I left the Outlands. I came here to get away from that judgment. To be in a place where I feel safe. I want you to understand what brought me here. I want you to stop looking at me the way you do."

"It's true I judged you," says Mercy, deciding that if Alyx has laid her soul bare then it's her turn to do the same. "But only because I'm jealous. I saw Luca visit you in your hut. I've seen the way he smiles at you. It was you he asked to look after the pods he caught."

"There's nothing for you to be jealous about." Alyx lets out a slow breath. "Believe me. It's you he cares for, not me. He visited my hut to talk to me. Like, actually talk. And he is teaching me about the pods to try to give me another option for my future. He's a good man. We have a history, but it's exactly that. History."

"History?" Mercy isn't sure if this is good news or bad, or even what it means.

Alyx nods. "Ask Luca if you want to know more. It's better coming from him."

"I've been trying to talk to him!" Mercy throws out her hands. "But he keeps running away! The guy hates me. You have it all wrong."

"Have you ever thought that he's keeping his distance for the exact opposite reason?" Alyx asks. "That maybe he's protecting you from people who might like to hurt him?"

Mercy reels back. This can't be true. Then she remembers

the tenderness of Luca's touch. The love that he poured into each kiss he placed on her lips. The way he looked at her in the moonlight like she was his sun and his stars. And she realizes she isn't sure what she believes anymore. Can somebody fake that kind of affection?

But just as she's about to make her denial, Sam breaks into the clearing.

And she's not alone.

Mercy has to blink to be sure she's seeing straight. "Ekon? What's he doing here?"

"Is he from Askala?" Alyx asks.

Mercy nods as she stands. Luca and Gust have already gone over to talk to him.

Alyx leaves her as she dashes away, and Mercy jogs over to the other Seekers, not wanting to miss a moment of whatever it is that Ekon has to say.

The first thing she notices is how distressed Sam looks. Her eyes are red and she's gripping onto Luca's arm like she needs his help to stand up.

"What's happening?" Mercy asks.

"Seb's sick," says Luca. "Ekon was sent to fetch Sam. She needs to go back."

"What about you?" Gust asks.

Luca shakes his head. "I need to stay here."

"But he's your brother, too," Mercy points out, trying to process what she's being told. Seb is always sick!

"It's Sam he's asking for," says Ekon. "We're worried he doesn't have long."

Sam lets out a wail at these words.

"He'll be okay," says Mercy. "He's always pulled through. You don't need to leave."

"She does." Ekon hangs his head, clearly hating being the bearer of such distressing news. "This time is different."

Mercy stands beside Sam, wanting to reach out to her but

knowing it's Luca's comfort she needs right now. This can't be happening. Seb is so young! He might be sickly but he's also full of life.

"It has to be a mistake," she says, unable to bear the thought of Sam leaving them. "A terrible mistake."

Ekon's silence is his answer. This is no mistake. Whatever has happened to Seb is serious. And it looks like Sam's made up her mind to go.

"I'm so sorry," Sam groans, her words muffled as she buries her face in Luca's chest. "I know I'm needed here."

"It's okay. Seb needs you, too." Luca drops a kiss on the top of her head, pain etched across his irritatingly handsome features.

People are coming out of their huts now to stare at Ekon whose face says he's a stranger but whose clothes tell them exactly where he's from.

Alyx emerges from Grace's hut with Corbin not far behind. Is that where she'd rushed off to so quickly? Mercy hadn't realized Alyx and Grace were so close.

Corbin has some kind of gash across his face that's dripping blood. He wipes it with the back of his hand and pushes in front of Grace.

"Who's this?" he asks, marching over to Ekon.

Luca lets go of Sam to position himself just a little in front of the others.

Mercy sees an opportunity and goes to Sam.

"Now's your chance," she whispers in her cousin's ear. "Go and see Hawk."

Sam's face lights up as her eyes widen.

"Hurry," says Mercy. "And be quick."

This could be Sam's only chance. And maybe if she sees Hawk, she'll realize that this is where she needs to stay. She can't go running back to Askala every time Seb gets sick. This has got to be Kian and Nova trying to guilt her into coming home. It doesn't matter what Ekon says! Seb will be fine. But maybe Hawk won't.

"I asked you who you are!" Corbin is in front of Ekon now and Mercy winces at the injury to his face. It looks like he just had an argument with a polar grizzly. Did Hawk wake up and do this? Is it possible he's not as asleep as they've been told?

"My name is Ekon. I come in peace." Ekon pulls back his broad shoulders and Mercy positions herself to cover for Sam as she slips away from the group.

Corbin sneers at him. "Listen here. We accepted this first lot of Sneakers." He pauses to laugh at his joke. "But that doesn't mean we're taking extra mouths to feed every time one of you lot decides you need a vacation."

Mercy glances to her left and sees Sam slip into Corbin's hut. She holds her breath, hoping she remains undetected.

"I came to deliver a message," says Ekon. "I don't intend to stay."

Mercy waves her hands, trying to get Ekon to be quiet. If he mentions Sam, then Corbin will wonder where she went. But Ekon doesn't seem to notice what Mercy's trying to tell him.

"And what message might that be?" Corbin asks.

"He came to tell me my brother's sick," says Mercy before anyone else can answer.

The Seekers all turn to her, well aware she doesn't have a brother. Then they seem to notice that the person who does have a brother is missing and they rush to cover up their surprise.

"That's right," says Ekon, glancing around. "Her brother is ill."

"You take us for fools!" Corbin roars. Mercy winces, pulling back slightly as she waits to see if she's going to be punished for her lie. She hadn't realized Corbin was so familiar with her family tree. "Nobody would risk their life to pass on a message. Not one of your people, anyway."

Mercy lets out a slow breath. Corbin has no reason to think she'd just lied. Although, it's going to be very difficult to explain why Sam wants to return home to visit Mercy's brother. Perhaps that hadn't been such a smart idea.

"You don't think we're brave?" asks Gust. "We had to fight off leatherskins to arrive here. We left everything we've ever known with no idea if you were going to kill us when we arrived."

Mercy glances at Corbin's hut hoping Sam emerges soon. It doesn't take that long to check on someone. What is she doing in there?

"Oh, you poor liddle babies," Corbin mocks, laughing as he swipes at his face, smudging blood across his bruised cheek. "We eat leatherskins for breakfast around here."

"You ate the fin off a leatherskin," corrects Gust. "And you ate it for dinner, not breakfast. Plus, we killed it for you."

"See what I have to put up with!" Corbin sneers at Gust, before shifting his gaze to Ekon. "Maybe you can take this one back with you. Leave the one who's easy on the eye."

Mercy blanches as Corbin leers at her, not wanting to be easy on any of these Newlanders' eyes. Especially Corbin's.

"But I dug the well!" Gust protests. "And I know how to build shelters. You need me here!"

"We don't need any of you here." Corbin stabs his finger into Gust's chest and Mercy lets out a breath to see Sam emerging from the hut and scurrying back toward them. Her face is pale, her eyes like saucers.

"Forgive me, Commander," says Mercy, bowing her head. "I lied to you just now."

Corbin leaves Gust and glares at Mercy, his anger magnified by the damaged state of his face.

"It's not my brother who's sick," she says, knowing he's going to find out if Sam chooses to leave, and not wanting Ekon to take the blame for Mercy's stupidity. "It's Sam's."

Sam looks up from the back of the group and it's like she never left their sides.

"I don't care whose brother is sick!" Corbin shouts. "Just tell me why he's really here. What are you planning? You're up to something."

"I come in peace." Ekon holds up his hands. "I swear it. I want no trouble."

Raiden chooses this moment to approach. Mercy hadn't even noticed him watching.

"If Sam's brother is sick, I'll take her back to him," he says.

"No, you won't." Luca steps forward now. "I'll take her."

"Kian asked me to bring her home myself," says Ekon.

"Stop it." Sam holds up her hand. "Nobody's taking me. I'm not going anywhere. The Newlands is my home now."

Mercy is desperate to drag Sam away and find out what she saw in the hut that changed her mind.

"But Seb's sick." Luca raises his eyebrows at Sam.

"We knew when we came here that people would get sick," says Sam, firmly. "Seb has family around him. And he knows I love him. My place is here."

Raiden sidles up to Sam and puts an arm around her shoulder. "I'm glad you feel that way."

Sam visibly cringes at Raiden's touch, and Mercy feels like tearing away his grubby hands. Isn't it enough that he has Nikita throwing herself at him? Can't he see that Sam's heart belongs to someone else? Someone who Mercy very much hopes is still alive, because looking at the total lack of color in Sam's face she's starting to wonder. Something in that hut spooked her.

Nikita bursts through the tree line at that moment.

"Outlanders!" she calls, her face red and her lungs heaving for breath. "Outlanders are approaching!"

"Where?" asks Grace.

"On the beach just now." Nikita runs to Raiden, frowning to

see his arm around Sam. "There are two boats about to land. Hurry!"

Corbin sticks his fingers in his mouth and lets out an ear-piercing whistle. His men emerge from the Round House and start to run.

"What do we do?" Mercy cries out.

"We stay together," says Luca, drawing them into a huddle. "And we get ready to fight."

LUCA

The Newlanders stand along the tree line, facing the beach. They hold their spears by their side, forming an angry, pointy-edged line of defense. Luca has the Seekers standing among the trees—close enough to see what's about to go down, but with enough distance to keep them out of the fray.

Please let them stay out of the fray.

His mind tries to plan how they can come out of this unscathed. There's hiding in the forest. Taking one of their boats out to the water.

Or fighting.

The arriving boats are almost at shore when Luca does another quick scan. Mercy and Sam are just behind him, Gust another step back behind them. Ekon is right at the back, where Luca asked him to stand. They need someone strong at the front if they have to turn and run, and Hawk's still healing.

Luca's lips flatten. Nikita's standing behind Raiden, amongst the Newlanders. Twice Luca's caught her eye. Twice she's looked away.

She's made her choice about who she's aligned with.

Crossing his arms, Luca narrows his focus on the approaching invaders. He's ready to do what it takes.

He needs to protect Mercy and Sam at all costs.

There's a slight shuffle and Luca sees Mercy come up beside him. He's about to hiss for her to get back when she lifts her chin, her gaze daring him to say something.

Not after he's done everything he can to avoid her.

Which he's been doing exactly for this reason. This close, everything this beautiful woman has become is inescapable.

Mercy is tough. Courageous.

She takes his breath away.

Another subtle crunch of leaf litter and Sam's on his other side. Luca doesn't need to look at her to know her own chin is angled for the sky. He wipes a hand down his face. Of course he had to team up with brave, determined females who have only got a taste of what they're up against.

Straightening, Luca focuses back on the rusty ocean, reaffirming his vow.

He'll protect them at all cost.

The first boat scrapes across sand, the second doing the same only moments later. Several Outlanders leap out, splashing through the shallows as they drag the boats up. All of them are men. All lean, muscled, and grimy.

Every one of them personifying the brutality and struggle of the Outlands.

The Newlanders shift subtly, their spears angling forward. One of the Outlanders notices, his eyes narrowing. He nudges the man beside him, indicating with his chin.

The second man scans the welcoming committee, as Corbin likes to call it. His lip curls in his tangled beard. He reaches into the boat and pulls something out. Something that has Luca's arms unwinding and his spine stiffening as other Newlanders do the same.

Every second Outlander is now carrying a flamethrower.

Images of Siena's agonizing death rise unwanted in Luca's mind, closely followed by the knowledge that Hawk's still in Grace's hut, recovering from the last time these people arrived on the shores of the Newlands.

The men fan out, walking away from the beached boats, the man with the beard spearheading them. As he comes closer, Luca sees the deep, rutted scar across the man's cheek, carving a white line through his dark facial hair.

The man stops in the center of the beach. "You look as foul tempered as always, Corbin," he calls out.

Sam draws in a sharp breath, but Luca's surprised at the man's words for a whole different reason. Rudeness like that in the Outlands is actually quite common.

Corbin crosses his arms. "That's because I have to look at your ugly face again, Marr."

Common between men who know each other.

Stepping forward into the light, Corbin spits in the sand. "You'd better have made it worth my while."

Marr waves to the bedraggled troops behind him. "The flamethrowers aren't enough?"

The men who are holding them jostle the weapons. Along with the tattered clothes and matted hair, they look wild and menacing.

The fact that this conversation has taken such an unexpected turn makes Luca even more nervous. These men are playing at something, and he doesn't know what.

"They're a good start," Corbin growls.

Marr turns to two men behind him, nodding once. They walk back to the boats, leaning over to lift something up.

"If we need to run, we run," mutters Luca.

With swift movements, the men yank their prizes up and above their heads. Timber rests in their palms, metal glints softly in the light.

Axes.

The people around Corbin break into a roar as they rush forward.

Luca watches the clash of bodies as the men bump chests and thump each other on the back. It's a better outcome than he was hoping for, but for some reason, it still makes him uneasy.

"They know each other," murmurs Mercy.

Luca nods, not taking his eyes off the men as they crowd around the axes. "It looks like they've brought supplies."

Sam frowns. "Then why did they greet them like that?"

Sam wouldn't understand that any greeting in the Outlands is about a show of strength. Weakness isn't tolerated, either from those who have staked a claim on a piece of land, or those approaching it.

"They were making sure that each side knew who they were dealing with," explains Mercy. "They don't want to be aligning themselves with someone weak."

But it seems Mercy does get it.

Ekon steps up beside them, taking in the way the men are jostling each other like old friends. "What does this mean for the Seekers?"

No one answers.

Because no one knows.

Sam squares her shoulders. "We should meet them. Show them we're residents here, too."

As much as Luca doesn't like the sound of that, he knows they need to. Hiding is seen as a weakness.

They exit the trees, Luca watching to see who will notice their arrival first.

For some reason, it's Grace who looks up, as if she'd been aware of their presence in the trees the whole time. The rest of the men are clueless, too busy fawning over their weapons and tools.

Marr flexes his sinewy arm. "Between the axes and these muscles, the next stage is—"

"Corbin," Grace says loudly. "The others are here."

The new Outlanders instantly contract, their gazes finding the Seekers and not letting go. Corbin barely glances at them. "Like a bad smell," he mutters.

Sam stiffens, probably taking exception to someone as foul-odored as Corbin calling them a bad smell. Her response only increases Luca's churning gut. Sam seems to have made it a personal quest that the more Corbin is rude to her, the nicer she'll be to him.

Just as he expected, Sam steps forward, smiling. "Welcome to the Newlands."

She glances at Corbin as if pointing out this is how a welcome should be done.

Marr scowls. "And you are?"

"Sam. Lovely to meet you. My friends and I are Seekers from Askala. We come in peace. We're working together to establish this colony."

At the mention of Askala, a ripple coils through the Outlanders. Marr looks at Corbin sharply, then Grace.

"They've dug a well, and helped us source food," she says.

"Have they now," murmurs Marr as he turns back to them. "Isn't that...helpful."

Sam's smile grows wider. "We like to think so."

But Marr isn't interested in Sam. His dark eyes scrutinize Luca and Ekon, no doubt noting their size and strength. Not for the first time, Luca wishes Hawk was here. Marr's gaze flickers past Gust then settles on Mercy.

And stays there.

For the first time, he smiles, the scar on his face twisting and stretching. "You a friend of Alyx's?"

Mercy opens her mouth to respond but Luca subtly steps in front of her. "She's a friend of mine."

Although Marr's smile stays in place, his gaze hardens. "Aren't we all friends, here?"

"We most certainly are," says Sam cheerily. "Just think of how much we can achieve together."

Suddenly, Raiden steps in, standing beside Sam. "Anything we put our mind to."

Corbin roars with laughter and Sam's face lights up. Luca's jaw is so tight his teeth are aching. He doesn't like this unexpected turn of events.

Corbin lifts his arms in the air, turning to face everyone. "We shall have a feast!"

There are cheers as more fists punch the sky. Gripping their flamethrowers and axes, the Outlanders follow the others to the trees. Raiden smiles at Sam, indicating they should follow. Sam hesitates for a moment but then joins him, glancing over her shoulder.

Luca tries to tell her to be careful without saying it, knowing Sam probably won't pick up on the signals.

A hand lands on his shoulder and Luca finds Ekon next to him. "I'll follow."

Luca nods, relieved. He hadn't realized how much he'd come to depend on Hawk to keep an eye on his trusting sister. Sam means well, but she believes everyone else does, too.

The beach is almost empty when Mercy strides past Luca, flicking her waterfall hair over her shoulder. Reflexively, Luca grabs her hand, only to quickly release it when their connection instantly flares to life.

But he needs to warn her.

"Mercy, I don't like this. You need to stay away from these new Outlanders."

She spins around, her eyes blazing. "So, now you're Mr. Protective again?"

Jamming his fingers through his hair, Luca wishes he could point out he's never stopped protecting her.

Caring for her.

He couldn't have stopped falling for her if he tried.

Hell, he did try!

"These men are dangerous. And the number of Outlanders here just grew."

The Seekers are even more outnumbered than they were before.

Mercy glances at where they just disappeared through the trees. "And Marr mentioned the next stage."

Luca was hoping she hadn't noticed that, although he should've realized that was a hopeless wish. There's very little that gets past Mercy.

Which is why he has to keep her at arm's length, no matter what.

"We're going to have to find out what that means," Luca mutters. "We have no idea what we're up against."

Mercy chews her lip. "Sam's so sure we're making progress."

"I hope she's right."

If anyone could prove his nagging suspicion wrong, it's Sammy. But until that moment happens, Luca's not letting his guard down.

Sam means too much to him.

And so does Mercy.

Knowing he needs to get out of here before his emotions get the better of him, Luca takes a step toward the trees. "We'd better see what's happening."

But this time, Mercy reaches out and grabs his hand. But unlike Luca, she doesn't let go.

And despite it all, he can't bring himself to pull away. Mercy's soft hand around his is the sweetest thing he's felt since he was forced to break both their hearts.

"We can't keep going on like this, Luca."

His gut winds itself into a knot. There's no way he can explain his actions to Mercy. "Then you need to let me go."

Something in Mercy's eyes flares—the same anger and hurt that's blazed before. As much as Luca hates it, he welcomes it.

It means Mercy doesn't want to be around him.

But then her hand tightens. "I've realized why that's so hard to do." Her gaze sharpens and softens all at once. "Because a part of you—the part that's standing here like my fingers just anchored you to the spot—doesn't want me to let go."

Dammit.

Luca knows he has to deny that. To push Mercy away, once and for all.

Except his muscles have locked. His throat is constricted.

And his heart is clamoring against his ribs, trying to get to her.

Mercy's lips part. Then angle up. Her eyes devour him like they've been apart too long.

Before either of them can move, sounds reach them from the village. Sounds which fracture the moment Luca couldn't escape.

"Oh, no," moans Mercy.

Luca's heart sinks, realizing what must be happening.

There's the sound of metal hitting wood.

There's the sound of crackling flames.

And neither of those are the sounds of progress.

HAWK

*T*he sun is bright outside the hut. Too bright. It's like hot spears are being poked into Hawk's eyes.

He blinks, lifting his arm to shield his face. But now it's the noise that's assaulting him.

There's shouting. Gasping. And a loud thumping noise like a drum.

But whatever's out here can't be worse than staying in that stifling hut for another moment. The last thing he can remember is the chilling realization that Grace drugged him. But he can't remember why she did it. Was it to help him heal? Another thought nags at his consciousness. There was more to it than that…

Looking down, he sees his chest in the sunlight, and gasps.

It's hard to tell what's a bruise and what's a tattoo but his torso is covered in black lines that are snaking their way across his skin in a series of patterns. He looks like his father, a man he'd be honored to be like. But he also looks like Corbin and his men…

Ashamed, he drops his arm to cover his chest and shakes his head, wondering why there are so many people in the clearing.

There's a wall of sweaty, skinny backs facing him. The Outlanders have formed a circle, and something is happening in the middle of it.

Hawk stumbles both left and right looking for an opening in this ring of human body odor so he can see what's happening.

A cheer ripples through the clearing and the men thump their spears on the ground, picking up a rhythm that spirals into the smoke-filled air.

"Hawk!"

He turns at the sound of Sam's voice, squinting as he tries to make sense of what's happening. Grace had told him something to do with Sam. But what was it?

She's beside him in an instant.

"What have they done to you?" she asks, her eyes glued to his chest.

"I'm sorry," he says, even though he played no part in the decision to mark his body in such a way.

"You're still Hawk." Sam slips her arms around his waist and presses herself gently against him.

He may not know what's going on, who all these people are, and how long he was asleep, but Sam steadies him like an anchor, holding him in place.

He's here.

She's here.

Which means they're both here together, and none of the other details matter.

"I don't care what they've made you look like," Sam says. "I'm just glad you're awake. I thought you were never going to wake up. You looked so fragile underneath that blanket. You scared me."

"You visited me?" His voice is like a rasp in his dry throat. He's certain he'd remember it if Sam had visited. Her absence had been a gaping cavity in his chest. Or was that just his broken ribs?

She lets go of him a little so she can look at him, and nods slowly, her eyes filling with tears. "When I saw you like that I just knew I couldn't leave you."

"You were going to leave me?" He tilts his head, trying to make sense of what she's saying. But it's hard with the beating of the spears on the earth, the roars of the men, the sunlight...so much sunlight. Why does it have to be so bright? His head is spinning, and for a moment he thinks he might faint.

Sam grips him tightly around the waist and leads him over to the other Seekers.

He focuses on her as he allows himself to be led.

Luca's there. And Gust. And Mercy, who instantly slips in beside Hawk and puts a hand on his back.

"Nice ink!" says Gust, seeming genuinely impressed as he gawks at Hawk's chest. "How do I get myself some of that?"

Hawk opens his mouth to answer, but something's not right. Nikita's missing. And Siena. And why is Ekon here? Ekon's not a Seeker.

He must still be asleep. That's what this is. A confusing dream that's not supposed to make any sense. He needs to stop trying so hard to fit the pieces together.

Then the memory of Siena's death crashes back with such pain that he knows he's very much awake. It wouldn't be possible for his heart to ache this much if he were asleep. The smell of Siena's charred remains is still lodged in his nostrils. It won't matter how much time passes, he's never going to forget that smell.

Luca reaches for Hawk and lifts up one of his half-closed eyelids with his thumb.

Hawk winces, but lets him, wondering what he's looking for.

"Check out the size of his pupils," says Luca to the others. "I don't know what he's been given, but he's drugged up to his eyeballs. Literally."

Hawk's not sure why Luca's talking to the Seekers and not to him, but he's glad as it saves him having to answer. His voice isn't keen on coming out of his mouth.

He giggles at the image of his voice having become a separate being that's hiding behind his tonsils.

"Hawk." Mercy squeezes him gently. "Are you okay?"

He smiles at his beautiful cousin.

"You're very clever," he tells her. "Not as clever as Sam, but you're still clever."

Mercy shakes her head and smiles. "I think it was a truth drug they gave him."

This is even funnier than his voice hiding behind his tonsils and Hawk tips back his head and laughs. It's more like a bellow. Or an intense chuckle.

The words *intense chuckle* make him laugh even harder, sending shooting pain from his ribs radiating across his chest.

Now, not only are the Seekers staring at him, but so is everyone else.

"Hawk!" calls Corbin.

He turns and sees Corbin walking toward him.

"Good to see you awake," says Corbin, his eyes on his chest. "Looking as strong as ever."

"Why did you do that to him?" asks Sam. "If Hawk wanted those tattoos, he'd have asked."

"Had to turn him into a real man for what I've got in mind for him." Corbin loops an arm around Hawk's shoulders and tries to lead him into the clearing. But Luca grips Hawk tightly on the arm.

"Leave him, Corbin," growls Luca. "He's not recovered. You've done enough."

"I'm recovered!" Hawk shouts to the faces that are all watching him, enjoying the way they cheer at him. Is he seeing double? There has to be at least twice as many men as there were the last time he saw everyone gathered here.

"Hawk! What are you doing?" Sam is trying to grab hold of him, too, but Hawk isn't sure what the fuss is all about.

He shakes off both Luca and Sam, and follows Corbin a few steps.

"He's not acting like himself," he hears Sam saying to the other Seekers. "We have to stop him."

Hawk turns to Sam, trying to walk back to her but his feet feel like they have polar grizzlies tied to them. This thought makes him laugh again and before he knows it, Corbin has led him into the center of the clearing.

Corbin lifts Hawk's hand high into the air and a huge cheer erupts from the crowd.

Hawk grins at the people. So many faces. All looking at him. Then he remembers he doesn't like people watching him. He's the one who likes to do the watching. A wave of shyness sweeps over him and he looks to the ground as a soberness invades his senses.

What is he doing out here?

Looking at Sam, he sees Luca holding her back. Each and every Seeker has a look of fear plastered to their face. He needs to pull himself together.

And fast!

Corbin taps Hawk's bare chest, and Hawk realizes that he'd walked out of the hut without his shirt. Thankfully, he seems to be wearing his pants.

"Who's game to take on this beast of a man?" Corbin shouts to the crowd. "His friends call him Hawk, but I call him *the* Hawk. A bird of prey or a man of iron? Who's brave enough to find out?"

Now that the haze has fallen from his eyes, Hawk sees a man covered in blood crumpled in one corner of the clearing. Is he dead? There are more men with bloodied faces and torn clothes, sneering at Hawk as they raise their fists.

And now he sees the clearing for what it is.

An arena.

And these men are gathered to fight. Is it for entertainment? Or are they trying to prove something to each other? Perhaps it's both those reasons. And Hawk wants neither to entertain or prove anything to anyone.

Now he knows why Luca tried to hold him back. And why Sam is now having to be restrained from running out to stop him.

Raiden is grinning at Hawk from the sidelines and a sick feeling slides down Hawk's spine as a memory comes rushing back. Grace wanted Hawk out of the way so that Raiden could marry Sam.

His Sam. The only girl he's ever loved.

"Him," says Hawk, pointing as unwanted jealousy bubbles in his gut. "I challenge Raiden."

This wipes the smile from Raiden's smarmy face.

"No!" shrieks Nikita from beside him.

Her voice echoes around the clearing as a hush blankets it. But Hawk holds firm. He's not in much of a state to fight anyone but if he's going to be forced into this, then let it be the guy trying to take away the only thing that means anything to him.

Let Raiden see what he's going up against. And better for Hawk to fight for what he wants, instead of lying helplessly in some kind of drugged-up coma while Raiden steals his girl.

"Are you afraid of our more experienced fighters?" asks Corbin, unable to keep the panic from his voice. "You chose yourself a boy?"

Raiden scowls and rushes forward, clearly not liking the picture his father just painted of him.

Hawk drags in a deep breath and steadies himself. He may be weak and dazed but he's bigger than this spineless mosquito.

"Choose again!" shouts Grace from the crowd. "The son of the Commander is ineligible to fight."

Hawk looks for her, scanning the faces until he sees her, watching him with eyes filled with fear. He doesn't blame her trying to protect her son. He doesn't even blame her for drugging him. Desperate people do desperate things. Grace isn't a bad person. She's just damaged.

"I choose Raiden," says Hawk, straightening his spine and ignoring the confusion that's gripping his skull. In some ways Grace has done him a favor, because he's certain that whatever it was that she put in his water is dulling his pain along with his senses.

If only someone could turn down the brightness of all this light.

"A Commander must know how to protect himself, is that not true?" Hawk asks, noticing Corbin has a black eye and wondering how he got it. "Let the future Commander prove his worth."

"My son knows how to protect himself," says Corbin.

"Prove it," sneers Hawk, unable to stand the confident look on Raiden's face.

"I accept the challenge," Raiden says through gritted teeth.

The circle of men around them bang their spears on the dry earth and Hawk tries to ignore the way the primal rhythm is vibrating inside his head. Each thump of a spear is like a dagger at his temples.

"He's injured!" Sam cries out. "This isn't a fair fight."

This only makes the Outlanders laugh. Hawk may be dazed but he knows why they're laughing. Fairness isn't a concept that exists out here. The strong triumph over the weak time and time again in these lands without mercy. A polar grizzly wouldn't stop short of eating a rabbit because it has an injured leg. It would seize that opportunity for what it is.

An advantage.

Hawk just needs to make sure that Raiden's advantage isn't enough to allow him to win.

Corbin looks at Raiden to confirm he's sure about this. Raiden gives him a curt nod in reply and Corbin goes to Grace, who's twisting her fingers through her hair, clearly unhappy about what's about to happen here.

Which leaves a problem… what is about to happen here?

Hawk knows he's strong. But he doesn't know how to fight. The Outlanders proved that to him right after they killed Siena. But is Raiden any better? Has Corbin taught his son in the way Hawk's own father failed?

He tries to focus. To block out the way the trees around the clearing are swaying. To forget the blurred faces of the ring of spectators. He's the son of Phoenix. He can do this. He can make his father proud.

Raiden holds up his palms to Hawk.

Hawk stares at Raiden's hands, wondering what he's waiting for.

"You need to show me your empty hands," Raiden hisses under his breath.

"Oh." Hawk holds up his hands, and Raiden nods his approval.

"Now take three steps back," says Raiden, drawing away from Hawk.

Hawk wobbles as he steps back, trying to keep himself steady, wondering how he ended up in this situation when it seems like only moments ago he'd been asleep in Grace's bed.

He reminds himself that it's better to get this over with now. To show each other what they have. Perhaps then Raiden will leave Sam alone. Because Hawk still has that interrupted kiss he needs to finish.

Hawk concentrates on not falling over as he takes his next two steps back. He plants his feet on the ground and decides to let Raiden make the first move. If he runs forward himself, there's a big risk he might fall over.

The energy from the ring of onlookers soars and lifts something inside Hawk. He can feel their excitement almost as if he owns it himself. Is this what attracts these primitive men to the sport of fighting?

"Let the Tournament begin!" calls a deep voice from the crowd.

Hawk raises his fists and waits.

There are a few things Hawk's learned over the years observing people. All those times when he used his eyes in place of his words. He can read people better than most. Which means he can tell that Raiden's scared.

He's not shaking. Nor does he seem to be breathing rapidly.

It's in his eyes. He's barely blinking, not shifting his gaze from his opponent for even a second. He's calculating his best first move.

Hawk holds steady. He can stand here all day in the blazing sun if he needs to, just like he did with the bucket test in his Proving. Perhaps that test was more appropriate for the Seekers than anyone realized at the time.

Raiden comes running at him. His movements are fast. Sudden. Almost like he thinks Hawk won't notice his approach. The beating of the spears picks up pace to match and Hawk grips the earth with his bare feet, bracing for impact.

Raiden lunges, grabbing him around the neck and forcing him to bend in half. Hawk's ribs scream at him as they reach the threshold of pain able to be blocked by Grace's elixir.

Hawk swings around, trying to send Raiden flying, but his grip is too firm, so instead Hawk pulls back his fist and slams it into Raiden's stomach as hard as he can.

The spears fall silent as if they, too, are shocked by the impact, and Grace's scream echoes around the clearing.

Raiden groans, stumbling back in shock.

Hawk steps forward again and delivers another blow, this one landing on Raiden's cheek.

Raiden howls, covering his face with his hands as blood pours from between his fingers.

"Stop!" he begs. "Please, stop."

Seeing his opportunity, Hawk draws back his fist again. He can finish this with one swift movement. Three strikes and the job will be done.

Then why is his hand hovering in the air? Are Grace's screams stopping him? Or is it the whimpering coming from his pathetic opponent?

"Hawk!" cries Sam, and he knows at that moment he's not going to hit Raiden. This might be a fight for the girl they both have their hopes pinned on, but that doesn't mean that the one who inflicts the most damage is the one who'll win.

It's the opposite.

Sam values compassion, not violence. A kind heart is so much more important to her than physical strength.

He shakes his head trying to bring back his senses. Sam's faith in him isn't misplaced. Because the truth is that he doesn't want to hurt Raiden. He doesn't want to hurt *anybody*. All he wants to do is show people that there's another way to live. He wants to save them from themselves just like Askala saved his father.

Which means he needs to show these people what kindness looks like. Sam will be his no matter who walks out of this fight as the victor. He has to believe that.

Letting his fist fall, Hawk goes to Raiden and drapes an arm around his shoulders in a gesture that he hopes is friendly. Raiden winces before realizing he means him no harm.

"Look up," Hawk whispers. "Don't let them see your weakness."

These people will never follow a Commander they don't respect. Raiden has no hope of taking over from Corbin one day if he finishes a fight like this.

Slowly, Raiden lowers his hands, revealing his injured face.

Hawk had no idea he could inflict that much damage with a single punch.

"That's it," says Hawk softly. "Show them your strength."

"Thank you," says Raiden.

The next thing Hawk knows, Raiden turns and slams his fists into Hawk's already broken ribs.

Raiden's face is full of menace and determination as he pummels a series of sharp blows, over and over and over. Hawk roars with agony as he's swallowed into a world of unexpected pain, catching another expression hidden beneath Raiden's scowl.

Joy.

Raiden is getting some kind of sick satisfaction out of the damage he's doing.

The crowd cheers loudly now, the beating of their spears slicing into the oblivion that Hawk's trying not to slip into.

Hawk lunges at Raiden, swiping for him, but misses as black spots cloud his vision.

Raiden dodges left, then right, then gets under Hawk's arms and continues to pound at his ribs. He's found Hawk's weak point and he exploits it time and time again, each punch gaining strength fueled by the success of the one that came before.

Hawk steps back, trying to avoid the next impact, blinking as he desperately tries to bring his vision back into focus.

Grace has fallen silent and it's Mercy he can hear now. A howling cry punctuated by Sam calling out for Raiden to stop.

But Raiden comes at him again with his fists. Hawk falls to the ground, a mistake he made when the Outlanders came, and one he bitterly regrets now as Raiden swaps his fists for his feet. He can't let this happen again.

He can't!

Raiden draws back his foot and Hawk sees a blur of movement as it swings toward his head. Reaching up, he grabs hold of Raiden's ankle and using every ounce of strength he has, he twists until he hears the bone break. Refusing to release the damaged limb, Hawk pulls and Raiden comes crashing to the ground beside him.

The screaming is as incessant as the punches Raiden was throwing at Hawk only a moment ago. This time, instead of them making Hawk feel sorry for him, they infuriate him.

Hawk could have ended this fight but had shown Raiden mercy. He'd tried to show kindness, and had received nothing but hot rage in return. This guy is a coward.

Rolling over, Hawk leaps up and straddles Raiden, putting his hands around his neck. It wouldn't take much to end this weasel's life.

"No!" howls Raiden. "No!

Hawk releases this pathetic excuse for a man and works his legs, trying to get himself into a stand. He doesn't want to kill Raiden. He never did. He's just not sure Raiden feels the same way. There's no doubt he'd have killed Hawk if given the chance.

Wobbling, Hawk raises a fist in the air, but all spears hold still, all mouths remain silent. This isn't the victory they want to celebrate.

Hawk can't see Sam to look at her. He can't even tell what direction she's in. His vision is blurred in the blinding sun, the pain riding through his body like a relentless tsunami.

There's a commotion behind him and he feels two sets of strong hands grip him. Hawk falls limp as the agony in his ribs slices his consciousness in half.

At last, the brightness of the sun is extinguished.

All he sees is night.

SAM

*a*s two men start to drag Hawk away, Luca finally releases Sam. She stumbles, having gone from straining to free in a blink. Pushing herself up, she doesn't let it slow her momentum.

She has to get to Hawk.

The men grip Hawk under the arms, his feet scraping two lines in the dirt as they make their way past the people still milling around the human arena. His head lolls to the side, his chest now shades of bruise on bruise underneath line on line of ink.

"Wait! Where are you taking him?" Sam calls out.

"The Commander said to throw him where he belongs," one of the men shouts over his shoulder as they both continue walking.

Sam catches up, unsure whether she should focus on being beside Hawk or trying to get these brutes to stop. "Please, he's hurt. Is there another way to move him?"

The man who spoke glares at Sam. "He picked the opponent. What did he think was going to happen?"

That Raiden would show Hawk the same level of compassion he was shown when Hawk could've won the fight.

That Raiden would show him mercy.

They reach the skeleton of their barely constructed hut and the men release Hawk's arms, letting his torso thump to the ground.

Sam cries out and rushes to kneel beside him. When she looks up a moment later, the men are already walking away, shaking their heads. Sam ignores their callousness. Hawk's injured. Seriously injured.

That's all she can focus on right now.

Shuffling over, Sam gently lifts his head and slips it onto her lap. "Oh, Hawk," she chokes.

Although his face was saved from the beating it received last time, the rest of his body has been battered. His chest, his abdomen, his arms, are all mottled with deep red and painful purple. His skin underneath is painted with yellow and blue—the bruises that had barely healed last time. Except now they're nestled between fresh lines of tattoos, made from a mixture of ash and water and injected under his skin as a permanent reminder of how helpless he'd been rendered.

His breath is shallow and raspy, no doubt because his ribs are fractured all over again. Sam traces a finger over his cheek, her own chest aching.

Hawk should never have fought, let alone picked Raiden as an opponent.

Nor can Sam pretend that she doesn't know why Hawk picked him. Whatever friendship she forged with Raiden is the reason Hawk did what he did.

His eyelids flutter, lifting slowly as if it's an effort. But once his eyes are open, they're instantly scanning. Searching. They connect with Sam, and Hawk relaxes. "Sam."

"Shh, I'm here. We're going to take care of you."

Although Hawk's blinking like his eyelids are weighed down with stones, his gaze doesn't leave Sam's. "Raiden..."

"It's okay. They took him to Grace's hut."

Hawk has probably fallen out of favor with her, now.

He swallows, his throat working. "Stay away from him," he rasps.

Sam strokes a curl back from Hawk's forehead. "He won't be going anywhere for a while." Leaning down, she continues before he can say anything else. "You don't need to worry about that right now. We need to get you better." She presses her hand to his cheek. "What can I do?"

Hawk's eyes flutter shut, turning his head so he presses more firmly against her palm. "Stay."

His body goes limp again as consciousness slips away but Sam doesn't remove her hand.

"Always," she whispers through a tight throat.

A shadow falls across them and Sam almost doesn't want to look up. What if it's Corbin? Will he want revenge for what happened to his son?

Mercy squats down, reaching out but then thinking twice before touching Hawk. "How is he?"

Sam can't answer straight away. Every bruise is a stamp of violence on Hawk's body. Each one feels like a strike to her own heart. She swallows, knowing she needs to get herself under control. Hawk needs her.

"Significant contusions. I suspect there are multiple fractures. I hope there isn't any internal bleeding."

Luca appears behind Mercy, Gust beside him. "Considering the guy's built of stone, I doubt it."

Mercy nods. "Luca's right. Hawk's tough. We'll get him through this."

Grasping their optimism and clinging to it, Sam blinks away her tears. "Of course we will."

There's no other option.

"First thing's first," Luca says. "We need to get him in the shade."

Gently placing his head down, Sam stands. As much as she just wants to sit here holding Hawk, Luca's right. She finally looks around. They're only a few feet outside their new hut. Their barely-built hut. The framework is there, and part of the roof, but little else.

Mercy dusts her hands off. "This will have to do for now. We need to move him quickly but gently."

As if some agreement's been reached between the two of them, Luca and Mercy each reach down and each slip an arm beneath Hawk's shoulders. Luca looks across at Mercy. "That's it, grip my arm. Once we lift, we can do the same with our other hands." Not breaking his gaze with her, he speaks again. "Sam and Gust, you guys take a leg each."

Obeying without question, Sam does as she's told, glad Gust does the same. She hopes Hawk stays unconscious for this part. Moving him is going to hurt.

As one, they lift Hawk, Gust grunting in surprise at the weight. Although Sam feels like she's carrying a tree trunk, she focuses on moving Hawk as smoothly as possible.

"Yep," huffs Luca. "Built of stone."

Slowly but surely, they move Hawk into the half-built hut, laying him under the section of roof. He doesn't stir, which Sam knows is a good thing for his pain, but has her frowning, nonetheless.

How long will it take Hawk to wake up?

Luca steps back, scanning their partially built hut. "We'll have to finish this shelter. He needs to be out of the elements."

Mercy moves in a circle, her hands on her hips. "If we could have the roof done by tonight, that will be a start."

Sam nods. She doesn't plan on leaving Hawk's side during the night so a roof is all they need. She's going to have to keep an eye out for a fever.

Gust nods resolutely. "Let's get to work."

Luca and Gust stride away into the forest, Luca instructing Gust on what materials they're going to need. For once, Gust agrees with everything that's being asked of him, paying attention intently.

It seems everyone wants Hawk to get better.

Sam's knees give out and she sinks beside him. Impossibly, it looks like the bruising is getting worse. How could someone do this to another human being? One who hurts and bleeds just like they do?

"What does he need, Sam?" Mercy asks quietly.

Sam shakes her head. Hawk needs proper medical care. He needs someone like her mother.

"Think, Sam."

"Zinc," she mutters without thinking. "And vitamin K. Zinc helps the body heal wounds and tissues. Vitamin K helps the blood clot."

Right now, Hawk's body is bleeding just beneath the skin, countless capillaries crushed and macerated.

"Yes," Mercy says urgently. "Where can we find them?"

In Askala. Where nutrient rich foods are grown and are easily accessible.

Where something like this would never happen.

But then Sam realizes something. "In plantain. And chickweed. Just like we collected in the fourth test."

Mercy's face lights with hope. "Do the forests here have them?"

"Plantain is most likely. It's a pioneer species—the plant species which first colonize new environments. They're hardy with long tap roots, breaking up the soil for future species—"

Mercy grips Sam's shoulders. "You need to go find some."

Sam's denial is instant. "No, I can't leave Hawk."

"You know what you're looking for." Mercy's hands tighten

around Sam's arms. "We can't afford for someone like me to bring back the wrong thing."

Sam shudders. Like the deadly nightshade that Hawk found. The same plant that killed Simon.

Mercy holds Sam's gaze. "I'll look after him. I love him, too."

Sam blinks. She's never denied that she loves Hawk. She's loved him all her life. But what she feels for him now is so much more than that. Her lip trembles. "I love him more than a best-friend."

Mercy nods, her face softening. "For once, there was something I knew before you did."

Knowing she needs to go source the plantain, Sam presses her face close to Hawk. "I'll be back. We're going to make you better," she promises fiercely.

Not giving herself time to think any further, Sam darts out the half-made doorway. Plantain lives in shaded areas. Hopefully, she won't have to go far into the forest to find some.

Skirting the outer huts of the village, Sam can see that although the Tournaments are over, the celebrations are still continuing. A thick plume of smoke rises from the center of the village, the same place where they had their arena. Sam's stomach recoils. It's like these people celebrate destruction.

People mill around, some coming in and out of the Round House, others talk and laugh. Sam can't hear what they're saying, but there's a whole lot of jostling and punching, as if they're reliving a fight.

Trying to remain unseen, Sam slips around the next hut. She's about to dart to the next one, when a word reaches her.

"Feast."

The smell of roasting meat has Sam frowning, but before she can wonder what the Outlanders are cooking she slams into a body. Stumbling backwards, Sam's wondering if she should run when she recognizes the person.

"Ekon, you startled me."

"Sorry, I've been keeping an eye on things. Looks like they're gearing up for quite a party." He frowns. "How's Hawk?"

Sam's hands twist in the hem of her shirt. "He has a lot of healing to do. I'm going to get him something to help with that."

"From the forest? On your own?"

"Of course from the forest. Beside the vegetable garden we planted, nothing grows in the village."

Ekon glances around. "The vegetable garden?"

Sam points to a clearing several yards ahead but then she sees what she's indicating toward.

The Outlanders have dumped the supplies they brought with them where the ploughed rows used to be. Now trampled, axes are leaning against large branches that have been hacked off.

Sam presses a hand to her mouth, stifling the gasp. The seeds were just starting to germinate. She doubts the Outlanders ever saw the fragile green shoots reaching up from the soil, seeking the sunlight that would help them grow strong.

Or even if they did, they wouldn't have cared.

Ekon shakes his head. "This is no place for you, Sam. Your parents were right."

"This is no place for anyone," Sam hisses. "That's why we're here."

"With Siena dead? With Hawk beaten to a bloody pulp?" He clenches his fists. "With your brother dying, his only wish is to see his sister again?"

Sam flinches. She never thought she'd be forced to choose like this. Being a Seeker was always about fighting *for* Askala. Not having to choose between the two.

She shakes her head, resolute. "I'm not leaving Hawk." Straightening her shoulders, she looks Ekon in the eye. "Or the progress we've made here."

Ekon sighs as if he's not surprised to hear that. "Your mother said you'd do what you thought was right." He glances over his shoulder. "At least let me come with you into the forest."

The tension unwinds a little. "Thank you, that would be appreciated." Two people collecting plantain are even quicker than one.

Sam's barely taken a step when a roar echoes from the center of the village. Sam freezes, worried she's been seen, but she quickly realizes what has the Outlanders celebrating.

And it's not spotting her.

Two men, one of them the scarred man called Marr, are entering the center. Between them, they're both shouldering a barrel.

The pod barrel.

Sam rushes forward, fury a hot flash through her veins. How much more can these people take?

"Stop, those are not to be eaten!"

The men turn to her, surprised, but their faces quickly soften to mirth when they see Sam coming toward them.

"What else are you supposed to do with them?" Marr asks with a sneer.

Sam stops beside the barrel, trying to hold onto her anger. "Of course they're to be eaten. But not now."

Marr's lip curls as he looks at her in disgust. "Tomorrow ain't guaranteed. Our stomachs know now is."

He punches his hand into the water, grasping for a few seconds before his face lights up. Lifting his fist victoriously, he greedily plops the wriggling pod into his mouth.

A cheer rises as the people rush forward, shoving and jostling to try and grab a pod of their own. Sam steps back, knowing her voice won't be heard.

Wondering if it ever was.

She turns around, the fire that was hurling all the black smoke into the atmosphere warming her even at this distance. It's the biggest she's ever seen, showing the axes have already been hard at work. Sam presses her hand to her chest, trying to contain the loss. The gardens. The pods. The trees.

She gasps when she discovers it doesn't end there. At the edge of the fire, coals have been raked aside. The bodies of several hares have been skewered onto spits, their meat glistening as it cooks.

Sam doesn't need to see the cages to know those breeders are gone, now, too.

Someone grabs her arm, and Sam looks up into Ekon's concerned gaze. "There is nothing more you can do. Your family needs you."

Sam's frown is fierce. "No." Not sure what she's denying, she jerks her arm away. "There's always something that can be done."

An idea strikes her. "Wait back where we were. I need to talk to Raiden."

Sam's gone before Ekon can object, racing toward Grace's hut. Raiden can't be aware that his hares have all been killed. That the pods are all gone.

He said he'd order people not to touch them.

Sam's almost reached the entry of the hut when the flap is pulled back and Nikita steps out, holding a clay jug.

Sam stops in her tracks. "What are you doing here?"

Nikita lifts her chin. "Grace is in the Round House. I'm looking after Raiden."

But Hawk's lying bruised and battered in a half-built hut…

"Did you come to gloat?" Nikita asks accusingly.

"I would never do that."

How could Nikita even think that?

Her hands tighten around the jug. "And yet this is all your fault."

Sam reels back. "I never—"

"You led Raiden on. You had Hawk worried he was losing you."

Sam shakes her head, guilt burning in her gut. "That was never my intention. I would never want to see anyone hurt."

"And yet here we are. Like it was inevitable."

"You're starting to sound like one of the Outlanders, Nikita," Sam says softly.

Like violence is unavoidable. Like nothing can be achieved without it.

"Do you know what's smart, Sam?" Nikita leans forward, her face tight. "Being here long enough to make a difference."

Sam shakes her head. "But you're forgetting what we stand for."

"I'm alive. I'm a Seeker who's working with the Newlanders. I'm doing better than Siena or Hawk."

Nikita's haughty gaze tells Sam she considers she's done better than any of them.

Raiden's voice carries from the hut. "Who's there, Nikita?"

"It's Sam. She was just leaving."

"Send her in," comes the immediate response. "And leave us."

The order is said sharply, making Nikita flinch, but with little more than a glance at Sam, she heads in the direction of the well.

Sam watches her walk away with her back straight, probably telling herself she still has some pride. She's going to get water. For Raiden. From the well dug by her fellow Seekers.

Sam frowns. How much are they supposed to give in order to make a difference here? Nikita's right. Siena paid the ultimate price. Hawk paid in blood and bruises.

But what has Nikita achieved by aligning herself so totally with everything the Newlanders stand for? She's ensured her own safety, and little else.

"Sam."

Raiden barks her name, making it a demand.

Sam's spine stiffens. Raiden may think he can talk to Nikita like that, but Sam is here to fight for what she believes in. Yanking back the material at the door, she strides in.

It takes a few seconds for her eyes to adjust to the gloom and smoke, but when Sam sees Raiden, she stops. He's lying on a mat, his face swollen and discolored above his puffy neck. His right foot is elevated on a flattened rock, partially dry clay encased around his ankle.

The memories of the fight assault her. Hawk, slamming his fist into Raiden's face with so much force that a bomb of blood detonated across his face. Hawk could've claimed victory shortly after, but instead he gave Raiden an opening.

And Raiden had targeted every one of Hawk's weaknesses, going straight for his barely-healed wounds.

"This is what your bastard Seeker did to me," rasps Raiden.

Although the sight of more pain has Sam's stomach clenching, she crosses her arms. "Would you have killed Hawk if you had the chance?"

"He challenged me! He's the one who wanted this."

Hawk never chose this. None of them would've.

Sam moves closer, kneeling down beside Raiden. "Would you have killed him?"

Raiden glares at her. "I can't believe you're even asking me this question."

Sam stills, knowing what she wants that answer to mean, but she's discovered her assumptions haven't been terribly reliable.

"Of course I would've! He was trying to humiliate me!"

The words are a slap even though they shouldn't be. Or maybe it's the hot hatred in Raiden's eyes. Either way, Sam's head spins.

Her mind is a whirlpool of anger. Hurt. So much confusion.

And yet she tries one more time.

"You need to stop this, Raiden. They've killed all the hares. They're eating the pods."

All the progress Sam was so sure they'd made...

"There are twice as many of us now," Raiden growls.

"I know you'd have to wait. But think of how much we could teach you if you just gave us a chance."

Raiden's lip curls. "There's nothing you don't have that we can't take."

"But why would you do that?" Sam cries. "We're trying to give it to you."

"As long as we play by your rules. And make ourselves as weak as you are," he spits.

Sam recoils, shuffling back. As she does so, she knocks over a plate that had been sitting on a low stool beside her.

The earthen plate hits the packed dirt, breaking into large shards. But it's not the broken pieces that have Sam gasping. Sitting in the dirt is a roasted chunk of hare.

And two pods.

"You idiot!" shouts Raiden, struggling to sit up. "I need to get my strength back!"

Sam stands even though her legs are wobbly. "Was I making any difference?" she whispers. "Why did you even bother listening to me?"

Raiden snorts as he lays back down, grimacing with the motion. He turns his head away, not bothering to answer.

He could probably use a dose of plantain himself. But Sam doesn't feel like collecting some for him, too. She doesn't even want to share the information with him.

A part of her wants him to hurt.

As she turns away, she feels sick to the pit of her stomach.

She hasn't made any progress.

In fact, all that's happened is she's done exactly what Nikita has.

She's become more like them.

MERCY

*M*ercy sits beside Hawk, her breath shallow in her chest as she watches him struggle to hold onto life. This isn't right. Hawk's the last person she thought would be wounded like this. He's so strong. But that's exactly why he's in this situation. Because his strength made him a target.

Sam is taking ages to return with any plantain. Not that Mercy minds. She knows Sam will be moving as quickly as she can. She won't want to be away from Hawk for a minute longer than necessary. And tending to Hawk is hardly a burden.

Although, it is heartbreaking.

Hawk's poor face is shadowed with bruises. Thankfully, the swelling from his first beating has subsided and the sap they'd brought with them from Askala is doing a good job of swiftly healing any cuts that might cause infection.

His chest is a whole different story. Covered in both bruises and tattoos it's hard to find any skin Hawk's normal color.

Mercy dips a cloth into some clean water from the well and squeezes it out, placing the cool fabric on Hawk's forehead. It's early evening now, which means the worst of the day's heat has gone.

"Hold on," she tells Hawk. "You're going to be fine. Just hold on."

"Sam," he groans.

"She's not far," Mercy tells him. "She's just getting a few things to help you. She'll be back any moment. I'm here. I won't leave you."

He moves his head in the slightest but enough to tell Mercy he understands.

"I love you, Hawk." She smiles at him as she adjusts the cloth on his forehead. "But if you don't pull through this, I swear I'm going to beat you up myself."

"Interesting strategy," says Luca from above her as he fixes some branches to the roof of the shelter. "Threatening him into recovery."

Mercy doesn't reply. If Luca thinks he can have anything like a normal conversation with her without explaining what the Terra is going on between them, then he's wrong.

"Just build the shelter," she tells him. "And keep your special comments to yourself."

"Yes, boss." Luca looks at Gust and shrugs, a gesture that Gust seems to find hilarious.

Mercy blocks them both out and focuses back on Hawk's face, unable to bear to look at his bruised chest.

"We're back!"

Mercy looks up to see Sam returning with Ekon close behind carrying an armful of what she can only assume is plantain.

"How is he?" Sam squats down on the other side of Hawk and her hands fly to his face.

"He's the same," says Mercy. "He asked for you once."

"I'm here, Hawk." Sam leans forward and kisses his cheek. "I'm right here. It's me. Sam."

Mercy smiles. Hawk would already know it's her.

"I might just go and wash myself up." Mercy stands and

stretches. She's a little sore from crouching over Hawk for so long. Not that she can complain. He must feel several million times worse.

"Want me to come with you?" asks Ekon, setting down the plantain and wiping his hands on his trousers. "It's not safe out there."

"I'm fine," says Mercy. "I've been going every day, and nothing's happened to me yet. I won't be long."

"Let him go with you." Luca pauses his work and looks at her like he actually cares.

"I said I'm fine!" Mercy plants her hands on her hips, more determined now than ever. "Give a girl some privacy, would you!"

Ekon holds up his palms. "Okay!"

"I'll be back before you know it," she huffs as she sets off to weave her way through the trees in what's becoming a familiar path to the beach. The Newlands will never feel like home in the same way as Askala, but this place no longer feels so foreign.

A home away from home.

She smiles at that thought, even though it's not entirely accurate. Just because something's familiar, doesn't make it a home. The Seekers still have more work they need to do. A lot more.

But right now, a quick dip in the ocean is exactly what this Seeker needs. A re-set, like there's a chance the acid might strip away the horror of everything she's experienced since she arrived here. Maybe then the Newlands can start to feel like a real home.

When she steps onto the sand with the setting sun behind her, she looks toward Askala, imagining what her parents are doing right now. Has Charity managed to fill part of the hole Mercy left in their hearts when she left? She hopes so. Because so far, nothing's managed to repair the damage she's feeling in her own heart.

She misses her home and her family with acute pain. She has to remind herself that if she'd stayed behind, she'd be missing her cousins with that same pain. She was never going to win.

Wandering closer to the water's edge, Mercy braces herself for the burst of energy it's going to take to get herself clean. A quick dash out into the deeper water and back again. That's all she needs to do.

The hair on the back of her neck bristles as she senses someone watching her.

Turning slowly, her heart stops when she sees who's behind her. It's Marr, the leader of this newest group of Outlanders who arrived with their boats loaded to the brim with destruction and misery. Hawk would be well on his way to recovery by now if they hadn't arrived, bringing those stupid Tournaments with them.

"Well, look what we have here." Marr rubs his hands together. "A gift."

Mercy's heart goes from dormant to a hammer that's pounding her ribs. She's in danger. Possibly the greatest danger she's faced since setting foot in the Newlands, and that includes the attack that stole Siena's life. Marr has done nothing but leer at Mercy since he first saw her.

"I didn't mean to disturb you." Mercy shoots Marr a polite smile and spins around, wondering if she could be so lucky as to find her way back without any further interaction with this revolting man.

Why hadn't she let Ekon come with her?

She takes a few steps back to the trees, smelling Marr's rank body odor before she feels him grip her upper arm. She looks him in the eye, trying to convey that she's not afraid, even though every cell in her body is screaming with terror.

"You sure you're not a friend of Alyx?" Marrs asks, the setting sun glinting off the oil that's coating his matted hair. "An honest man like me is happy to pay for what he wants."

Mercy shakes her head. "I'm sure Alyx would be happy to talk to you."

Marr runs his tongue over his bottom lip, catching the bristles of his dark beard. "Problem is that Alyx isn't my type. Too skinny. I like myself a real woman."

His eyes are glued to Mercy's chest and she knows this is exactly what her dad had been worried would happen to her. This is why her mom taught her where and how to jam her knee to have the most impact. But she also knows that as soon as she makes the first move, the fight will be on. And what hope does she realistically have against a guy twice her size?

It's not just about choosing the right move. It's about deciding when's the right time to use it.

"What's the matter?" Marr asks. "You think I don't have anything to pay with?"

"You're hurting me." Mercy moves her arm, trying to get him to release his grip.

"It's you people who can't be trusted," he says, ignoring her. "Not me. I always pay my debts. Unlike that scum friend of yours."

Mercy flinches, trying to figure out who he's talking about.

"My friends aren't scum." She might be in danger here, but she's not prepared to listen to him say anything bad about her friends.

"What about the daughter of that asswipe, Gritt?" he asks. "I heard she smelled like roast grizzly when she got barbecued by Bohr's men. Shame I couldn't be there to see it."

Mercy blanches, wanting to be as far away from this revolting man as humanly possible. But he's holding on far too tightly. She doesn't have a hope of getting away from someone so much stronger than her. Her only hope is to try to talk her way out of this.

"How do you know about that?" she asks. There's something

not fitting together quite right about all of this, but she can't quite work out what it is. Her fear for her safety is overriding any logic her brain's wrestling with right now.

"Bohr came sniffling back saying all his men were dead," Marr says. "That you scum Seekers killed them all."

"We didn't kill any of them!" Mercy leans back trying to avoid the stench of his breath. Why would Bohr have said that? Was that the deal Corbin struck with him? That he'd let him go as long as history was rewritten in the process?

"Told you that you couldn't be trusted." He jerks her arm and pulls her closer. "Lying to me as well, now. Bohr had no reason to make that up. All he wanted was Gritt's whore of a daughter. She was owed to him. Good men didn't have to die for that."

Mercy tips up her chin, trying her best to hold onto whatever power she has left. Then something falls into place. How has she not thought to ask this before?

"How did Bohr know Gritt's daughter was here?" She glares at him as the last of the day's light threatens to fade and leave them standing here in the dark. "Who told him?"

"You think I'm going to tell you that?" He spits as he talks and Mercy flinches when a droplet lands on her cheek. "It's none of your business who talks to who around here."

"Someone sent a message," says Mercy. "Someone sold Siena out. Tell me who it was."

"That information is worth something, I reckon." Marr sniffs deeply as he runs his slug of a tongue over his lips. "And you've got something I've been wanting ever since I saw your pretty little ass swaying as you walk."

Mercy shakes her head, struggling against his grip now.

"You think a girl like you can tease a man and not get what's coming to her?" He grips her other arm now and draws her even closer, his face only inches from hers. "I've seen you looking at me. You want it just as much as I do."

233

"It's not a trade," says Mercy, feeling the sweat bead on her forehead as her legs start to shake. "I don't accept."

"Too late." Marr brings his lips to hers, and Mercy freezes as terror slides through her body. The rancid taste of him, the harshness of his bristles, and the unwanted intrusion of his tongue in her mouth is overwhelming. She bites down.

Hard.

"Bitch!" Marr pulls back as he lets go of her with one hand to wipe at his mouth. If he can still talk then it seems she didn't bite hard enough.

He raises his free hand and swipes it through the air, preparing to slap her across her face, but Mercy ducks and all he manages to collect is a few mosquitos.

Now! she tells herself. It has to be now. This is the moment to act.

She brings up her knee and slams it to Marr's groin in just the way her mom taught her.

Marr howls, instinctively letting go of Mercy for a split second. But it's enough time and Mercy takes it. Twisting away from him, she digs her heels into the sand and runs, keeping to the wet sand as she tries to put some distance between them.

With her heart beating faster than it ever has before, Mercy pushes forward, thanking her mom, thanking the universe, thanking whatever it was that helped her get away from that revolting excuse for a man.

She's managed to get a few yards, when she's grabbed by the back of her shirt and slammed to the ground so hard the air is knocked out of her lungs. Trying to drag in another breath is impossible. Her whole chest is constricted, although she's not sure if it's from the force of the impact, her pure terror, or because Marr is now on top of her.

He tears at her shirt and the fabric rips, exposing her chest and Mercy's glad for the darkness shrouding her humiliation.

"Luca!" she screams, knowing there's no way he can hear her. But she has to try.

Marr's hands are everywhere, his rough skin clawing at her and she squirms as she tries to dislodge herself. He's not going to get what he wants without a fight. She'll poke both his eyes out before she willingly submits to a creep like him.

Bringing her hands to his face, she tries to do exactly that. But Marr grips her by her wrists and twists them until she's left shrieking in agony.

"Lie still," he snarls. "It's easier that way."

Mercy spits in his face, using the only defense she has left. Except, he doesn't seem to care. Her anger is only spurring him on.

"Don't do this," she begs, a feeling of helplessness consuming her. "Please, don't do this. Let me go."

"Quiet, bitch," he snarls, jamming his fingers across her mouth. She tries to bite at them as his other hand slides down below her waist. But she can't get a grip with her teeth. He has her pinned and there's literally nothing left that she can do.

It's no wonder Alyx escaped the Outlands when this happened to her. Mercy feels like running to the other end of the Earth. Anything to get away from where she is now. She should never have come down to the beach alone.

Foolish! She'd been so incredibly foolish.

"Ekon!" Her cry is muffled by Marr's hand. "Ekon!"

"Nobody can hear you," Marr growls, yanking at the fabric of her trousers.

Mercy yelps as she holds onto the thought of Alyx like a lifeline. If she could survive her trauma then so can Mercy. If she can't get away, then she will learn to get past this.

If only she had a Falcon like Alyx had the first time she was attacked.

But the Falcon's dead.

And Mercy knows that soon there will be a part of her that will be equally as dead.

She should never have come to the Newlands. It's not a home away from home.

This place is a living hell.

LUCA

"*L*uca!"

His name. Screamed once. Drenched with terror.

Luca had gone from stomping through the forest, telling himself he needs to stop following Mercy everywhere or she's never going to give up, to running. No, racing through the forest. Wishing he could fly.

Hoping he's there in time.

"Mercy!" he shouts.

But there's no reply.

"Mercy! Hold on!"

Please let him be there in time.

Luca breaks through the trees just as the moon slips from behind a cloud. He sees her. Them. His stomach jackknifes to his throat.

A filthy Outlander is on top of her.

His feet feel like they barely touch the sand. His heart has stopped and is pounding all at once.

"You bastard!" he screams.

The man looks up and Luca recognizes him.

Marr.

A split-second later he ploughs his fist into the man's face.

Marr rockets backward, slamming onto his back as his nose explodes with the impact. He howls as blood gushes down his face, seeping into his matted beard. Mercy scrabbles backward, frantically bringing together the remnants of her top.

Luca grinds out two words. "Run, Mercy."

The scar on Marr's face is a testament to how many fights he's been in. He stands, shaking his head as droplets of red flick onto the sand, then levels his gaze at Luca.

"You're not keeping her all to yourself," he spits through blood covered lips.

Luca steps in front of Mercy. "She's no one's to have."

Marr rushes at him, just like Luca expected him to. He's faced too many men like him in the Outlands.

And the outcome has always been the same.

Marr slams into Luca, wrapping his arms around his chest. Luca grunts, absorbing the impact as he's shoved backward. The tip of a wave brushes his foot.

Slamming his fists down on Marr's shoulders releases the pressure around his chest as Marr's arms slip down. A quick uppercut and he's free.

Stepping back, Luca sizes up his opponent in the gloom as the water laps at his ankles. Marr's eyes glint with venom, the lower half of his face smeared with blood. "Once you're dead, she'll be mine."

Another step backward has Marr's face lighting with premature victory. This time when he comes at Luca, he raises his fist.

"Luca!" Mercy screams, the sound ricocheting through the dark.

But Luca waits.

As Marr's fist is about to strike Luca's head, he spins, grabbing his hand and jerking. Marr stumbles, water splashing wildly, then crashes into the shallow water. Still holding the

Outlander's hand, Luca twists it backward. Any roar of pain is cut off as Luca pushes down.

Hard.

Marr thrashes as he finds his torso pinned in the acidic sea. His filthy body jerks and flails, the night concealing the way his blood would be dispersing in the already-red ocean.

The water starts to foam, Marr's free hand trying to push himself up, his legs kicking wildly. Desperate to get his face out of the suffocating water.

But Luca lifts a foot and presses it between Marr's shoulder blades, slamming his face into the sand.

The sight of Mercy, fighting to get Marr off her even though she knew it was useless, hovers before Luca. He tightens his grip on Marr's hand. He pushes his foot down further, grinding the man's face into the ground.

"Luca, stop."

Luca doesn't look up even though Mercy must be standing right beside him. "He's a waste of air. I'm not giving him another lungful."

"You're better than this."

Shaking his head, Luca doesn't take his gaze off Marr. The man's already losing strength, his desperate struggles just as helpless as Mercy's were. "He's not the first man I've killed."

Mercy presses a hand to his arm. "But the others would've been in self-defense."

Marr's hand twitches in his and Luca knows he's close to death. He finally looks up, seeing the pleading in Mercy's eyes, even in the dark. "We need to keep the peace."

Luca releases Marr's arm, dropping it in disgust. Instantly, Marr pushes himself up, gulping air in harsh gasps.

Luca kicks him, knocking him over onto his side in the water. "You never touch her again. Or any other woman, for that matter."

Marr scrabbles through the water to the wet sand, repeatedly stumbling, but pushing himself up the moment he can gain traction. Mercy quickly moves out of the way, the white in her eyes multiplying. Without looking back, Marr half-runs, half-staggers toward the trees.

Within moments, he's swallowed by the darkness. The sounds of him lurching through the trees is all that remains.

Luca stands in the shallows, breathing heavily. A part of him still wants to run after Marr and finish him.

A big part.

"Luca..."

He can only just make Mercy out, standing at the edge of the water, holding her tattered shirt tight around her.

"He... He was going to..."

Mercy's voice chokes. Breaks. Then fractures on a cracked sob.

She's in Luca's arms before her knees give out. He lifts her, moving her further away from the water. "It's okay. You're safe now."

Mercy's arms wrap around his neck, trembling yet clinging with the strength of someone who's not letting go anytime soon. She tucks her head in, burying her face in his neck.

A few more steps and they're out of reach of the waves. Luca sits down, his own legs suddenly weak, keeping Mercy in his lap.

She curls up as if she's trying to disappear inside him. Luca wraps his arms around her, hauling her close and holding her tight.

"I've got you."

That seems to be all Mercy needs to hear. Great, wracking sobs convulse through her, each one like a punch to his chest. Luca holds her. Strokes her hair. Presses his lips to her forehead.

And lets her pour out the injustice of what almost happened to her.

Sooner than he expected, the sobs dissolve into hiccups and

shuddering gasps. Mercy's hands move to her face. "I can...I can still smell him on me."

Wordlessly, Luca stands, Mercy still in his arms. He walks toward the ocean, the water quickly lapping at his ankles. "Then let's get rid of that bastard."

Luca walks until the water is at his waist, then lowers Mercy into the water.

Instantly, Mercy starts scrubbing herself. Her arms. Her face. Every inch of her skin. She even rinses her mouth out with the toxic water. She's just finished her right leg when she starts all over again.

When she looks like she's going to it a third time, Luca grabs her hands. "He's gone, Mercy."

Her skin would have to be stinging from the acid and the friction. If she keeps this up, there'll be none left.

She pauses, nodding, but then looks around, like she's lost as to what to do next. Luca scoops her up, carrying her out of the water. Once they're back on dry sand, he places her down. He yanks off his shirt, pulling it over Mercy's head. She pulls away at the remaining tatters of her own shirt then pushes her arms through the sleeves, pulling it tight around her as she inhales deeply.

"Are you okay to walk back?" He needs to get her back to their hut. To the safety of the other Seekers.

But Mercy steps forward, slipping her arms around his waist. "This is where I feel safe."

"Mercy..."

But he doesn't know what he wants to say.

We can't do this...

I'll always keep you safe.

Always.

Reflexively, his arms draw her in, holding her as if he has the luxury of being able to keep her there.

Mercy pulls back enough to look up at him. "Kiss me, Luca,"

she whispers, her voice barely louder than the waves. "Remind me there's good in this world."

Luca's powerless to refuse. With a barely-there groan of his own, his mouth sinks to hers. He brushes his lips across hers softly, tenderly. Showing her the preciousness that he's discovered exists when they touch.

Mercy's breath shudders, coming out on a sigh. She pushes up, seeking more contact.

The next touch of lips is a meld. A blending of mouths. A tangling of breathless silence.

This kiss is gentle and sweet, a contrast to the blazing passion that they've shared up until now. It's a testament to everything beautiful that exists between them. That aches to be acknowledged.

Mercy's body melts against his and his arms tighten.

This feels so right.

So perfect.

Luca draws back, resting his forehead against hers. Their breathing synchronizes. It feels like their hearts are beating in unison.

"Thank you, Luca," Mercy whispers.

"Is this a good time to suggest you go back to Askala?"

Mercy jerks back with a gasp and Luca winces. He might've destroyed the mood, but Mercy's just learned what the world beyond Askala is really like. They need to have this talk.

But rather than the surge of anger he was expecting, Mercy shakes her head. "I can't."

"What? Why not?"

Mercy takes a step back, her fingers pressing to her temples. "Askala," she repeats. "Marr said something, before... He was talking about Bohr, saying that he told them the Seekers killed his men." She gasps. "We should have realized it earlier. The Outlanders knew Siena was here! Someone sold her out!"

Luca draws in a sharp breath. They knew the Newlanders were in contact with the Outlanders. But they've been betraying the Seekers. First, they told them that Siena was here. And then, the Newlanders sent back false information.

Mercy's pacing, unaware of how resilient she's being. It's hard to believe it's the same girl who fell apart in his arms not long ago.

"Marr wouldn't tell me who, but he knew. He wanted to trade for the information."

Except Mercy would've refused. So the bastard tried to take it, anyway. Luca pushes the thought away. Marr will have what's coming to him.

Apparently, all Luca has to do is make it look like self-defense.

Luca rubs his chin. "They never wanted us here."

The Newlanders have tolerated them rather than welcomed them.

"But we are here," says Mercy with a frown. "It's like there's something they want from us. Like they've been using us."

The uneasiness that has lived in Luca's gut since the moment they arrived multiplies, becoming a slithering, black weight. "On the day the Outlanders rocked up, Marr mentioned the next stage before he was cut off."

Mercy stills. "And stage one is complete."

The uneasiness stops moving. It sinks as it morphs to weighted, jagged dread. "They're planning something."

"Which is why we can't leave. We have to find out what."

Luca's jaw feels so tight it could crack. The Newlands are becoming more and more dangerous. How long before another one of them loses their life?

And just like last time, Luca can't stop it.

Mercy steps in close, taking Luca's hand. "What if... What if Askala's in danger?"

Luca's glad it's dark. It means Mercy can't see that those words have already occurred to him.

That although he wants to deny it, he knows she's right.

They can't leave.

They have to find out if the home they love, the very place they came to champion, is under threat.

HAWK

*H*awk is awake with his eyes closed. Not so much because he's pretending to sleep, but because he wants a moment to figure out how he's feeling before Sam and Mercy start fussing over him.

He's okay, he thinks. His chest is sore, both on the surface where Corbin drove in that needle hundreds, if not thousands of times, and deep within. His skin will heal faster than his bones, yet that's the part of him that will retain a permanent reminder of what he's been through here in the Newlands. The irony isn't lost on him.

Rain is falling gently on a roof. It's usually one of Hawk's favorite sounds but right now it's confusing him. Where is he? Their hut burned down. He remembers that much at least.

Opening his eyes just a crack, he looks up to see a roof made from branches in Luca's trademark style. He must have built a new shelter. Although, Hawk can't hear the ocean so he must have built it somewhere else. Surely, not in the clearing? The Outlanders would never allow that.

Letting his eyes close again, he listens to the patter of the rain, pretending he's home in Askala with Dove digging her heels into his back. Whose bed is she sneaking into when she has a bad dream now? Robin wriggles too much when she sleeps and Starling snores too loudly, despite being only two feet tall. And Lark and Swan aren't old enough yet to share anyone's bed for fear of getting squashed.

He really didn't think he'd miss his tribe of sisters.

But he does. And it's causing him greater pain than any of his ribs.

"Seekers," hisses Luca. "Wake up. We need to talk."

"What time is it?" moans Sam from beside Hawk.

"Early," says Luca. "This might be our only chance to talk before the Outlanders get up. It's important."

"Can't it wait?" asks Gust, his voice croaky. "I'm tired from building the shelter. Practically alone toward the end, might I add."

"Luca had to check on Mercy," says an unfamiliar deep voice. "And I helped you. You were hardly alone."

"Thanks, Ekon," says Luca.

Ekon? What's he doing here?

Something scratches at the back of Hawk's skull. He thought he'd dreamed that Ekon was here. All his memories of waking up in Grace's hut then the fight that followed are muddled up. He can't quite figure out what he dreamed and what actually happened.

But it seems that Ekon's arrival was real.

"It's important we talk," says Mercy. "We learned some things last night that change everything."

"What happened?" Sam's voice is no longer sleepy. She's on full alert now. "Why didn't you tell us last night?"

"Too many ears," says Luca, keeping his voice low. "And half of you were asleep by the time we returned. And I'd hoped Hawk might be awake to hear this."

Hawk contemplates letting him know that he's listening but

holds still for now. Whatever Luca has to say shouldn't need his input.

Sam slips her hand into Hawk's and holds it as they wait for Luca and Mercy to explain.

"I ran into Marr at the water last night," says Mercy in a strange tone that Hawk can't figure out without seeing her face.

"Did he hurt you?" asks Sam, her grip on Hawk tightening.

"He tried to." Mercy's voice wobbles and anger rises inside Hawk. "But Luca intervened in time. We should all be wary of him in future."

"You woke us up to tell us that?" grumbles Gust. "We already knew not to trust any of those Outlanders. Especially the new ones."

"Marr said some things to Mercy," says Luca. "He confirmed that someone here sent a message to the Outlands about Siena being here."

"How could they!" gasps Sam. "She was innocent. Her father's debts aren't her own."

She's squeezing Hawk's hand so hard that it would probably hurt if she had more strength. But instead, he finds it a comfort.

His eyes open so he can look at her. Except, her focus is so firmly on Luca that she doesn't notice. Nobody does.

"Who do you think it was?" asks Ekon. "Any suspects?"

"We have no idea," says Mercy. "But we need to find out."

"There's more," adds Luca. "Remember how when Marr and his men arrived they said something about the next stage?"

"Corbin cut him off," says Sam, jiggling beside Hawk. "Did he tell you what it was?"

"No." Mercy sounds disappointed with herself. "But Luca and I talked it over and we agree it doesn't sound good. We think it might have something to do with Askala."

"Sweet Terra!" breathes Sam. "Our families could be in danger."

The thought of Hawk's innocent sisters, still so fresh in his mind, has him closing his eyes again as he pictures their sweet faces.

He has to get better. He must regain his strength so he can protect them. So he can protect everyone.

"Have you got a plan?" asks Gust. "I'm assuming you're telling us because you have some idea what you want to do next."

"We do," says Luca. "As of today, our role as Seekers has changed. Our focus is no longer on protecting the future of this island. It's about protecting Askala and the people who live there. The people we love."

"We need to become spies." Mercy's voice is low but filled with possibility. "Our role is to find out what's going on and use that information to put a stop to whatever they're planning."

"They're not going to tell us anything," says Gust. "Why would they? I wouldn't tell us anything if I were them."

"They seem to like Hawk," says Ekon. "The Commander even made him look like one of them. Maybe we wait for him to wake up."

Hawk's breath catches in his throat as he becomes aware the Seekers are looking at him.

"Not anymore," says Sam. "They may have had plans for him, but the moment he chose Raiden as his opponent in the Tournaments, those plans were done. Hawk's made his loyalties clear. You saw how they cast him aside, leaving him for dead once Raiden was finished with him."

"True," Ekon agrees. "What about Nikita then? I've barely seen her since I arrived. She could find out from Raiden exactly what's going on."

"We can't trust her." Luca's voice is full of betrayal. "Her loyalties have also been made clear. She's one of them now."

"It has to be Sam," says Mercy. "Think about it. She's the only one with any kind of connection to them. If she wins Raiden's favor back, he'll talk to her. It's our best hope."

Sam sighs. "I'll do it."

These words don't just have Hawk's eyes springing open, they have him struggling to sit up.

"No!" he hisses, trying but failing to keep his voice low. "Not Sam."

"Hawk, you're awake!" Sam leans over him, letting go of his hand to trail her fingertips over his cheek. "How are you?"

"I was okay until I heard you agree to talk to Raiden!" He tries to prop himself up on his elbows but pain shoots through his chest, so he lies back down. "Do you know how dangerous that is?"

"Of course, I know," Sam huffs. "I only have to look at you to know how dangerous these people are. But Mercy's right. I'm the only Seeker who's managed to form any kind of relationship with these people. It has to be me."

"No." Hawk blinks up at Sam, remembering the bruise Corbin had given her when they first arrived. And having seen what Corbin did to Grace's face, he knows that was just a warmup. "No, Sam. No."

"I know what I'm doing, Hawk." Sam slips her hand into his once more. "Don't underestimate me."

"I've never underestimated you," he says. "It's you who's underestimating them. I have things to tell you, too. Things I was told when I was in Grace's hut."

"What things?" asks Luca.

Hawk blinks. It was almost like he'd forgotten the others were there. Sam has that effect on him. It's always like she's the only other person in the room.

"Grace wants Sam to marry Raiden." Hawk hates the knowledge that these words will hurt Sam to hear. "She wants her son to marry the daughter of who they believe is the leader of Askala."

"But Kian's not the leader," says Gust. "We have many leaders."

Sam nods solemnly. "Raiden's mentioned this before. He believes my dad is the leader. I couldn't convince him otherwise. But...marry him? Surely, you misunderstood?"

Hawk runs his thumb across Sam's hand. "Grace said that you marrying Raiden would unite Askala and the Newlands."

"Polar grizzly's ass it will!" fumes Luca. "We will never unite with the Newlands! Not under those terms."

"Unless we're forced to," says Sam. "With the Newlands in control."

"Stage two," says Mercy. "An invasion. It has to be an invasion."

"So, if we already know this, then why do you need Sam to talk to Raiden?" Hawk asks.

Luca shuffles closer. "I don't like this idea any more than you do. But, think about it. We don't know anything for certain. We don't know how they plan to invade and when. If we can find these things out, maybe we can put a stop to it. Without that information we're at even more of a disadvantage."

"I'll be careful, Hawk," says Sam. "Raiden's never hurt me. I don't think he's like that."

"Umm, did you actually see what he did to your boyfriend out there?" Gust points to the clearing. "Because I'm pretty sure Raiden has a lot more violence in him than you're giving him credit for."

"You're not helping, Gust," scowls Mercy.

"Luca, can you help me sit up?" Hawk asks, not wanting to have this argument lying down. He feels so pathetic, but there's no way he can sit up on his own.

Luca gets up without hesitation and slides his hands under Hawk's shoulders.

"There's no gentle way to do this," he says. "Take a deep breath and count to three."

Hawk nods. "One, two—"

Luca heaves and Hawk can't believe he fell for that old trick. But it works, and a few excruciating seconds later, Luca has Hawk seated upright and leaning against one of the hut's supports.

"I'm not so sure that was such a good idea." Sam scurries over beside him. "What if he has internal damage?"

"I'm fine," he says. "I've recovered."

"No offence." Gust raises his eyebrows. "But the last time we heard you say that, it didn't end very well."

"I just need a little more time," Hawk protests. "I'm fine."

"Enough, Gust." Sam holds up her hand. "In fact, enough from everyone. Do you guys mind making yourselves scarce for a few minutes so I can talk to Hawk alone?"

"Sure," Mercy and Luca say almost at once.

"No problem." Ekon smiles at them.

"But it's raining!" says Gust.

Hawk wipes the sweat that's beaded on his forehead and pushes down his pain. Sam wants to talk to him alone. Which is perfect. Because he needs to talk to her, too. If there's one thing he's learned over the last few days, it's that he needs to get better at seizing the moment.

Because you never know when it's going to be your last.

"Come on," says Luca. "We'll collect some branches to build our walls. Think of the rain as a shower, Gust."

This doesn't seem to make him any happier, but he heads off anyway, using his hands to shelter him.

Hawk breathes out a sigh.

"Sam," he says, not willing to wait for her to speak. "I need you to know something."

"It's okay, Hawk." Sam shifts a little closer to him, turning to look into his eyes. "I know."

"I don't think you do." He can't leave room here for any misunderstanding. He has to be clearer with her than he's ever been. "Sam, I—"

"You love me," she finishes. "I know, Hawk. I know you love me. And I love you, too."

"Not just as a friend," he adds, unsure if she gets it. Like, *really* gets it. "Sam, I'm in love with you. I've been in love with you for the longest time."

"I know, Hawk." She sits forward and cups his face gently in her hands. "I'm in love with you, too. It's always been you. I just needed some time to catch up."

Relief floods Hawk. He'd dared to hope she felt the same. Everything had pointed to it. But hearing her say it is something else altogether.

Sam brings her face closer to Hawk's. "I've been—"

"No." He holds a finger to her lips. He doesn't want to hear her say a bad word about herself. "It doesn't matter it took you longer than me. I don't care how long it took. All I care is that you're here now."

"I'm here," she whispers as she closes the gap between them and presses her lips to his.

Sam's kiss is like one of Grace's magic elixirs as all pain leaves his body. He's not aware of any of his injuries. All he can feel is Sam, the warmth of her molding her mouth against his, like this was exactly what they were born to do.

She's being gentle with him like she's afraid she's going to break him. He slides his fingers into her hair and draws her closer, wanting more of her.

So. Much. More.

"Hawk." Sam breathes his name as she breaks away ever so slightly.

But he's not ready to let her go. He's waited for this kiss his whole life and the excitement is lighting inside him like wildfire.

And it seems she's not ready to let go just yet, either. She leans into him and deepens their kiss, letting out a small moan as their mouths explore and meld in exactly the way he'd been dreaming of.

"Hawk," she giggles against his lips. "We can't. There are no walls. Everyone can see us!"

"We're just kissing." He tries to coax her lips back.

"That is not *just* kissing," she says. "Kissing you could never be *just* kissing."

She gives into him and this time her mouth is filled with heat. Desire. And it adds a whole lot of fuel to the fire that's burning bright between them.

"I love you, Sam." He breaks away before the fire becomes an inferno that's impossible to put out, and trails his fingertips from her hair to her face, marveling at how beautiful she is. "I want to kiss you every second of every day, forever."

"Technically that's not actually possible," she says. "The human body—"

"Ouch!" Hawk had leaned forward in an attempt to cut Sam off with another kiss, only for pain to explode through his chest. It seems not every injury can be kissed better.

"Did I hurt you?" Sam's face fills with concern. "Are you okay?"

"It's that guy you want to talk to who hurt me," he huffs, remembering why he's so worried about her. "He's more dangerous than you think. For once, Gust is right."

"I know how to handle him." Sam visibly draws back.

"It's not your job to save everyone," he tells her. "This isn't all on your shoulders."

"But it is, Hawk." She shakes her head. "Can't you see it's what makes the best sense?"

"There are other options." He reaches for her hand and holds it, needing the closeness of her once more. "Luca could talk to Alyx. I could talk to Grace."

Sam rolls her eyes. "I'm not sure you're in Grace's good books after what happened with Raiden."

"Let me try," he says. "Let me talk to her. If it goes well then there's no need for you to speak to Raiden."

"It won't go well." She studies him like she thinks he's gone mad.

"Would you bring her to me?" He lifts his hand even though it sends pain rolling through his chest and trails his thumb down her cheek. "Please?"

This is his one chance to save Sam from that creep she thinks she knows how to handle. And it *will* go well. Mainly, because it has to.

"Okay," she says. "I'll get her. But only because I think we need to follow all our leads. You should talk to her, just like Luca should talk to Alyx. We should also talk to Nikita and see if she knows anything. And I should talk to Raiden..."

He sighs, wishing she hadn't added that last bit.

"Can you just do me one favor before you get her?" he asks, shifting on the base of the hut, trying to get more comfortable.

"Do you need some water?" Sam looks around. "Some food? You must be hungry."

"Just another kiss." He has to try. That last kiss wasn't enough. A thousand more wouldn't even begin to sate his desire.

Sam laughs but doesn't hesitate. She leans forward and kisses him far more tenderly than he'd like but it's the most beautiful thing he's ever felt. Her last kiss had been filled with promise but this one is undoubtedly filled with love.

It's with huge reluctance that he lets her pull away. She presses her lips to his forehead before she disappears from the shelter, heading in the direction of Grace's hut.

Hawk touches his lips, trying to capture the feeling of Sam so he can store it away for later. It's hard to believe that right while all their dreams as Seekers have fallen apart, his hopes for a future with Sam have come together. She loves him. Not just as a friend but as so much more.

And no matter what happens in the future, he knows that's the only thing he needs to make him happy. Which is why he needs to handle this conversation with Grace carefully. So much is riding on it.

"You wanted to see me?"

At the sound of Grace's voice, Hawk tries to turn. But that's not possible with a chest cavity filled with broken ribs.

"Grace," he says, waiting for her to enter the hut and stand somewhere he can see her.

She sits down a few feet away, folding her legs underneath her. Her long dark hair hasn't been tied into its usual braid and is flowing over her shoulders. The bruise on her cheek has faded, replaced by circles under her eyes.

She looks as tired as she looks vulnerable.

"How's Raiden?" he asks, not caring in the slightest how that snake of a son of hers is but knowing it's polite to ask.

"You broke his ankle." Her voice is hard. "I had trouble setting it. He's in a lot of pain."

"Thank you for seeing me." He can't comment on Raiden's ankle. He can't even apologize for it. That would be taking things too far. Because he's never been less sorry for anything in his life.

"I don't want Corbin to see me talking to you." Grace's gaze dips to his newly inked chest but she drags it straight back up to his eyes.

"Why did he do this to me?" Hawk asks, pointing to his chest. "Why did he want me to look like one of his men?"

"You saw why." Her voice softens. "He thought you'd make a good fighter in his Tournaments."

"So, these Tournaments are a regular thing?" he asks, surprised. For some reason, he'd thought it had been a one off.

"In the Outlands they are. Those were the first Tournaments we've had here."

"You know why I chose Raiden, don't you?" he asks, praying

that she's not going to storm out. "It was because of what you told me. About Sam. I was jealous."

She thinks about this for a while.

"Maybe I'm the jealous one." She looks to the floor as a pink color rises to her cheeks.

"I don't understand." He leans forward but when it hurts too much, he sits back.

"Hawk, you must have noticed how I feel." She lifts her eyes to his. "I don't know if it's just because you're so strong and I'm in need of protection, or if it's something else. But I just feel this connection to you. I felt it the first time I saw you. I've tried to make it go away, but it won't. I'm so ashamed to admit it but even when you were fighting my son there was a small part of me that was rooting for you."

Hawk blinks, trying to take this in. He'd noticed her looking at his naked torso before. He's seen her shyness. And he remembers the way she'd cared for him in her hut. All of that had screamed at him that she felt something more, but he'd been so blinded by his feelings for Sam, he hadn't really given it a lot of thought.

"You're with Corbin," he says. "And I'm with Sam. I'm also younger than you."

"I know." Her voice is a whisper. "I know it's wrong. Why then does it feel so right? Age is just a number, Hawk. It means nothing. Tell me you love me, too. Please, I need to hear it. Even if we can't act on it, I have to know you feel the same way."

Hawk's jaw drops. This conversation isn't going anything like what he'd expected. Or what he'd needed. How does he keep Grace on side enough for her to tell him all the Commander's secrets yet remain true to himself? And to Sam.

"You're a beautiful woman," he says. "Corbin's a very lucky man."

"You don't feel it, do you?" Grace bites her lip as she blinks back tears. "I'm not good enough for you. I'll never be good enough for anyone."

"Grace! Don't talk like that." He reaches for her hand, but she pulls back. "You're good enough. Too good for the likes of Corbin. You deserve so much better than him."

"But I don't deserve you. That's what you're saying, isn't it?"

"My heart belongs to someone else." He regrets the words as soon as he says them even though they're true. Rejecting her isn't the way to get her to talk. He's failing miserably here. He just doesn't know what else to do.

"I'm not asking you to marry me," she says, attempting a smile. "Just to visit me occasionally. Nobody else has to know. It can be our secret."

Hawk groans. Any man would be flattered to receive the attention of a woman as beautiful as Grace. If he'd never known Sam then maybe it's possible he'd be flattered, too. But he has met her. Which means that he feels awkward instead.

"I have a lot of secrets," Grace says, shuffling forward and resting a hand on his thigh. "If you share a little of yourself with me, there's a lot I could share with you."

Hawk lets his head tip back until it's resting on hard timber.

So, this is what it comes down to. He can quite possibly find out everything the Seekers need to know. All he has to do is the impossible.

Give himself to Grace in exactly the way he dreams of giving himself to Sam.

The choice should be easy. The Seekers' mission should be his number one priority.

Except, it's not.

"What do you think?" Grace moves her hand higher up his thigh and smiles at him as she waits for his answer.

He takes a deep breath and fights between the response he knows he should give and the one he knows he can live with.

"Well?" She tilts her head, sending waves of soft hair falling over her shoulders.

And he gives her the only answer he knows will keep Sam safe.

SAM

*I*s this how Sam's parents felt when they finally said *the* words?

When they finally *heard* them?

A feeling that defies description. Classification. The ability to be encompassed.

Love.

Sam *loves* Hawk. With every part of her being. It's like her feelings for him are spun through her DNA just like every other part of her. It's like when her heart formed, Hawk was already in there. Being with him is as natural as blinking, as her next breath, as inevitable as a seed unfurling and growing the moment moisture touches it.

And the amazing part is Hawk loves Sam, too.

Which only makes what she has to do next all the more vital. They need to find out what they're up against. For Hawk and Sam's future. Quite possibly for the future of Askala.

Sam swallows, glancing around the village she's making her way through. There are twice as many people now. Mostly men. All covered in dirt and scars. All covered in poverty and violence.

Are they planning an attack on Askala?

It's a terrifying hypothesis.

Sam straightens her shoulders, angling toward Raiden's hut. If Hawk's doing his part to find out what he can, then it's only fair she does the same. And if she gets the talk with Raiden over and done with, then it saves the clash of opinions with Hawk. Sam's in no more danger than any of the other Seekers when it comes to trying to uncover what's going on.

And as it turns out, Grace was already on her way to their hut, which was lucky timing. In fact, she almost seemed to rush forward when she saw Sam exit, her smile instantaneous when Sam asked if Grace had a moment to talk to Hawk.

It appears she has a forgiving heart, which is promising.

And genetics dictate that positive trait is likely to have been passed onto her son.

Nikita's sitting outside Raiden's hut, but this time Sam was expecting that. What she doesn't expect to find is Nikita sharpening a spear.

Sam stops in front of her, waiting for Nikita to look up. But Nikita simply continues to abrade the tip of the thick stick with the flat stone she's holding. "You're just going to make things worse," she mutters, telling Sam she knows she's here.

"Do you know, Nikita?" Sam asks quietly. "Do you know what they're planning?"

Nikita looks up, her brow crinkled. "Of course, I do."

Sam's eyes dart to the leather-covered entry behind Nikita. "And you didn't think to warn us?"

Nikita goes back to sanding away layers of wood, focused on making the tip as sharp as possible. A sick feeling burns through Sam's gut. Could that spear be used to kill a Seeker one day? Maybe even the people of Askala?

"Raiden hasn't told you?" Nikita asks, lifting her chin haughtily.

"I didn't realize there was anything like that I needed to know."

"That's your problem, Sam. You think you know everything."

Sam squats down, unsure where this animosity has come from, but they don't have time for it. Too much is hanging in the balance. "What are they planning, Nikita?"

"They're going to make themselves strong. Strong enough to build a place where we can live the way we deserve. Strong enough to go find new lands to live on. We'll be respected in ways you can't even imagine."

"And you want to be part of this?" Sam asks incredulously.

"As opposed to being one of the masses in Askala? As some simpering, faceless weakling?"

Sam draws back. Nikita's been fed words she wanted to hear. Words that have made her feel...powerful. The image she just painted has her eyes flashing with anticipation.

Sam straightens. Doesn't Nikita realize that by helping make the Newlanders strong, they're also making them more of a threat to Askala?

Sweet Terra. Except that's what Sam's been doing, too.

"Askala makes every one of us great," she says quietly. "That's something you should've known."

Nikita glances away, looking annoyed, and goes back to sharpening the spear. Sam walks past her and into the hut, deciding she's not going to give Raiden the opportunity to refuse her entry.

Inside, Sam pauses as her eyes adjust to the smoky room. Raiden's where he was last time she was here, but this time he's sitting up. He straightens when he sees who's just barged in, but then quickly relaxes. "Hey, Sam."

Surprised at the warm welcome, Sam stops where she is, unsure whether to trust it.

Raiden smiles. "I was hoping you'd be back sooner rather than later."

He stretches and flexes his arms as he puts his hands behind his head, drawing Sam's eyes to his bare chest. It's decorated with a new tattoo, this one larger and more ornate than the one Hawk has, the dramatic lines curling around his pectorals and spearing toward his biceps and abdominal muscles.

Sam takes another step closer, studying it. "You got that after the fight, didn't you?"

"For winning my first Tournament." Raiden grins, watching her closely.

Anger ignites deep in Sam's belly. Hawk's going to take weeks to recover from the unnecessary violence Raiden inflicted on him. Those marks on his chest celebrate that.

But she can't afford to get Raiden offside. The information they need is too valuable.

Which means Sam has to do the one thing she's never been good at. Lie.

Walking toward Raiden, she nods. "And that's where all the men's tattoos come from?"

"Mostly." Raiden watches as Sam lowers herself onto the stool beside him, his eyes twinkling in the flickering light given off by the fire. "Some men will get them in anticipation of a fight."

Like Hawk did. Whether he wanted it or not.

"They're telling every guy in the Tournaments they're ready to take them on."

Which is the last thing Hawk would've wanted to convey. Recognizing that Raiden is waiting to see how she'll respond to his goading, Sam clasps her hands in her lap. "And yet you won anyway," she says quietly, ignoring the bad taste in her mouth.

Raiden's chest puffs out. "Yes, I did." His smile grows. "I knew you'd start to understand our ways. It's that smart brain of yours."

Even though that's exactly what Sam wants Raiden to think,

it makes her nauseous. "I've always wanted to understand you and your people."

His face softens. "I know. That's why we chose you."

Sam doesn't like the sound of that—we? Chose her for what? But Raiden no longer has any of the animosity and anger that was there last time they spoke, and she can't afford for their conversation to deteriorate back there.

So, Sam shoves down her questions and uneasiness and tries to draw up a smile. "I'm glad you did."

Right now, it's their best chance of finding out what they're up against.

Raiden shuffles as he sits up a little straighter. "Yep, you're one smart girl, Sam." He moves a little closer. "Pretty, too."

Sam wants to pull back more than anything. The hut suddenly feels smaller, the smoke more cloying. But she stays where she is. "I was just talking to Nikita. She said you're planning on strengthening your people, of extending to new lands."

Raiden stills. "Yes, that's what I told her. If the Newlands have been exposed, who knows what else is out there. Food. Water. Shelter."

Sam nods. That makes sense. And if the Newlanders are just trying to make themselves strong, then they're not planning on attacking Askala. Except she can't keep making those sorts of assumptions.

"And you want to make yourself strong."

"Of course we do. The strong are the ones who survive."

"And what then?" Sam asks, holding her breath, knowing the answer will dictate what the Seekers will do next. "Once you're strong, what do you do then?"

Raiden shrugs. "We get stronger."

"But what about Earth? All the resources you're going to need to become strong?"

More vegetation cleared.

More fires.

More destruction.

Raiden rolls his eyes. "We need that stuff to become stronger." He shakes his head. "This is another one of your stupid moments, Sam."

Ignoring the jibe, Sam leans forward. "It doesn't have to be this way, Raiden. Askala is strong, we can show you how your people *and* Earth can thrive."

Raiden snorts. "Not if everyone in Askala is dead."

Sam reels back. "What?"

But Raiden grins, grabbing her hand before she can pull away too far. "Just joking. What I meant is, Askala is the weakest of them all. One attack and your society is gone." Raiden's hand tightens around hers. "Although, you could protect Askala from that, Sam."

Trying to steady her spiking heart rate, Sam holds herself still. She waits, dread like coal in her gut.

Raiden reaches forward, his tattoo shifting and stretching as he lifts a hand to stroke Sam's cheek. "Marry me. Unite the Newlanders and Askala."

"What?" Sam barely breathes the word, but Raiden's gaze has dipped to her lips. He follows the motion as he registers the single word.

"The son of the Commander marrying the daughter of Kian. Our people, armed with knowledge and strength, would be unstoppable."

Sweet Terra, Hawk was telling the truth. Unsure whether she should move, Sam decides to try and reason with Raiden.

"I told you, my father isn't the sole leader of Askala."

"That's a technicality, Nikita told me. Everyone follows your father." Raiden's hand cups her cheek, but it feels more like a clamp rather than an affectionate gesture. More like a trap. "This is what I want, Sam. You can't deny you like me."

Sam tries to shake her head, only to find Raiden's hand stopping her. "I do, but I like everyone."

Hawk's the only one who ever sparked more than that.

Raiden's gaze drops to her lips again. "That's enough for me. Once we're married, the Newlanders can continue to grow in numbers thanks to everything you know." His calloused thumb scrapes over her jaw. "And Askala will be safe."

Although Raiden says the words softly, all they sound like is a threat.

No, worse than that.

An empty promise.

Askala wouldn't be safe from the Newlanders. The Newlanders would be stronger, increasing in numbers. And they'd know more and more about the fertile island that everyone wants.

Sam yanks back. "Never. You just want to use me like you have from the beginning."

Raiden's hand clenches in midair before dropping to his side. With great effort, he turns around, placing his clay-packed foot on the ground. He shakes his head. "Another stupid decision, Sam."

She can't help but try one more time. "You don't need to marry me. I was sharing my knowledge with you, anyway. We all were." She frowns. "Although, now I'm not sure you're using that information in the way it was intended."

"Which is what we thought would happen. That's why marriage is necessary. We need you tied to me."

And that's what she'd be. Tied to Raiden. Bound.

Even more powerless than she is now.

Sam knows tact isn't her strong point. She knows she needs to refuse this offer in a way that won't cause conflict. Desperately, she hopes she isn't about to make things worse.

"I'm sorry, Raiden. But the answer is no."

Raiden's face hardens, suddenly looking far more like Corbin. His upper lip curls as his shoulders expand. "That's not an option. If you refuse me, the Seekers will be told to leave."

Sam shoots to her feet. "What?"

"You heard me. If you say no, you and your friends will no longer be welcome here."

"You're blackmailing me?"

"I'm ensuring my people's survival." His gaze sweeps over her body. "Your looks are a pleasant bonus."

Sam takes an involuntary step back. Staying has never been more important. They need to find out what the Newlanders are planning on doing with their newfound strength.

But to stay as Raiden's wife? No other thought has ever made Sam feel so ill.

Hawk would never accept it.

Her soul would shrivel up and die.

Sam's hands clench. "The Seekers won't leave. It's too important that we stay."

Raiden watches her for long moments through narrowed eyes. "I had a feeling you'd say that." He turns his head toward the door. "Nikita," he shouts. "Bring me my walking stick."

Relief wants to wash through Sam, but something stops it. Raiden's face isn't the face of someone who's accepted defeat.

In fact, his face is of someone who's resolute.

And Sam has no idea what course of action he just committed to.

The flap over the door pulls back, spilling in harsh sunshine as Nikita enters. She stops, the spear in her hand as she looks from Raiden, sitting on the makeshift bed, to Sam, standing a few feet away.

She holds out the stick, the tip pointing to the roof. "Here, both ends are done, now."

As she passes it over, Sam realizes each end of the spear has been sharpened to a point.

Raiden stands, putting his weight on his good foot. He jams it into the soil as he leans on it. "Great. It'll grip far better now."

That's Raiden's walking stick? A double-edged spear?

Nikita ducks her head, a small smile climbing up. "I'm glad it'll help you."

Sam's about to take a step to the side, hoping this is a cue for her to leave, when Raiden jabs the spear into the ground again.

"Nikita, there's something we need to talk about." He glances at Sam. "As it turns out, this isn't going to work. The Seekers are going to have to leave."

Nikita's face morphs from confusion to shock. "What? No!" She spins to face Sam. "See? I told you you'd only make it worse. You're always so clueless!"

Sam winces. "I told Raiden the Seekers won't leave."

Nikita rushes toward Raiden. "She's right. I won't leave. You said we'd be together." She presses her hands to Raiden's chest, stepping even closer. "You know how I feel about you," she whispers.

Sam looks away, wanting to be anywhere but in this hut. Is Nikita in love with Raiden, or the power he represents?

One step and Raiden's voice cracks through the air. "Stay."

Sam freezes. The barely restrained anger in Raiden's voice meant the word shot out like a bullet.

It's Nikita who moves, taking a few hesitant steps back. "Raiden?" she asks tentatively.

"So if we tell you to leave, you'll refuse?" he demands.

Retreat can't be an option. They'll never know how real this threat to Askala is.

How big.

Nikita's head drops. "I don't want to leave you."

Raiden's gaze shifts to Sam. "That's your answer?"

Sam raises her chin. Nikita wants to stay for a different reason. "The Newlands aren't yours to claim as your own."

Instead of becoming even more angry, Raiden's eyes light up. He almost looks like he's...smiling. "Then this is what will happen."

With one swift move, Raiden lifts the spear and jabs it forward, his face twisted with the effort.

The spear lances through Nikita's chest.

In the silence that follows, there's the sound of bone crunching and sinew tearing. Of Nikita's muffled gasp.

Of her blood rushing up her throat to cut it short.

"No!" Sam screams as she dashes forward.

She catches Nikita as her legs give out and they both crumple to the ground. Sam tries to cushion Nikita's fall, but the hands she wraps around her middle are instantly soaked in slick blood. Nikita slips to the ground, landing propped at an awkward angle thanks to the length of wood skewered through her.

"No, no, no," Sam whispers desperately.

But Nikita's head lolls to the side, her sightless eyes staring blankly at the wall. Falling back onto her knees, Sam's bloodied hands fall useless onto her lap.

Nikita's dead.

And Sam caused it.

Raiden steps past her, gripping the end pointing up and jerking the spear back out. With a sickening wheeze through the hole in her chest, Nikita's dead body slumps onto the dirt.

Sam's not sure what to feel first. The deep sadness. The overwhelming powerlessness.

The undeniable fury.

She looks up to find Raiden wiping his spear. He shrugs callously. "I need my walking stick."

Pushing to her feet, Sam's head swims. She goes to press her fingers to her temples, only to see how covered in blood they are.

Blood that no matter how much she washes, the stain will never go away.

The stain of guilt.

Raiden straightens, jamming his spear back into the ground.

"This is why you need to marry me, Sam. If the Seekers refuse to leave, they'll suffer the same fate."

Sam doesn't move. It feels like if she does, she'll shatter. She can't cry. Tears are useless. They won't wash away how naïve she's been.

But despite what she tells herself, a single drop of saltwater trickles down her cheek. "You leave me no choice," she chokes out.

Raiden relaxes, looking pleased with himself. "There's my smart girl."

Sam wants to vomit. She wants to scream at Raiden that he's a murderer. She wants to crumple beside Nikita and say she's sorry.

Instead, she moves her wooden legs toward the door. "I need to tell the others of my decision."

She needs to tell Hawk.

"I'm not going to wait long," warns Raiden. "We will make this official today."

Their marriage. The ceremony which will forever tie her to him. Ensuring the Newlanders protection because Sam's parents would never allow her to come to any harm.

But if she doesn't, the Seekers will be ordered to leave. And be killed when they refuse.

Outside, the sun's rays seem to pierce right through her, exposing every one of her shortcomings. Wrapping her arms around herself so she can hide her hands, Sam hurries through the village. Head down, she doesn't look at anyone. Tries to pretend she's invisible.

Like she should've from the beginning.

Reaching their hut, she finds Luca and Mercy outside, still working on the walls.

Mercy turns around, hearing her arrival. "Oh, I thought you were Gust and Ekon coming back with the water." She stills, looking more closely at Sam. "Are you okay?"

Luca's by her side in an instant. "Here, you need to sit down."

But Sam shakes her head. There are things she needs to do first. "Nikita. She's dead."

Mercy gasps while Luca curses. "The bastards."

Sam swallows, glad her arms are still wrapped around herself. Her chest feels like it's about to explode, there's so much pain in there. "She told Raiden she wanted to leave," Sam lies. "That she's had enough."

Mercy moves in closer, wrapping an arm around Sam's shoulder. "So they killed her. That's...horrible."

Sam turns back to look at Luca. "Do you believe me?"

They need to understand what will happen if they try to leave. Because if they leave then all of this was for nothing. It's Sam who's the problem here, not them.

"Of course I believe you. That's exactly the sort of thing these people do. I'm just sorry you had to see it."

It was the most brutal lesson Sam's learned about how unprepared to be a Seeker she really was.

"Can you...can you go get her? She deserves a proper farewell."

Luca nods grimly.

Mercy's arm tightens around Sam's shoulder. "I'll stay here. You've had quite a shock."

"No!" Sam quickly modulates her tone. "I just want to talk to Hawk. You go with Luca." Desperation creeps into her voice. She needs to be alone with Hawk. "You have to stay safe, Mercy."

Frowning, Luca nods. "Okay, Mercy can come with me. But you stay here with Hawk, okay? Gust and Ekon will be back shortly."

Sam nods, wondering how she could lie so much in one day.

But deeply grateful that the others are assuming her honesty is still intact.

With Luca and Mercy gone, Sam faces the door. She doesn't have much time.

And yet her feet are rooted to the ground.

But what has to happen next isn't a choice. It's the only solution.

Stepping into the hut, Sam's gaze falls on Hawk. He's sitting up in the same way she left him. Like he was waiting for her. Like he couldn't go back to sleep until he knew she was okay.

His face lights up when he sees Sam standing there. So handsome. So strong.

So full of love.

Sam's heart screams for her to go to him. But the garish hole in Nikita's chest hangs over her like the silent threat it was designed to be.

She swallows down the bile climbing up her throat, staying where she is. "Raiden just killed Nikita."

"No," Hawk breathes. He tries to push himself up only to groan and slump backwards again. "Come here, let me hold you."

Sam shakes her head. "I thought we were making progress. I...I can't do this, Hawk."

Hawk tries to move again, only for his face to twist in pain. "Yes, you can, Sam. Don't let the doubts get to you. You're strong in ways the rest of us aren't."

"I also make us vulnerable in ways none of you have."

And it's put everyone in danger.

"We can do this together. Like we always have."

Sam's chest feels like it's fracturing. Hawk's not going to give up.

But he has to.

Taking a step back, Sam can't hold his gaze. "I'm sorry, Hawk." She pulls in her own painful breath. "But the kiss...it showed me something."

Now, Hawk's as unmoving as she is. His raspy breath

filtering through his broken chest becomes the only noise that fills the hut.

"There was no...spark. It showed me I don't love you like that. You're my best friend, and that's all you can ever be."

"Oh."

One word. One syllable.

An ocean of pain.

"I'm so sorry." Sam whispers before stumbling out of the hut.

Hawk doesn't follow her, and although that's exactly what she wanted, Sam still clasps her hand to her mouth, trying to contain the agony.

The lie has left the taste of ash in her mouth.

Ahead, Gust and Ekon appear, each carrying a bucket. Sam straightens, drawing together the pieces that she's barely holding together, watching them approach.

Gust peers at her as they come closer. "Have you eaten something bad again?"

Sam ignores him. She turns to Ekon. "I need to go down to the beach. Would you come with me?"

"Of course," says Ekon, concern etched into his features.

Sam turns slowly but deliberately, focusing on each movement. Ekon falls into step as she draws one foot in front of the other.

Leaving Hawk holding the lies she just told him.

"We're going to look for some more plantain?" asks Ekon.

Sam waits until her feet are sinking into sand before she responds. Ahead, the boats they arrived in are resting above the tide line.

"We're going back to Askala."

Because the best thing she can do for the Seekers—the only way she can save their lives—is to no longer be one herself.

Which is probably the way it should always have been.

"But—"

"And we're leaving now."

MERCY

*N*ikita is dead. Dead. Like never going to wake up ever again kind of dead. Gone forever, just like Siena. This can't be happening!

Mercy shakes her head. If she thought things were bad before, they're catastrophic now. The level of danger they're in just went from ten out of ten, to a billion. The Seekers need to make a plan. Urgently. Preferably one that doesn't involve anyone else dying.

When she steps into Raiden's hut, the coppery smell of death wraps around Mercy like an unwanted blanket she can't shake off. She turns to Luca, who seems more accustomed to the sight of someone who'd once been a friend lying on the dirt in a puddle of their own blood.

Raiden is sitting on the bed glaring at Nikita's body like it's offending him.

"You were the one who killed her?" Mercy's jaw drops. When Sam had said Nikita had been murdered after telling Raiden she wanted to leave, she never expected he'd have been the one to do it.

"She needed to learn a lesson." Raiden's voice is impassive.

To think when they'd arrived here, they'd thought he was one of the good guys! It seems the blood he shares with his father runs thick in his veins.

Mercy blanches at the thought of more blood.

"This isn't how you make people stay," says Mercy as Luca squats down and lifts Nikita, cradling her body to his chest.

"You're staying?" Raiden seems surprised.

"Of course, we're staying," snaps Mercy.

Raiden taps his spear on the ground and Mercy can't help but notice the end of it is stained a deep red. "I knew she'd make the right decision."

"Who?" asks Mercy.

"Let's keep moving." Luca takes a step toward the door.

"Bring my future wife to me," Raiden demands.

Luca clutches Nikita a little closer to his chest. "Not a chance!"

"We're taking her out to sea." Mercy crosses her arms, not taking her eye off that spear in case Raiden decides to stain the other pointy end with the color of her own blood.

"Not *her*." Raiden pulls his face into a disgusted scowl. "I mean Sam. We're going to unite the Newlands with Askala. With our marriage."

"You're lying," says Luca. "Sam would never agree to that."

"Go and ask her yourself." Raiden crosses his arms. "The wedding is this afternoon."

"We don't believe you." Mercy pulls back the leather flap at the door for Luca to pass through. The sooner they get out of here, the better.

"Oh, and don't think you're getting off that easy, loverboy Luca!" Raiden calls after them. "There's talk of you marrying Charity as soon as she's old enough. Then our families really will be united."

"Come on," Mercy says to Luca, trying to usher him out before he responds and makes things worse. There's even less chance of Luca marrying Charity than Sam marrying Raiden.

Thankfully, Luca listens and they step out of Raiden's hut into the bright morning sun.

"Let's go straight to the beach," says Mercy.

"Will the other Seekers want the chance to come with us?" Luca asks.

"It's not like Hawk can," says Mercy. "Sam's already upset enough. And I'm not sure that Ekon or Gust would really mind. Let's just send her off on our own. Keep it peaceful."

Luca nods, taking the path to the beach.

"Is she heavy?" Mercy asks, even though Nikita looks like a small child in Luca's arms.

Luca shakes his head.

As they pass near their hut, they see Hawk still sitting against the pole with his arm covering his face as if he's trying to block out the sun.

"Where's Sam?" Mercy calls out.

Hawk lowers his arm. His face is pale. It almost looks like he's been crying.

"The beach," he shouts back.

Mercy hesitates, wondering if she should stay with Hawk. Helping the living is undoubtedly more important than helping the dead.

"Go after her!" calls Hawk. "Make sure she's okay."

"What's with that?" Mercy asks Luca, only to see he's already at least a yard away.

She picks up her pace to catch him. It's hard to know what fire to put out first, so many of them are popping up.

"I don't know." Luca sighs. "But let's give Nikita a respectful send-off and then we can sort out everyone else."

Mercy nods. Nikita may have defected to the Newlanders' side, but she hadn't deserved what happened to her. This is the least they can do.

"I don't believe Sam," says Mercy. "She was lying when she said Nikita told Raiden she wanted to leave."

"What?" Luca's frown deepens. "But it makes sense. Why else would he have killed her?"

"I'm not sure yet. I'm just telling you that Sam was lying," says Mercy. "Her lower lip always twitches when she's not telling the truth. Just a fraction. You only really notice it if you're looking for it."

"Why didn't you say anything at the time?" Luca asks as they step into the trees heading for the beach.

"Because I'm still trying to figure it all out!" Mercy throws out her hands. "Sam must've had her reasons. I mean, she didn't exactly tell us that she's getting married this afternoon, did she?"

"That's because she's not!" Luca's voice is like thunder. "She's not marrying that murderous slimeball."

"He seems to think she's agreed to it," says Mercy, her brain hurting from trying to fit all the pieces together. "Maybe he killed Nikita to clear the way to marry Sam. Nikita was never going to be happy about it. I don't know why, but she loved Raiden."

Luca seems to turn this over in his mind. "Do you think that's why Hawk was upset just now? Because Sam told him she's marrying Raiden? Although, I just can't buy that she'd agree to that."

"She would if he threatened her with something," Mercy says carefully.

"Like killing us all?" Luca looks down at Nikita.

"It makes sense, Luca. Raiden killed Nikita to show Sam he was serious. He was threatening her. You know she'd agree to anything if she thought he might do the same to you or me. Or Hawk."

Mercy keeps close to Luca's side as they walk, trying to give him what little comfort she can. Not an easy task given he's carrying a Seeker's body in his arms.

They reach the sand and make their way down to the water-line, Mercy filling her pockets with stones along the way. It's a brutally hot day and the sun is beating down on them like it's joining Raiden in its threat to take them down.

"You wait here," Luca says as he steps into the water. "I can do this."

"Not a chance." This isn't a task anyone should have to do alone. Not even someone as toughened to the world as Luca.

They wade out until the water reaches Mercy's waist and Luca pauses. Mercy removes the stones from her pockets and tucks them into Nikita's clothes.

"Goodbye, Seeker," she says. "Travel well, wherever it is you've gone."

Luca lowers Nikita into the acidic depths of the water and they watch as she sinks from sight, her dark hair the last part of her to cling to the surface before being sucked under. It's hard to believe that in a few hours there will be nothing of her left.

"Nikita," Mercy whispers, holding her fingers to her lips.

Luca ducks into the water, washing the blood from his hands and clothes. Mercy decides to do the same. After what happened with Marr on the beach, she can't get clean enough. She'd wanted to scrub the skin off her body when it first happened. It's still not such an unappealing idea.

Once they're both soaked through, they wade back to the shoreline and wring out their clothes, knowing the sun will make fast work of drying the rest of them.

"So much for Sam being down here," says Mercy, scanning the beach.

Luca shakes his damp hair in such a way that has Mercy's stomach clenching. He's still the most annoyingly good-looking guy she's ever seen. But out of respect for Nikita for once she doesn't do anything about her feelings. It just wouldn't be right.

"What's that?" asks Mercy, squinting into the distance as something catches her eye in the water.

Luca follows her gaze and frowns as he tries to focus on what they're looking at. "It's a boat."

"Not more Outlanders," Mercy groans. They already have their hands full with the ones who are here. They'll be done for if more of them arrive.

"It's not coming here," Luca says. "It's headed out to sea. In the direction of Askala."

"The invasion," Mercy gasps. They've taken too long to find out what's going on and now Askala is about to be attacked while the Seekers are all standing right here.

"One of our boats is missing." Luca points to the two remaining ones sitting on the sand. "The one Ekon arrived in."

"They took our boat!" Mercy is aghast even though it should be no surprise that these people would steal from them.

"Mercy, for a girl who notices everything, why can't you see what's going on here?" Luca jams his fingers into his hair as if he wants to tear it from his scalp. "That's Sam and Ekon on the boat. It has to be!"

"We need to go after them!" Mercy runs toward the boats on the shore.

Luca is right behind her.

"No!" he cries when he leans over the edge of one of them to look inside. "They've been sabotaged."

Mercy looks into the boats and sees what he's talking about. A hole has been smashed into the bottom of each boat. The timber could be replaced, but not in a hurry. It will take time to fix this.

"What was she thinking?" Luca kicks the side of the vessel, his gaze returning to the small boat on the horizon.

"That Raiden can't force her to marry him if she's in Askala." Mercy puts a hand on Luca's arm. "That our lives will be spared if she's not here to disobey the Newlanders."

"We could all have left together," Luca points out.

"Hawk could never make the journey," says Mercy. "He's far

too ill. And if we all left, what does that mean for our work as Seekers. That it's all for nothing?"

"But it already is all for nothing! Mercy, we've failed. Not just a little bit. We've failed spectacularly!" Luca's hands bunch at his sides. "Everything we've done has played right into the Outlanders' hands."

"Then we need a new plan." Mercy's voice is low, like even she doesn't believe what she's saying is possible. "We need to talk to Alyx."

Luca turns to her. "Why Alyx?"

"She's our last hope. Who else can we trust?"

"Okay, I'll talk to her. See what she knows."

Mercy shakes her head. "Let me talk to her first. Woman to woman. She really opened up to me last time we spoke."

"But we have history," Luca protests. "She trusts me."

It's exactly this history that worries Mercy. One day she'd like to find out exactly what that history entails. But right now she needs to talk to Alyx. Because she *is* the best person to talk to her. If anyone knows how to read people and get information from them, it's Mercy. The Proving was evidence of that. If this isn't Mercy's strength, she doesn't know what is!

"Please, Luca. Let me speak with her," she pleads. "This is what I'm good at. I'll come and get you when I'm finished and then you can talk to her if we still need you to. You can look for some timber for the boats in the meantime. Or check on Hawk. He looked so upset."

"Poor guy," says Luca.

"Remember the days when you didn't like him?" Mercy asks.

Luca shakes his head. "Never happened. He's a good guy."

Mercy gives him a smile. "I'll be back as soon as I can. We're going to fix this, Luca. We'll repair the boats and figure something out."

He catches her hand as she steps away and pulls her back. Her heart leaps as for a moment she thinks he's going to kiss her. But, instead, he just looks deep into her eyes as if he's trying to tell her something but doesn't have the words.

"What?" she asks, holding onto his hand.

"I'm sorry, Mercy." His voice breaks with emotion as he lets go of her. "Go talk to Alyx. Find out what you can."

Stepping up on her tiptoes, she kisses Luca's cheek. "I'm sorry, too." She knows she pushed too hard. Expected too much. Drove him away when all she wanted was to draw him close. Maybe once all this is over, they can try again. Slower. So that the rising of the tides can catch up to the beating of their hearts.

She turns and walks back down the beach. If she lined up all her days in a row in order of the best to the worst, this would have to come close to being the worst. It's definitely the second worst after that time Luca smashed her heart to pieces.

Nikita's dead.

Siena is, too.

Sam's gone.

Now it's just Mercy, Luca, Hawk and Gust.

Hawk's only barely hanging on. Gust is more of a hindrance than a help. And Luca...

Mercy sighs. Luca is Luca, which means she doesn't quite know what he is. But he did apologize for wronging her, which is a start. It's something to build on at least.

Weaving through the forest, Mercy makes her way to Alyx's hut. She takes the long way to avoid Hawk, knowing that's not going to be a short conversation when it happens. He's no longer just nursing broken ribs. He'll also have a broken heart.

"Hello?" she calls from Alyx's door, hoping she doesn't have any visitors.

"Mercy!" Tarquin peels back the flap and throws herself at Mercy. "I missed you, Mercy!"

Mercy hugs the little girl back, certain she only just saw her the day before.

"Is your sister home?" she asks.

Tarquin grips her hand and drags her inside. "Alyx! Mercy is here!"

"I'm right here," Alyx laughs. "I can see for myself."

Mercy blinks in the dimly-lit hut. Tarquin pulls back the door and ties it with a leather strap to allow more sunlight in.

"I was hoping we could talk," says Mercy, as Alyx indicates for her to sit on a mat on the floor. Tarquin tucks herself in beside Mercy as she sits. As much as Mercy loves this little girl, she'd been hoping to talk to Alyx alone.

"Anything you want to say can be said in front of Tarquin." Alyx sits opposite her and gives a reassuring smile. "Sadly, I can't shelter her from the world we live in."

Mercy pauses as she decides where to start. It doesn't feel right just to launch straight in with an inquisition. Better to try to find some common ground first.

"I was attacked on the beach last night." Mercy swallows. "By Marr. He tried to…"

"Oh, Mercy." Alyx leans forward sending her blonde hair spilling over her shoulders and Tarquin puts a small hand on Mercy's back. "Were you able to fight him off?"

Mercy shakes her head. "I tried to, but he was too strong. It made me think of the story you told me about a similar thing happening. When the Falcon saved you. Except, it wasn't the Falcon who saved me. It was Luca."

"This is why I need to be the Falcon," says Tarquin sitting up straight like there's a rod in her spine. "People need the Falcon."

"Hush now." Alyx waves a hand at her sister. "You're only the size of a mosquito, Tarquin. If Mercy couldn't fight him off, what hope do you think you'd have?"

"I'm growing every day," says Tarquin indignantly.

"I feel so dirty." Mercy rubs at her arms. "Like I can't wash the smell of him off me. I was hoping you might have some advice."

Alyx lets out a long sigh. "Life is tough in the Outlands. But it's toughest of all for the women. We may have proven over the years that we match the men in brains, but sadly, we will never match them in strength. And as you've fast learned, strength is everything out here."

"So, how do we beat them?" Mercy asks. "What do we do to protect ourselves?"

Alyx's face hardens. "There's nothing we can do. Mercy, do you think the way I live my life is because I'm a winner? Nobody wins in the Outlands. All you can do is accept that this is the way it is. And if you can earn a living out of it then it's all the better than being forced to give it for free. Either way it's going to be taken from you."

A sick feeling wraps its way around Mercy's gut. Alyx is talking in code for Tarquin's benefit, although her meaning is clear.

"You need to learn to put yourself first," Alyx says, an edge to her voice. "You can't spend your life trying to save everyone else when your own life is the one at risk."

"Not me," whispers Tarquin. "The Falcon saves people. He showed us it's possible."

"And look what happened to him," snaps Alyx.

Mercy puts her fingers to her temples and rubs them. She'd thought Alyx might be able to give her some strategies for how to survive out here with her dignity intact. But it seems she doesn't have the answers. Or at least the answers she has aren't the one Mercy wants. Which brings her to the real reason she came here. To find out what Alyx knows.

"They killed Nikita," says Mercy. "I think Corbin wants us all dead."

Alyx puts a hand on Mercy's knee. "Get out of here, while you can, Mercy. Go home to your people. It's not going to end well if you stay here."

"What do you know?" Mercy asks. "There's talk of an invasion. Of a stage two. What can you tell me?"

Alyx flinches. It's enough to tell Mercy she's hit a nerve. But will she be able to turn that nerve into a betrayal of the Outlanders? Will Alyx tell her what she knows?

"That sounds like nonsense to me." Alyx gives her an unconvincing smile. "Dangerous nonsense. Go home, Mercy. I mean it, go back while you can."

Mercy stands, knowing she's not going to get more out of Alyx right now. Luca was right. He's the one she trusts. And she clearly knows something.

"Luca wants to talk to you," she says. "Are you going to be here for a while?"

Alyx stiffens but quickly nods. "Sure. But Mercy, you think about what I said, okay?"

Mercy steps out of the hut without answering, not all that surprised to find Tarquin follows her.

"Want to help me find Luca?" Mercy asks. "I think he's down at the beach."

Tarquin nods enthusiastically as they take a few steps away.

"I think you'll make a great Falcon," says Mercy, not wanting this complicated little girl to let go of her dreams of helping people. "The best Falcon the Outlands has ever seen."

Tarquin skips ahead and does a somersault before running back to Mercy. "Do you really think so?"

"I know so. Never let go of your dream to help people, Tarquin." Mercy smiles as Tarquin slips her hand into Mercy's and they walk into the trees. "I love your plan for your future."

"Alyx doesn't." Tarquin pulls a face and pokes out her tongue. "But she says we're going to be *just fine.* She's made sure we're going to be safe."

"Really?" Mercy wonders just how she's managed to do that. Safety isn't easy to come by out here.

"Really, beally, super teally!" Tarquin laughs. "Alyx and me are going to be *just fine!*"

"Alyx and I," Mercy corrects.

Tarquin groans, letting go of Mercy's hand to run ahead again, this time practicing a series of leaps through the air.

"Careful!" laughs Mercy. "You'll twist your—"

Tarquin falls heavily and tumbles on the forest floor, letting out a squeal as she sits up and grabs her ankle.

Mercy runs to her and crouches down beside her. "Are you okay?"

Tears spill down Tarquin's cheeks. "I hurt myself. I'm a terrible Falcon."

"Oh, Tarquin you're not." She hugs the small girl to her chest. "Even the strongest people sometimes make mistakes."

Giving Tarquin a few minutes to pull herself together, Mercy sits quietly, soothing her. When she thinks she's ready, she helps Tarquin to her feet, quickly realizing she won't be able to walk far on that ankle. At least it's not broken like Raiden's. She'll be okay once she's given it a rest.

"Let me take you back to Alyx." She squats down and Tarquin climbs onto her back. "Hey, you're heavy! You weren't joking about growing."

Tarquin rests her head on Mercy's shoulder. "I'm growing every day."

"You are." Mercy turns and walks back in the direction of Alyx's hut. She'll have to go and look for Luca alone.

But as they break through the trees into the clearing, she sees there's no need for that. Luca is already talking to Alyx outside her hut.

He seems agitated. If only he'd stuck to the plan and waited for her, Mercy could have told him that she's certain Alyx knows something.

Luca glances around, and for a moment Mercy thinks he sees her approaching.

But he mustn't. Because he seems to decide that the coast is clear.

Luca dips his head in that familiar way of his.

And kisses Alyx.

It's a long, passionate kiss. The sort Mercy had hoped was reserved for her.

Mercy almost drops Tarquin as the heart she'd only just pieced back together shatters like it's made from glass. How could he do this to her? This day just went from the second most terrible, to the worst day she could ever think up.

Feeling her distress, Tarquin strengthens her grip around Mercy's neck and whispers in her ear. "Even the strongest people sometimes make mistakes."

Mercy sets Tarquin down on the ground and runs into the trees. Tarquin may have been talking about Luca, but she's exactly right.

Falling for Luca was the biggest mistake of Mercy's life.

LUCA

*L*uca pushes Alyx away the moment silence follows Mercy's departure. He has to control himself not to shove her almost violently. Disgust is twisting his stomach into knots.

Not that he can feel it.

Fury is burning him from the inside out.

Alyx raises her hand to her lips. "Not the response I was expecting to the news I just gave you."

Luca spins around, making sure Mercy is as gone as those fleeing footsteps sounded. The forest is empty apart from rows of trees, all silent witnesses to the betrayal he just enacted.

Turning back to Alyx, Luca doesn't know what to do with his hands.

He wants to shake her.

He wants to wipe away the stain of their kiss.

He clenches them into hot fists.

He wants to punch fate.

All he can gasp out are two words. "You what?"

Alyx's hand falls away. So does her gaze. "I thought I should tell you."

"Like you're doing me a favor?" Luca asks incredulously.

Luca steps backward, realizing Alyx is no different to anyone else born in the Outlands. He should never have trusted her.

Alyx frowns. "You're the one who made me realize I had to do this."

"Don't even think of putting this on me, Alyx. You're the one who told them."

"It was the pods!" Alyx's gaze returns to his, wide and fierce like a cornered animal. "You showed me there could be another way." She deflates. "And then they were taken away."

Luca's fingers spear through his hair, gripping so hard it makes his eyes sting. "Do you know what this means?"

He already does. He knew the moment she told him.

It's why he had to kiss Alyx when he saw Mercy approaching them.

"Of course I know what this means! This wasn't an easy decision to make, Luca!"

"You've signed my death sentence," he grinds out.

And anyone who knows him.

Alyx shakes her head desperately. "Not if you get away. That's why I told you. So you can disappear before they get here."

Alyx takes a step forward as she reaches out, but Luca retreats. He doubts he'll ever want Alyx touching him again.

Her hands fall to her side. "Don't you understand? I had to tell them the Falcon is still alive. I did it for Tarquin. To give her a chance at a life that's more"—she waves her hand toward the hut where she sees the men who pay her—"than this..."

The reward.

It progressively went up the more the Falcon took from those not willing to share.

It's the promise of enough food and materials for anyone to be able to live independently.

Like Alyx.

And Tarquin.

The fury dies. Morals are the luxury of the rich.

Not vulnerable women trying to raise their little sister in a harsh, violent world.

There's a gasp and they both spin around to find Tarquin standing at the door of the hut. How could they have forgotten she's here? She grips the side of the doorway. "The Falcon's still alive?"

Alyx rushes forward. "No, that's not what I said—"

Tarquin frowns ferociously. "That's exactly what you said." She jerks her arm back as Alyx tries to grasp it. "You let me believe he was dead."

"It was better for everyone to believe that," Luca states flatly.

Alyx winces and Luca hates the small shot of satisfaction that follows it. He might understand why Alyx did what she did.

But there's no way he's ever going to be okay with it.

Tarquin glares at him. "But he's not."

No. The Falcon was never dead.

But now that Alyx has told the leaders of the Outlands that the Falcon's alive, they're going to do everything they can to rectify that.

Luca spins on his heel, his body feeling like it's made of wood. Wood that's been fractured and split.

And is seeping sap.

"Where are you going?" Tarquin calls after him.

Luca doesn't look back. "I have to organize something."

A way to make sure the Seekers are safe when more Outlanders arrive. Baying for blood.

As he strides through the trees, regret stabs him in the gut like a hot knife. He's already taken the first step.

He's ensured Mercy will never want to be near him again. Ever.

Now, he has to protect the others.

Gust isn't in the hut when Luca arrives, which is a relief. That means fewer questions.

Fewer lies that masquerade as answers.

But Hawk's there. Looking broken in spirit far more than body. Luca pauses. Hawk deserves to know that Sam's gone.

He squats down beside the man he used to consider competition. Probably a threat. That feels like such a long time ago.

Now, all he feels for Hawk is respect.

If things were different, one day they could've been friends.

"Is Sam okay?" he croaks.

Luca almost smiles. In spite of it all, that's Hawk's first question.

But it never has a chance to gain life. "She's gone, Hawk. Sam's sailed back to Askala."

Hawk's eyes drift closed. His face twists with more pain than Luca's seen since their arrival in the Outlands. Despite a violent attack at the hands of several Outlanders.

Despite a barely-healed body being beaten all over again by a glory-seeking bastard.

A wheezy, agony-filled breath seeps through his lips. "That's probably a good thing. She'll be safe this way."

"She should never have come here." Luca's naïve, self-sacrificing sister will finally be back where she belongs.

Hawk's eyes fly open, flashing with anger. "Sam achieved far more than any of us did."

Luca clasps his shoulder, acknowledging Hawk sees Sam in a way he's never been able to. "You're right. She did." He watches Hawk carefully. "What are you going to do now?"

"I'm going to find out what the Newlanders are planning," says Hawk, his voice hard.

Luca nods. Remaining is going to be dangerous. But it's the only way they can find out what Askala is up against.

"Good. Make sure Mercy's okay, will you?"

Hawk's eyes narrow. "Have you two had a fight again?"

"Mercy and I are..." How can he say over? They never really had a chance to begin.

Luca pushes to his feet. "Let's just say she's going to need a friend."

"Where are you going?"

Hawk sounds tired. Like he's realized there are parts of him that are never going to heal.

Luca knows how he feels.

On his way out, he grabs the tool pouch beside the door. "I've got some boats to fix."

Leaving before Hawk can ask anymore, Luca makes his way to the beach. He stops beside the boats that Ekon and Sam sabotaged. Just like he thought—only one plank has been damaged.

Luca picks up the rock that Ekon would've used and throws it into the trees. It's late afternoon, which means he has to work fast. Going to the other boat, Luca quickly pries off the plank of wood he's going to need.

Moving back to the first boat, he finds it's a little too wide. Glad for the opportunity, Luca picks up the hammer. He has to hold back from hitting too hard as he taps the plank into place. There's a rage in him that's screaming for an out. To beat and batter the wood as if it's responsible for all the choices that have brought him here.

But he does exactly what Phoenix taught him. His muscles strain as he keeps the taps even and light, working around the edge of the timber that's being added. The reality is, as he's repairing the boat, he's smashing the future he was foolish enough to envisage, anyway.

Panting, Luca steps back to survey his work. The hole no longer exists. All he needs is some sap to seal the joins. It won't have enough time to dry adequately, but the water will seep slowly enough for him to bail it out.

Walking along the beach, Luca heads east for several minutes before turning into the forest to collect the sap. He doesn't want to see Alyx. He doesn't want to have to endure saying goodbye to Tarquin. The Seekers are going to have to learn to move forward without him.

Hours pass. The sun slowly sets on the day he destroyed any chance of having love in his life.

Luca stays away from the village.

From the hut.

He stays away from Mercy.

And as the light darkens and deepens, Luca pushes the boat out to the water. The Outlands are closer than they've ever been. A few hours and he'll be back on the scorched soil that he traversed looking for his mother.

He'll face the Outlanders and end this, once and for all.

Jabbing his oar into the blood-colored water, Luca grits his teeth. This time, the regret is like a fiery blade trying to shred him.

But this is what he has to do.

To keep the Seekers safe.

To protect the girl he should never have fallen in love with. The girl who's tough and determined and will always follow her heart.

Which is why Mercy can never know that Luca's the Falcon.

THE END

Ready for the next installment in The Thaw Chronicles?
Check out Book 7, EXILE, now!
http://mybook.to/ExileThaw

BOOK SEVEN - EXILE

BEYOND THE THAW

Only the chosen shall seek.

Sam, Hawk, Luca and Mercy.

Four teens no longer sure what they're seeking. Four teens no longer sure whether it can be found.

They were supposed to be building a new world. One where the Earth is respected as much as the people who depend on it for survival. One where the benefits of Askala could be shared by all.

Except instead of bringing people together, Sam, Hawk, Luca and Mercy are more divided than ever. Sam has returned to Askala, learning exactly how vulnerable her home is. Hawk is trapped, forced to fight for his life to save those around him. Luca has returned to the Outlands to right his wrongs. Mercy is determined to find out the truth at any cost.

In the struggle to repair the world from the ravages of global warming, the fight to reunite is going to be their greatest battle yet. Because no matter where they are, treachery is far closer than they ever realized.

Living has never been more deadly.

Lovers of Divergent and The Hunger Games will be blown away by the next installment in the bestselling series, The Thaw Chronicles, from USA Today best-selling author Tamar Sloan and award-winning author Heidi Catherine.

Grab your copy now!
http://mybook.to/ExileThaw

WANT TO STAY IN TOUCH?

If you'd like to be the first for to hear all the news from Tamar and Heidi, be sure to sign up to our newsletter. Subscribers receive bonus content, early cover reveals and sneaky snippets of upcoming books. We'd love you to join us!

SIGN UP HERE:

https://sendfox.com/tamarandheidi

ABOUT THE AUTHORS

Tamar Sloan hasn't decided whether she's a psychologist who loves writing, or a writer with a lifelong fascination with psychology. She must have been someone pretty awesome in a previous life (past life regression indicated a Care Bear), because she gets to do both. When not reading, writing or working with teens, Tamar can be found with her husband and two children enjoying country life in their small slice of the Australian bush.

Heidi Catherine loves the way her books give her the opportunity to escape into worlds vastly different to her own life in the burbs. While she quite enjoys killing her characters (especially the awful ones), she promises she's far better behaved in real life. Other than writing and reading, Heidi's current obsessions include watching far too much reality TV with the excuse that it's research for her books.

MORE SERIES TO FALL IN LOVE WITH...

ALSO BY TAMAR SLOAN AND HEIDI CATHERINE

The Sovereign Code

Elemental Games

ALSO BY TAMAR SLOAN

Keepers of the Grail

Keepers of the Light

Keepers of the Chalice

Keepers of Excalibur

Zodiac Guardians

Descendants of the Gods

Prime Prophecy

ALSO BY HEIDI CATHERINE

The Kingdoms of Evernow

The Soulweaver

www.ingramcontent.com/pod-product-compliance
Lightning Source LLC
Chambersburg PA
CBHW031556240626
47153CB00002B/530